# BASEBALL & A GIRL

### RICKY CANÓ

# ALSO BY RICKY CANÓ

Identical The Switch - Book One

BASEBALL & A GIRL

A 3-0 count doesn't mean you'll get a fastball.

Sit back on the change-up.

Don't chase the curve.

By

RICKY CANÓ

# BASEBALL & A GIRL

It's okay if you think Baseball is boring. It's kind of a smart person's sport.

*First and foremost, Thank you, God, for allowing me to wake up and see another day.*

*I want to thank Dr. Noran, Dr. Gary Johnshon, Beverly, the entire Gamma Knife department, and the entire 6INC crew for saving my life.*

*And last but not least, my speech pathologist, Amy. Thank you for your patience and your help.*

*Because of all of you, I am able to live a normal life.*

A brain arteriovenous malformation (AVM) is a tangle of blood vessels that connect arteries and veins in the brain. The arteries take oxygen-rich blood from the heart to the brain. Veins carry the oxygen-depleted blood back to the lungs and heart. A brain AVM disrupts the vital process. Signs and symptoms of a brain AVM may begin at any age but usually emerge between ages 10 and 40. Brain AVMs can damage brain tissue over time. The effects slowly build and often cause symptoms in early adulthood.

I was 20 years old when a previously undetected AVM ruptured, temporarily ending my ability to walk, compute language, and have long-term memories… Recovery from a brain AVM is exhausting and complicated.

"This level of brain injury is still not talked about. Services and care are not prioritized, even for the young people who might be able to give back to their communities and societies in a very manful way in the future" - Clemency Burton-Hill

# *INTRODUCTION*



*In My Own Words*

The stark reality of Dr. Woo's words hit me like a ton of bricks. No sugar coating, just a blunt proclamation that shattered any illusions of a normal future. I couldn't believe it – "You're going to die. People with your condition who have gone through this type of brain hemorrhage usually do not make it to age twenty-eight, let alone live to see thirty."

Dr. Woo, this short, thin Asian guy with surprising hairy knuckles and a loud, direct voice, delivered the verdict in his 7th-floor office. The sun beamed through the window, casting a glare on his glasses as he dropped the bombshell.

*I'm going to be eighteen soon*, I thought, feeling the weight of my mortality pressing down on me. I was just given a death date – ten to twelve years to live, max.

"But - but I play baseball," I stammered after what felt like an eternity of silence.

"That doesn't matter. You won't be able to play base-ball anymore," Dr. Woo replied, his voice as loud as ever. "You're a walking critical condition. It doesn't matter how good you feel post-surgery. You're not okay. Whatever life you had before your massive brain bleed, you have to leave it behind if you have any chance of beating these odds."

I sat there, broken but trying to hold it together. "I'm a baseball player," I insisted.

"Not anymore. Not anymore," Dr. Woo repeated, like a harsh mantra sealing my fate.

The room, once a familiar place where I discussed rehab and recovery, now felt like a battleground. The plaques on the wall seemed irrelevant, and the sunlight that used to inspire hope only highlighted the harsh reality. Dr. Woo's appearance, with his black hair and hairy knuckles, was just details – inconsequential against the ticking clock now governing my life.

In the face of this life-altering prognosis, I clung to the remnants of who I used to be. A young adult thrust into a reality where the familiar rhythms of life were disrupted by the persistent drumbeat of impending mortality. The doctor's loud voice, once annoying, became a tool to hammer home the gravity of the situation, echoing in the silence that followed.

As I grappled with the enormity of my fate, the resilience that kept me stoic hinted at a strength within. The future was uncertain, and Dr. Woo's words lingered, shaping the contours of a young adult life now constrained by a narrow window of time. A ticking clock, reminding me that the once boundless possibilities of the future were now replaced by a need to reimagine what it meant to live with urgency and purpose.

# PROLOGUE

Hearing the doctor say that my son would die if he didn't act soon was the worst moment of my life. The feeling was unexplainable. I felt like I couldn't breathe, but I had to remain calm for my ex-wife, Betsy, my son's mother.

You hear and read about the terrible stories children go through—cancer, rare diseases, freak accidents, catching stray bullets, etc. You never stop to think that this, too, can happen to your child.

"It's not looking good," Doctor Ogni told Betsy and me. Reiterating what he had previously stated, his tone was more urgent. "I need to put the stent in his brain now, or he will die."

Betsy and I couldn't comprehend how this happened. Our son was a perfectly healthy teenager. Other than occasional headaches, there weren't any signs of a deadly brain condition. We witnessed this kid play baseball almost daily since he was five. Little league, AAU travel ball, junior high, high school, double headers three times a week during the summer, showcases, all-stars, etc. How could this happen to such a strong and healthy kid?

Betsy and I consented and allowed Dr. Ogni to perform the emergency procedure on our son.

Suddenly, his baseball dreams didn't matter. The college scouts didn't matter. The choice between staying close to home or playing down south didn't matter. All that mattered was him. We didn't, well, at least I didn't stop to think what kind of person he would become after all this. How was this going to affect him emotionally, physiologically, and physically?

That was a good sign. I know it probably made me sound like a selfish parent for thinking that at the time. See, the thing is that a certain sense of calm came over me. I didn't think he was going to die anymore. I couldn't and still can't put it into words, but I knew he would make it. My worry for him now was what type of person he'd be after potentially having his dreams shattered. How would he handle adjusting and learning to be a new version of himself after carrying a specific identity all his life? And most importantly, was he physically and neurologically able to?

Betsy slept in his hospital room every night. He was in critical condition despite my belief, and the doctors had yet to give any promising news. I convinced Betsy to go home and assured her I'd call her if anything changed. That night, I watched my son lying asleep with a tube-like drain inserted into his head, draining out red fluid. I couldn't help but notice an eight-by-11-inch piece of paper on his bedside table.

My son's essay was another reminder of how life can change in the blink of an eye.

Jonathan Machado

Mrs. Viking

ENGL

1 SEPTEMBER 2022

Baseball & A Girl

I dig my cleats into the dirt of the batter's box. One, two, three, three more times, I dig my feet into the ground as I get into my batting stance. I tightly grip my bat's handle with fresh, all-white batting gloves. I focus my undivided attention on a too-familiar face, the pitcher.

Jackson was and looked like the prototype American white boy, with medium-length, shaggy blonde hair that quickly peaked out of his baseball cap. His 6'3, two-hundred-pound frame towered over my 5'11ish 175-pound body. Jackson's blue eyes and baseball abilities capped off the quote-unquote hottest guy in the school check box.

I was the little guy. I wasn't supposed to be here. A medium to dark-skinned Dominican American kid from the inner city wasn't supposed to be playing in one of the best AAU baseball tournaments in the country against other seventeen-year-old kids who already had commitments to the top baseball colleges in the country. Yet, I faced a rival, not just on the baseball field.

My dad, a former college player himself, compared baseball to love. I'm only seventeen years old. What do I know about love? I like to believe that I know a thing or two. See, that's what Jackson and I have in common. That's what makes us true rivals.

Vanity is her name. She had coco skin, wavy black hair, pearly white teeth, and full lips. She was the only person I knew who had a unique mixture of Cambodian and Hawaiian. See, Vanity went to Metropolitan West High School in Cranston with Jackson and my younger brother in an upper-class section of Rhode Island. I went to Central High, in the heart of the over-populated and broken Providence, Rhode Island.

Jackson and Vanity, to my current knowledge, were high school royalty. Kids would label them a power couple. They were inseparable. They held hands in the hallways and kissed one another before heading into their separate classes; their friends all stuck together during lunch and even hung out on the weekends. In terms of popularity, they were in the upper echelon.

To Jackson and everyone else, Vanity was perfect. Her mother is a dentist. Her father is a judge. She drives a BMW to school. When was the last time you saw a seventeen-year-old drive, let alone own, a 2021 BMW? When it came to college, she knew exactly where she was headed. With her grades, she could go to any school, but she's attracted to Rutgers because it stands among America's highest-ranked, most diverse public research universities. Again, Vanity was perfect.

Jackson had the perfect girl by his side.

Today's temperature said today's high would be 90 degrees. We were penciled in for the 9 a.m. game. As I stood in the batter's box waiting for Jackson to deliver his first pitch of the seventh and final inning, it felt like we were lying in 105-degree weather. We were down 3-2 in the bottom of the inning. There were two outs. My good friend Derek was on second base as the tying run. Jackson was brought in to close the inning out. When Derek hit a double to get on base, the stage was set to take the rivalry between Jackson and me to another level.

Although everyone was fascinated with Vanity's unintentional mirage, I knew what most people didn't. I was neighbors with her cousin John. John was a year older than me. He was a gangster. He dropped out of school, sold drugs, and, to my current knowledge, was part of a street gang. John is shorter than me, standing around 5'6. His complexion was identical to Vanity. He didn't have any unique mixture to him. He was 100% full Cambodian, and his facial features showed it.

I met Vanity during one of John's mother's birthday parties. Despite her son being a criminal, John's mother was a lovely woman. When I first saw Vanity, I was instantly drawn to her. She was something I'd never seen before. The moment we were introduced to one another, I felt a connection. She felt the same.

What was then once a month turned into her coming into Providence every weekend. It was like a ritual. We'd sit on John's front stoop or my front porch and talk for hours at night. I got to know her likes, dislikes, dreams, and fears, and she got to know mine. I got to know the dynamics of her family. She was the only person to understand how strained my relationship with my father and grandfather was, and she encouraged me to try to tell my dad to fix it. She's the one. This is the person I was going to grow old with.

A few weeks ago, when I finally told my father about her after we disputed over something small, he said, "Save her for later." I was angered. Why would my father say that? Why would he say something like that to me, knowing I was falling for her?

I was aware of Vanity's situation with Jackson. She was done with him. She didn't connect with Jackson the way we did. He was just a high school sweetheart. I was the real deal. She broke it off with him. She was now my girl. This wasn't my intention. I didn't plan on coming between a relationship. It just happened. I felt bad for Jackson. At the same time, I didn't. Everyone at Cranston West hated me so much that they sometimes gave my brother trouble, underestimating how fiery my brother was. They cheered when their star pitcher drilled me when we played them at the beginning of the high school season.

"Just because you believe something doesn't make it true." My father said to me.

What the hell is that supposed to mean? I hated it

when he used metaphors. Was he talking about me or himself? The answer was clear: He was talking about us both.

My father resented my mother for not lasting longer in the major leagues. He didn't have to say it. I just knew.

I want to play College Baseball at the University of Miami, but Vanity wants me to join her at Rutgers. I didn't tell Vanity this, but Rutgers's bench coach visited my house last weekend and expressed how Rutgers wanted me as their shortstop.

It's a great opportunity when you sit back and think about it. I could play college ball and be with Vanity. I verbally committed to Rutgers. I told my father. I chose not to tell anyone else. Not yet, at least. I knew heading into this tournament all the top scouts would be here. So here I was, at the bottom of the seventh, with the game on the line, facing the nation's top high school closer, with Miami University's scout having a front-row seat to this matchup.

Jackson nodded, signaling his catcher that he knew what pitch he wanted to throw. Jackson hates me. He hates me for taking his girl. With first base vacant, he should pitch around me. His pride has gotten the best of me. He's going to challenge me with his best pitch. He wants to prove to his verbally committed school and Vanity, who's in attendance, that he's the better man.

Vanity is Jackson's end game. That's who he wants. Like me, Jackson verbally committed to Rutgers. Unlike me, it wasn't for baseball. He did it for her. Deep down, a part of me knows Vanity loves this. Her ex not going down without a fight, trying to prove his love for her, is somewhat poetic to her.

My father told me, "There's going to be a girl. At times, there may be more than one girl. You're better than I was at your age. You're going to be better than me in college. So, you're going to be faced with a decision. Your future may come down to Baseball and a girl."

With all the nation's top scouts in attendance, Jackson threw his pitch. And with a swing of the bat, I hit a two-run home run, delivering my team the win.

I skipped the traditional bat toss. My mind was racing. The crowd went wild. My teammates and coaches ran out of our dugout. I trotted toward first base.

My father's voice drowned out the loud cheers of the crowd. "Baseball is like love. Think about it. What's getting to first base with a girl? A kiss?"

When I trotted towards second base, my team was huddled at home plate, cheering me on. I glanced over at our opponent's dugout. Jackson was sitting on the bench. He was gripping a towel, pressing it against his face. His father, who had made his way into their dugout, patted him on the back. I assume that he was bawling his eyes out. Who wouldn't after blowing a big game in front of such important people?

"Second base is feeling a girl's breast over her shirt, right?" My father often spoke without a filter.

When I touched third, I could see Vanity in the stands. She was cheering me on, but I could see a slight sadness in her eyes. I knew she felt bad for Jackson. Who wouldn't? He's head over heels in love with her.

She breaks his heart and starts to date his rival. Then, Jackson loses the biggest game of his AAU career to that same kid. I'd feel bad for him too. Truthfully, I did.

My father's voice came to me again. "Third base is you're feeling under her shirt. She has her hands in your pants, right?"

I make my way home. My team is ecstatic. Everything now is moving in slow motion. For the last time, my father's voice came to me again.

"Getting home is sex. Let's take it from the top because I was talking about sex. You're facing the pitcher. That's the girl. You're getting to know her with every pitch she throws at you. If you get to first base, let's say she likes you and you like her. If you make it second, let's say you guys are dating. Third, oh, it's getting serious. You guys have the potential to go somewhere. Then, you manage to make it home. That's the final step. You guys made it. You're in love. This is it."

I'm now fifteen feet away from home plate, and my teammates are jumping up and down with excitement.

"It's up to you to know if home plate is love or lust. If your dream destination comes knocking at your door, are you willing to go another route because the other route offers you love?" My father's voice spoke to me for the last time.

I'm now five feet away from four, three, two, one. I jump up, landing with both feet on home plate, as my teammates huddle around me, jumping up and down with me.

We won the game. We beat our rivals. We're heading into the championship round. But most importantly, that home run answered the lingering question.

# CHAPTER ONE

Penn Station, A Train & A Girl

K elvin was tired from the long weekend. Frankly, he was quite on the fence about this whole Amtrak thing.

Not because he didn't like the long ride. (He did. He *loved* traveling. Traveling comes with baseball.) He'd been used to the door-to-door Dominican bus line buses that dropped you off at your doorstep. That type of bus line was and still is a bus line where it didn't matter if the bus fit twelve people; they'd squeeze in fourteen, fifteen max. The bus driver played his music of choice, mostly *bachata*. The music would only be turned down to a moderate to low volume to discuss politics in the Dominican Republic. The passengers were always a mixture of a handful of women in their mid-fifties to sixties, two loud-mouthed men in their forties, two annoyed pre-teens traveling with their mom in her thirties, a quiet male teen sitting in the back, wearing his headphones (*Kelvin*), and an active drunk, who's still drinking. These passengers always made the trips feel homey despite not knowing anyone.

The last bus back to Providence, Rhode Island, had left at nine o'clock, and Kelvin had to be back home for tomorrow's game. His mother was right when she told him that traveling to play in Long Island for the weekend on his cousin's AAU team to try to make it back at a reasonable time for school and a game wouldn't be a good idea. Of course, he didn't listen. What seventeen-year-old young man does? So, he was at Penn Station at ten o'clock, waiting for his train.

Surprisingly, even at this time, this train seemed like it would reach total capacity as passengers filled Penn Station's Amtrak waiting room. After playing two games yesterday and three this evening, the tile flooring at Penn Station wasn't doing the exhausted Kelvin any favors.

The five-foot-eight, facial hairless, skinny, broad-shouldered, wide-backed, traditional medium brown Caribbean skin-toned kid was carrying his baseball bag and backpack. He was so tired that he thought about sitting on the floor after giving his seat to an older woman traveling with her daughter. He was just about to sit on the floor until he saw her.

She was beautiful. She couldn't have been taller than five foot one or maybe foot two. She was a shade lighter than Kelvin, with long curly hair and dark but gentle eyes. Light freckles on her cheeks and full pinkish lips wrapped up this beauty. She stood about a foot away from a young couple that appeared to be in their early twenties. Because of the resemblance, Kelvin assumed the slightly older woman girl (*woman*) had to be her big sister. The girl wore light blue jeans, sneakers, and a green jacket over her blouse.

Suddenly, the urge to sit on the floor escaped his mind. He didn't notice, but he was staring. Suddenly, the girl turned her head and locked eyes with him. Embarrassed, he quickly looked away and stared straight ahead.

Finally, the announcement to board the train came. Kelvin and the rest of the passengers boarded the train. The Amtrak train was large with panoramic windows, where you could relax and enjoy the view. The seating was four at a time, in case you traveled in groups. Passengers had someone sitting beside them and someone facing them. The seats were comfortable and positioned so each passenger had leg rest and far more space than on an airplane.

Kelvin sat by himself on the outer seat, leaving the window seat next to him vacant, with his back facing the rear of the train. Alone in the four-seater, he quietly and shallowly wished away undesirable strangers looking for seats. Every stranger briefly made eye contact with Kelvin before continuing their search for the perfect travel seat.

Suddenly, the beautiful girl's sister and the guy she was with slid into the seating for four next to him, directly across the narrow aisle. Kelvin looked over for a quick second. The girl's sister took the window seat. The guy sat next to her. Kelvin knew the beautiful girl would be seated before the young couple. He would have the perfect view of her and her of him. On the one hand, he'd have a pretty face to look at during the ride.

On the other hand, what if she caught him staring? What would he say? What would she say? Then, there she was, approaching down the aisle. Her face was as serious as ever. If she were a cartoon, her character would blow smoke out of her nose.

He gave a quick, innocent smile, but it was in vain because she still looked angry. Feeling the rush of embarrassment running through him, Kelvin looked down before rotating his head to stare out the window.

Suddenly, to his surprise, he could see the beautiful girl stopped short of her sister from the corner of his eye. Her eyes quickly glanced over at Kelvin, then back to her sister. Instead of sitting with her sister, she slid in and took the window seat before Kelvin's bags to ride with the nice boy who gave up his seat to the older woman.

Her sister said to her from across the aisle, "Are you sure you wanna play it like this?"

"Yeah," the girl replied without looking at her sister.

The girl was upset about something. Kelvin noticed her eyeballing his backpack and baseball bag occupying the window seat directly across from her. He felt confused but chose to remain quiet.

"You know, I don't even know why you're making a big deal about this," her sister said.

The girl didn't bother replying to her sister. She quickly directed an annoyed look at Kelvin.

"Hi. Do you mind keeping me company during this trip?" The girl asked Kelvin. "My sister and this dude are going to be talking a lot of shit, and I don't wanna be in the middle of it. I could sit here silent, but then I'd be forced to listen to their shit. So, do you mind talking to me?... What's your name, by the way?" Her voice was soft yet firm.

Kelvin's eyes quickly rolled over toward the girl's sister. Her sister sucked her teeth and crossed her arms. Now locking eyes with this beautiful girl, Kelvin replied.

"Kelvin. My name is Kelvin. What's yours?"

"Analis."

"Nice to meet you, Analis."

"Nice to meet you too, Kelvin."

Analis's sister's boyfriend spoke from across the aisle, "You're immature."

"Excuse me. I'm having a conversation," Analis replied with more base in her voice.

Everyone sat in awkward silence as passengers occupied their seats. Soon after, the train started to move.

Through the first hour of the ride, Analis and Kelvin small-talked. Their topics were their current residence, ages, and what each other was listening to in their headphones. Analis listened to *reggaeton,* while Kelvin listened to *hip-hop.* Finally, Kelvin learned that Analis's mother was Dominican, her father was Puerto Rican, and she was a seventeen-year-old senior attending Classical High School in the heart of Providence, Rhode Island.

Throughout their school conversation, there was a particular interest in Analis on why Kelvin was a junior and not a senior like herself.

"It's cause of my birthday...My birthday is in

October after the school year starts. So, I started school one year behind in Miami," Kelvin explained.

"Miami?"

"Yeah. We moved around a lot because of my father."

"Oh… and the baseball bag?" Analis gestured to Kelvin's bags by slightly nodding her head toward the direction of his bag.

"Oh, I was playing in a baseball tournament."

"Did you win?"

"Lost the championship game."

"Oh, sorry."

"It's okay. I was a fill-in. I have a game tomorrow."

Analis smirked. It wasn't a smirk like she heard something funny. It was one of those smirks that people make when they realize something was said that has gone over their heads.

"Wait, who decides to fill in for a tournament before he has to play for his team the next day?" Analis asked.

"I do." Kelvin flashed a smile. It was the first confident smile he flashed while conversing with Analis. "I love baseball. It's what I do."

Analis had the eerie feeling of a set of eyeballs on her. Despite discretely arguing with one another, Analis's sister and her boyfriend have been glancing over at Analis. Analis had been so preoccupied with her music and her conversation with Kelvin that she hadn't realized the glances at her until now. Kelvin quickly noticed the discomfort on her face and wasn't sure what to say or do. This beauty was a stranger to him. He'd been having an experience one only sees in a movie, and he didn't want to do anything to mess this up.

Now, the problem was that Analis's mood was about to change. He didn't want that to happen.

"Do you mind if I sit next to you?" Kelvin asked.

He felt stupid for asking because Analis seemed to have sudden hesitation. Her eyes widened slightly, her lips suddenly appeared dry, and she straightened herself up in her seat. *Damn, why did I think I could be some cool guy here.* Kelvin was about to take back his offer, but to his surprise, Analis nodded.

"Yeah. Sure."

Kelvin felt a pang in his chest. It was a good pang. A pang that could be described as feeling happy when the girl you wanted to ask out to prom says yes. Still surprised, Kelvin tentatively rose and scooted out of his seat, glancing across the aisle toward Anais's sister and her boyfriend. They were still bickering in a lower, angry whisper as their gaze transitioned toward Kelvin. Analis was quietly surprised at Kelvin's *skinny-ish* but wide frame as he stood in the middle of the aisle. To her, he appeared to be on the far shorter side as he sat in front of her. With Kelvin standing up, she could see he was pleasantly taller than her. Although slimmer than the average junior and senior high school athletes, he was *cute*. It's funny what height does to a boy.

Kelvin scooted in and sat beside Analis, now feeling her older sister's gaze. He slightly turned left and stared out the window of the moving train. Analis did the same. Her scent mesmerized Kelvin, smelling fresh with a hint of coconut. Kelvin didn't know if the scent was coming from her hair or body lotion, but he loved how she smelled.

"Can I ask you a question?... Is that your sister sitting next to that guy?"

"Yeah," Analis replied.

"What up with her and that guy?"

Analis broke her gaze away from the window and met Kelvin's eyes. She could make out the brown in his dark eyes.

"That's her boyfriend. I saw him trying to kick it to another girl. My grandmother once told me that if you see something, it's best to keep it to yourself because you won't like the result nine out of ten times."

Kelvin knew what that meant. "You told her, she forgave him, and now you look like the asshole."

"Yeah. It's a shame, too, because she doesn't really know what she wants."

"And what do you want, Analis?"

"For starters, not someone who's for everybody."

There was something about the way she talked. Maybe it was the hint of the inner-city *Spanish* accent or the honesty in her voice. Kelvin didn't know what it was, but it was there in how she spoke. Precise. Truthful. Deep. Unlike anyone else. Familiar – impossibly so.

"I feel you," Kelvin said, trying not to accept that this may be love at first sight after hearing her laugh, watching her smile, and going through almost every emotion during the trip.

Throughout the rest of the trip, Kelvin and Analis learned more about each other. Likes, dislikes, home life, hobbies. She had learned Kelvin played varsity baseball for Metropolitan West High. Not only was his older brother a senior, starting shortstop for Central High in Providence, with multiple college offers already, but he was Kelvin's Irish twin, ten months and a half older. Being a shortstop himself, he knew he'd never see playing time playing on his brother's team. So, he used his father's address in Cranston to be able to play and start for a somewhat rival school.

Analis was an honor student and the youngest of four. Her mother was a secretarial clerk in judicial courthouses, and her father was a lieutenant in the Providence Fire Department. Although she wasn't involved in sports like the girls Kelvin knew back home, Analis knew precisely what she wanted to do. She wanted to study sports medicine. To Kelvin's disappointment, Analis was in a *situation-ship* that she was thinking of ending and didn't feel right about giving Kelvin her phone number. At least not yet.

Disappointment struck when their ride came to an end. After gathering their travel bags, Kelvin and Analis slowly exited the train station to Gaspee St in Providence, Rhode Island. Gaspee St. was located between the train station, the State House, and the city's largest Mall, just outside Downtown. Usually, this street was a traffic nightmare. But at this hour, 1:15 in the morning, the place was a ghost town with only a couple dozen cars parked outside. Analis's sister and her boyfriend were ten yards ahead, crossing the street to meet their ride on the State House side of Gaspee St.

Kelvin spotted his father's car a few cars behind Analis's ride.

"So, it was nice meeting you, Analis."

"It was nice meeting you too... Good luck in your game tomorrow."

Kelvin flashed a quick smile. "Thank you… If we never see each other again-"

"Then I look forward to reading about you or watching you on SportsCenter," she interjected. She met his eyes with hers and felt something funny. *What was happening?* She anticipated his response and decided to speak up again. "If we ever meet again, let's just hope I'm not treating you for any injury."

Kelvin smiled again. "You take care of yourself, Analis Ruiz."

"You too, Kelvin Machado."

# CHAPTER TWO

<u>New Count</u>

"Wait a minute." Ryan tilted his head. His smile was still in place, but his gaze became sharper, and his focus on Kelvin was less superficial. "Did you happen to tell her about Carrie...?"

Kelvin froze with the baseball still in his hand. The two had been warming up, tossing the baseball to one another in the infield between second and third base, fully dressed in white home uniforms with *"West"* written across the chest. Ryan was the starting third baseman for Metropolitan West High. The six-foot, dirty blonde-haired, green-eyed, Caucasian junior was Kelvin's best friend in school.

Like each other, the rest of the teammates were warming up before the game. The outfielders long tossed to each other. The second and first basemen threw the baseball to each other on the other side of the infield, and pitchers and catchers warmed up in their bullpen.

The pre-game stretches and slow-paced laps around the field were completed on this calm, sunny afternoon. Tossing the baseball to one another to keep their arms warm was the only brief time Kelvin and his teammates had to socialize under the strict regime of their head coach.

"No... I didn't mention Carrie," Kelvin replied before he threw the ball back to Ryan.

"What if Carrie finds out you had some kind of connection with this train girl?"

"How is she going to find out? We didn't exchange numbers. And I ain't stupid enough to confess that to Carrie."

Carrie was Kelvin's girlfriend. Kids in school labeled them a *power couple*, mainly because of their status. Kelvin, the starting shortstop, was dating the heartthrob female soccer player. Carrie was gorgeous and perfectly aligned with *strong is the new sexy*. Her legs were strong and toned, and she was starting to develop a six-pack. She had dark green eyes and long blonde hair.

With every teenage boy jumping on the fitness bandwagon, whether it was weightlifting or CrossFit, how dare Kelvin talk to another girl?

There was a loud whistle coming from their dugout. "Bring it in." It was their coach.

———

Later, at 6:45 p.m.

Bottom of the 7th

Score: 2-2. There were two outs, runners on second and third base, and Kelvin was up to bat.

———

The air had cooled off, causing those attending the game to layer up in their sweatshirts.

Kelvin has had a mediocre game with two walks, three assisted out, and turning three double plays, but a critical error that allowed the tying run to cross home hampered his game. And Ryan wasn't afraid to let him know about it.

"Hey, don't let that shitty glove ruin this game for us," Ryan playfully barked at Kelvin as Kelvin made his way to home plate, causing some in the crowd to laugh.

Kelvin calmly stepped into the batter's box. All afternoon, he hadn't gotten a good pitch to hit, which complements his discipline. Too often, kids step into the batter's box feeling anxious and like they must be the hero. Kelvin dug his cleats in the dirt several times before settling into his batting stance.

The pitcher, a cross-town closer at Park East High, darted his eyes to home plate, waiting for his signs from his catcher. Kelvin was familiar with the kid looking to strike him out, having been on the same travel AAU travel team just last summer.

The pitcher nodded in agreement with the sign his catcher gave him. Kelvin calmly blocked everything: the cheers of the home and away crowd, the sudden wind kicking up dirt from the infield, and people stomping on the bleachers. Most importantly, his strict baseball dad, watching, leaning forward, and pressing his forearms on the short outfield fence.

*Finally! Here it is.*

It was the pitch Kelvin had been looking for. A *get me over fastball*, slightly on the inside corner. Kelvin raised his lead foot slightly, quickly rotated his hips, and kept his hands back throughout his fast-swinging motion. Finally, he pivoted his back foot, keeping his back leg nice and strong. He caught the ball perfectly with the bat's barrel, making his aluminum bat sound like a wooden bat when it made a cracking sound at a professional baseball game. The ball jumped off Kelvin's bat as his school's crowd rose off their seats on the bleachers. It was a no-doubter.

After completing his swing and making firm contact with the ball, Kelvin knew he had just hit a *walk-off home run* (A home run to win the game). He watched the ball skyrocket for a few seconds toward the left-center field as the opposing outfielder didn't attempt to track the ball down. Once he started to make his home run trot, he pointed at his dugout, which was going wild, non-verbally saying, *I told you so.*

During Kelvin's home run trot, the crowd noise grew louder. He made quick eye contact with the opposing in-fielders. He exchanged head nods with Gregory, the opposing second baseman, his cousin, and a teammate on his travel team, and Alex, one of his closest friends who was labeled the *next big thing coming out of Rhode Island* because of his baseball superiority.

Upon reaching home plate, Kelvin's teammates enthusiastically greeted him at home plate. Most were jumping up and down, rowdy, and screaming for joy. Some were hollering encouraging words in explicit language and knew their coaches would talk to them after the game, and some just flat-out clapped. As soon as Kelvin touched home, all his teammates patted him on his helmet and continued their celebration.

Kelvin, being humble, held in his excitement a bit. He just flashed a big smile and high-fived his teammates as he met his coaches outside his dugout. His home crowd had started to vacate the bleachers and began to walk toward the fences next to their dugout. Kelvin looked up at the same group, trying to locate *him*. His father, Sandy, stood at the top of the bleachers, clapping with a smirk.

———

Half an hour later, the team was free to go after the head coach's speech in the dugout. The temperature had gotten cooler again, and the sun had started to set. Kelvin walked towards his father through the crowd by the fencing just outside the dugout.

Kelvin wondered what critique his father had in mind. His father always showed how proud he was but always had a comment. *You were early on that inside pitch. Use your hips more. Don't rely on your strong arm; charge the ball.* Kelvin wondered what comment his father would say after taking a ball that may have been a strike, which resulted in his second walk for the evening. He knew deep down that, had it been his older brother, Jonathan, he would have swung.

As Kelvin got closer to his father, Carrie stopped

him in his trail by jumping in front of him. Her eyes sparked with joy. She smiled from ear to ear, exposing a dimple on each cheek as she opened her arms to bear hug Kelvin. She was short. Not that Kelvin was considered one of the taller kids, but standing next to Kelvin's wired-framed, Carrie appeared shorter and compact. She wore a pair of slightly thigh-high gym shorts and a grey hooded sweatshirt, and her hair was in a messy bun. Kelvin dropped his baseball bag and wrapped his hands around her waist as she wrapped her arms around his neck. Knowing he wasn't a big fan of PDA (public display of affection), Carrie purposely planted a big kiss on Kelvin's lips.

Kelvin quickly met his father's eyes before slightly grinning at the amused Carrie.

"Baby, you were so good," Carrie said, trying to contain her laugh. She studied Kelvin's eyes for a quick second and knew he felt his father's presence. "Go ahead and talk to your dad. We'll catch up in a bit."

Kelvin smiled at Carrie, kissed her forehead, picked up his baseball bag, and headed toward his father.

Kelvin's father, Sandy, was a young dad, having just turned 37 years old, and looked even younger than his age. Kelvin resembled his father a bit but looked more like his mother. His brother Jonathan was the one who identically looked like a younger version of his father. Sandy stood around five foot ten, kept a low haircut to disguise the beginning stages of a receding hairline, and had the muscular body that most high school dads don't. The shape of his body resembled Kelvin's, with a broad back. Still, it also displayed what Kelvin's body could look like when it matured adequately with the proper nutrition and weightlifting regimen. Sandy was a shade darker than his son with dark eyes and always stood up straight, making him seem taller than his height.

As Kelvin approached his father again, something else caught his eye. Just a few feet behind Kelvin's father stood a familiar face. Could it be? It couldn't. She wore fitted, ripped, light blue jeans, a blue jean jacket over her tan blouse, and white low-top sneakers. She wore her curly hair out and wore a backpack. She appeared to be with a small entourage. Kelvin could quietly count five people with her. Four of the five were guys who seemed to be around his age range, although one was older. The girl standing next to her was on the taller side and familiar. Maybe a female basketball player. He couldn't quite pinpoint her, but there was no denying who caught his attention. She didn't break eye contact with him as she shook her head, unapologetically displaying the disappointment on her face.

Suddenly, Kelvin felt a slight pang in his heart. It wasn't a good one, pang. It was the feeling you get when you let down the people you love. Why did he feel like this? It was a confusing feeling. The way she shook her head at him, she must have felt the same. Did she? Kelvin didn't understand it. He barely knew her. Last night was just an innocent train ride, talking to a nice person. Why did he instantly care why Analis seemed so dissatisfied with him?

# CHAPTER THREE

<u>Strike One</u>

After vaguely explaining to his father why he'd be back, Kelvin spotted Analis in the school's dirt lot, a couple of feet away from batting cages. He felt eyes on him from familiar faces, parents of teammates, and faculty members, all wanting to congratulate him on his game. But there wasn't any time for that. He was on a mission. He picked up his pace and jogged into a little run just as Analis reached the car she had arrived in.

"Hey!" Kelvin called out to Analis.

His cleats were making a loud crunching sound on the pavement just before reaching the dirt lot. Analis stopped short of her ride and turned around to face Kelvin. Her friends proceeded to enter the SUV they all arrived in. Other cars were pulling off and leaving, kicking up dirt and dust, making Analis shield her eyes.

"Nice game."

"Thank you… I didn't think I'd see you again."

"Well, it should have stayed that way."

Kelvin was confused by the comment. He inched closer to Analis and looked into her eyes, but she remained stoic. Like any innocent seventeen-year-old kid, Kelvin was clueless.

It's a known fact that girls mature far faster than boys. Hence, high girls often date a grade or two higher. It's not a known fact, but it is a theory. Analis met Kelvin's eyes and saw him trying to decipher what she meant nonverbally. She didn't have to dumb it down for him, but her gut instructed her to do so.

"You're a talented kid, Machado, but you're just like every other guy… You're a for everybody."

*Ohh.* "She must have seen me with Carrie," Kelvin internally said to himself. *Ohhhhh.* She explained her *situationship* to Kelvin, but he hadn't disclosed anything about having a girlfriend. Analis was a hopeless romantic like him. Wait, no. He was with Carrie. He wasn't hopeless. How could he? They were currently *goals* for everyone else. Carrie was a 10 out of 10. There's no way he fell under the hopeless romantic. *Hope* and *less* didn't belong together when it came to him. So why, all of a sudden, did he feel this enormous knot in his stomach? His palms felt as sweaty as ever, and his heartbeat increased by the femtosecond as he stood and watched Analis give him a crooked smile before getting into her ride.

About a half hour later, Kelvin and Sandy walked into the restaurant Sophia's Cafe, owned by Kelvin's uncle French. French, real name *Francelin,* wasn't Kelvin's uncle per se. He was, in fact, Sandy's cousin. But Hispanics have the tradition of calling their parents cousins tío and tía (uncle and aunt) because they are raised like uncles and aunts. French was not only Kelvin's uncle but also his Godfather.

French was on the slimmer side with a very animated personality. Loud, funny, and very expressive. One was never confused about how French felt in a specific situation. His skin complexion was a shade darker than Sandy's; he kept his haircut low and a clean-shaved face.

Although all the food was freshly cooked and prepared, Sophia's Cafe was traditionally meant to be a grab-and-go type of restaurant. Their menu was full of hot sandwiches ranging from simple ham and cheeses to *Cubans, Chimis* (Dominican genre burgers), and New York's very own chop cheese. Designed and painted on the wall, the menu faced you upon entering the relatively small establishment. *Pastelitos* ranging from ham and cheese, chicken, and ground beef were pre-made and placed in a transparent heater near the front counter, although French and his partner spent all day cooking *pastelitos* since those were always in high demand.

Hot sandwiches and *pastelitos* were hardly the only items on the menu. Other items included chicken wings, French fries, onion rings, salads, salmon, *bola de yuca* (another Dominican type of food), breakfast sandwiches, coffee, sodas, and organic juices.

French was behind the counter, attending to a customer. Sandy and Kelvin sat at one of Sophia's cafe's only dine-in tables, eating Cuban sandwiches.

"So, what time is your next game?" Sandy asked.

"At 4:45 on Wednesday."

"You let that three-two slider go in the fourth. It was a close pitch from my angle."

*Here we go again. He's always got something to say.*

"But you had a better look at it. Good job getting on the base. That pitcher was tough. I hear he's going straight to draft. He's projected to go in the second round. He couldn't get you out." Sandy added. "I think you're reaching the point where you no longer need my baseball advice."

"Dad, come on. I'll always need your baseball advice."

"That's what makes a good ball player. He never stops learning."

Kelvin smiled as he took another bite into his *Cuban*.

"So, who was that girl I saw you go after? *La Dominican, oh es Boricua*?"

"She's both… She's a friend, I guess."

"A friend?" Sandy asked with a smirk on his face. "I thought you only liked *gringitas*."

Kelvin sucked his teeth before taking the final bite of his Cuban.

"But for real, Kelvin, who is she?"

Kelvin finished chewing his food and finished his red Dominican soda. His father patiently waited for his response.

"I met her last night on the train ride over here."

Sandy's eyes opened wide in amazement.

"And she came to see you?"

"I don't know… But she was there."

"And what about Carrie?"

"What about her? We're still together."

"I mean, did she see you go after that other girl?"

*Shit! I hadn't thought of that.* Kelvin's pale-faced, worried look told his father all he needed to know. Sandy finishes the rest of his Cuban.

"Don't worry about it," Sandy said with a smirk. "She probably didn't see anything. If she did, I'm sure you can come up with a good explanation."

Sandy finished the rest of his soda and studied Kelvin's face, wondering if Carrie had seen him going after Analis. Sandy switched topics to distract his son from focusing on a girl.

"So, did you tell your mother you plan on moving back in after the school year?"

"Yeah. She wants to know if I'm going to Central after Jonathan leaves or if you'll pay for Lasalle or Hendrcken since the rumor is they want me after their short stops leave."

"Do you want to know why I wanted you and your brother to play for public schools like I did instead of private schools?"

"The culture and toughness," Kelvin interjected.

"The culture, yes. Even though there's not much Dominican or inner-city culture in your school, you're both better players than I was. I had the potential to be in the Hall of Fame. So, if my sons can outshine all these other kids in prep and private schools coming from public schools, then sky's the limit. Obviously, this sport is a team sport, and I always want you to be great teammates instead of individuals. But if you can be the captains of your respective teams and put up great numbers against these stacked schools, the number of opportunities would be endless… I mean, look at your brother with multiple D-1 offers. Yours are coming. Just like your brother, you being the reason a public school knocks off those powerhouse private schools, you'll play for the college you want."

Kelvin smirked at his father's encouraging analysis.

"So, no Private School then?" Kelvin sarcastically asked, knowing the answer.

Sandy playfully threw his used napkin at Kelvin and chuckled.

"But for real, Kelvin. I believe in character first. I don't want to sound like a broken record, but your grandmother did her best with me. I went to public school, and we competed against all the private and top upper-class public schools. One thing that I noticed was that most of those kids were and acted like entitled spoiled punks. Me and my teammates we were grounded. We had to be. We came from lower class, and most of the time, we lived in single-parent homes, worrying about whether mom could make ends meet. Instead of turning to the streets, like most of our friends, we stayed grounded and rode out whatever storm we were going through. Everything we saw in our neighborhoods prepped us for the real world. We didn't have Mommy and Daddy's money to save us. We had to do that on our own… I'm proud of the young men you and your brother have become.

Just like I told him a year ago, sitting right here, whatever you wanna do, I won't stop you, and I'll support you."

Kelvin couldn't contain his smirk.

Honestly, he was happy that his father was always there and was more effective than his grandfather. Kelvin and Jonathan couldn't have asked for a better role model, even though Sandy hardly saw himself as one.

"I'll decide after Jonathan's senior night after we play his team."

Now Sandy is the one who couldn't contain his smirk.

"I know where you're going. You ain't gotta confirm my feelings...."

"Did Jonathan tell Vanity he's picking Miami over Rutgers and URI?" Kelvin asked.

"I don't know. What I want to know is, did you tell Carrie that you're leaving West?"

---

Vanity wrapped her arms around her knees, tucking them into her chest. She sat on her front steps next to Jonathan, who had just delivered the devastating verbal blow. The sun had fully set, and a slight breeze was in west Cranston, Rhode Island. Vanity's parents' mini-mansion didn't have a single tree in front of the yard, so the air always felt a bit brisker at her home than at others.

She wore a pair of black shorts and a crewneck grey sweatshirt with West High printed in red letters on the chest part of the sweater. Jonathan wore light grey sweatpants and a plain black long-sleeve shirt.

In her limiting lighting street, Vanity stared straight ahead at the house facing hers. Jonathan chose to stay silent for now, allowing Vanity to process what he had just said to her. He knew whatever he tried to say next wouldn't help.

"So, Miami then?" Vanity asked although it was more of a confirmation statement.

"Yeah."

"Why Miami? Out of all the schools, why there?"

Vanity slightly tilted her head, now locking eyes with Jonathan.

"Why so far away from me?" Vanity asked again. "Miami is a great baseball school. Don't you think you'll shine more at URI, BC, or Rutgers?"

"It's not about shining more, babe... It's that Miami is where I was destined to be at."

"Why?"

Vanity now had tears in her eyes. Not bothering to fight them back, a couple of tears started to run down her face.

"When my father got traded to Boston and spent most of his life in triple-A playing in Pawtucket, every-thing turned to shit. We were the happiest when he played and started in Miami... I feel like life will be better in Miami," Jonathan said.

Vanity started to wipe away some tears.

"Do you understand that you're not your father? The fact that he and your mom divorced has nothing to do with the change of scenery and professional status... You understand that, right?"

Jonathan chose not to answer.

"Why don't you come down to Miami with me? You can transfer there after a year."

Vanity scoffed. "I'm not going to Miami, Jonathan." Vanity rose to her feet. "If you wanted me to go down to Miami, you would have told me long ago that Miami was your targeted school."

Jonathan opened his mouth to speak, but nothing came out. Vanity turned around and started to walk towards her front door. Jonathan quickly rose off his feet. With one hand, he reached out to Vanity. When Vanity felt Jonathan's hand touching hers, she slapped it away.

Without turning around, she told Jonathan, "I need some space. I'll talk to you when I'm ready… Good night, Jonathan."

# JOURNAL ENTRY

*Our First Time*

*Kelvin*

"I never had sex before. This was my first time," she said. "So, since we just did this, and I never planned on doing this, we go together now."

Despite putting up a brave face, she begged me with her drowning eyes not to hurt her. She sat on my low dresser with her back pressed against my window.

Nobody prepares you for what comes after the first time you have sex, especially teenagers. We don't lay together under the covers and talk. We don't get to walk around naked, wrapped in sheets, and watch TV together. Last but not least, we don't do a second round. We just put our clothes back on as fast as possible, mainly because we hope not to get caught. So, in the end, we're left with awkward silence. Though she probably wouldn't escape the awkwardness, Carrie wasn't all for silence.

"I agree," I said. "You're my girl, and I'm your man."

She smiled from ear to ear, exposing her deep dimples and pearly white teeth. She wore those spandex-like black thigh-high shorts that drove me wildly crazy and a plain white T-shirt.

We were still at a loss for words. What do you say after your first time? My first initial thought was, was I big enough? Did she get a good look at it to determine if it was big enough? How many minutes did I last? If my mother found out I was doing this, she'd kill me.

I quickly walked over to my bedroom door and opened it before my father got home. He's a lot more understanding than my mother, but still, I didn't want to put Carrie in an awkward position.

When we arrived at the front of her house, her family was out back, seated on their back deck. I could smell burgers on the grille.

Good. Company. Maybe talking sports with her brother could get me talking like my usual self again, while her sister did the same with Carrie. As we walked up to the front door of her bricked-colored mini-mansion, she swiftly turned around, faced me, wrapped her arms around my neck, and kissed me hard.

I fell into the kiss, but my conciseness of knowing her parents could see us pulled me back. Her eyes landed on mine, and she said, "I love you, Kelvin."

———

As I lay on my bed, softly tossing a baseball up in the air and catching it, I couldn't help but think just how bad of a guy I was, well, am. I didn't say I love you back to her. And now, well now, for some reason, I can't stop thinking about Analis, the girl I met on the train.

How can life change this drastically in ten months? But in reality, all the signs were right there in front of me. I didn't feel those butterflies we all hear about when it came to Carrie. She wasn't the last face I pictured before I went to sleep. I mean, I care about her a lot, and I'm happy that I'm with her. But after seeing Analis there and how I reacted, did this make me a bad guy?

Oddly, Carrie hadn't texted me since my game. Did she actually see me run after Analis, as my father hinted? If so, I'm dreading what awaits me tomorrow.

# CHAPTER FOUR

<u>Strike Two</u>

Kelvin downed a couple of 500-milligram Tylenol tablets with a chug of water at his locker before homeroom started. As soon as he temporarily placed his bottled water on his locker's top shelf so he could transition his books from his backpack into his locker, the voice of the raging Vanity surprised him.

"Miami! You couldn't tell me he was headed to Miami, Kelvin?"

Kelvin closed his locker to make sure his eyes matched what his ears were hearing. Vanity was walking with a purpose directly toward him. She wore blue jean shorts, all-white tennis sneakers, and a navy blue crewneck sweater. Her hair was no-nonsense, up in a long ponytail, and she skipped the makeup for the day, showing how naturally beautiful she was.

"Why couldn't you warn me that your brother was going to Miami? I thought we were friends, Kelvin."

*Friends? We're friends?* Kelvin thought to himself. He just always took Vanity as his brother's girlfriend. The pounding headache prevented Kelvin from having his natural base in his voice. Some students gathered around in the hallway like some cheesy pre-teens show. *Why hasn't the bell for the homeroom rung yet?*

Vanity was now standing inches away from Kelvin. He could see the heartbreak in her eyes. The confident, popular, rich, and beautiful girl that every guy wanted and every young high school girl aspired to be suddenly looked like a wounded puppy.

"I didn't know about Miami, Vanity," Kelvin replied.

Vanity squinted her already slanted eyes. From afar, it appeared like she was sizing Kelvin up. She was trying to read him. But could she? She didn't know anything about him. All she knew was that Kelvin was her soon-to-be ex-boyfriend's younger brother and that he was a teammate of her current ex-boyfriend, Jackson.

Kelvin stared back at Vanity. He didn't know why. He wasn't trying to read her. He could honestly care less. This was Jonathan's mess. He had his own problems. And right now, his primary concern is getting rid of this headache before classes start.

"Look, Vanity. I didn't know where his head was. I ain't gonna front. Was Miami on his radar? Of course. That's where we both always wanted to go. I didn't know they were looking at him like that. I play here and live with my pops, and he goes to Central and lives with my moms. We don't really talk about baseball when we're together."

Vanity's eyes welled up with tears again. She looked left then right, trying to hold in tears. The large hall-ways were getting more crowded by the second. The last thing she wanted was for her classmates to see her lose control. She needed to be in control. She always needed to be in control. Kelvin felt bad. He did. His wide shoulders slumped, feeling a soft spot for Vanity's predicament.

"But aren't you happy for him, though?" Kelvin asked.

"Of course, I'm happy for your stupid brother," she replied after sucking her teeth. She was now making eye contact with Kelvin again. "It's just that I had planned for us to go to the same school."

"Can't you go with him to Miami?"

"Kelvin, it's too late. I have already been accepted by URI and Rutgers. We graduate in a few weeks."

"You can't apply late or transfer after a year? I mean-"

"Don't you get it, Kelvin?" Vanity raised her voice. There was heartbreak in her tone. "If he wanted me with him, he would have told me to apply there from the start."

Vanity shook her head, realizing there was no point to this.

"This is stupid. Look, I just came to see if you knew. That's all. I thought lying ran in the family."

Kelvin squinted his eyes in confusion. *Lying? What is she talking about?*

"Carrie is on her way to see you," Vanity said. "I hear you met some girl on a train."

Kelvin's eyes widen in complete shock. His heart started to race so fast it felt like it would pop out of his chest. Suddenly, the bell for homeroom rang.

"You bought yourself some time," Vanity said to him with a sad smile. "You better come up with an excuse."

# CHAPTER FIVE

Strike Three

Two periods had passed. English and Calculus had intensified Kelvin's headache. The Tylenol hadn't worked, and it was too soon to take another dose. So, walking into the school's enormous cafeteria would worsen his condition.

Kelvin hadn't uttered more than a couple dozen words throughout the day. He and Ryan didn't have class together until lunch, and he only shared the last school period with Carrie. So, staying quiet throughout the first two classes was a norm.

He pushed open the right side of the double door, entering the school's cafeteria, where the place was always loud. Today, of all days, felt deafening. The cafeteria looked like any other high school cafeteria. Even when the lights weren't turned on, numerous big windows illuminated the space, and countless long tables were positioned in rows in the cafeteria's center, left and right. The tile flooring looked like it was waxed weekly, the tan walls between the windows were always spotless, and the thermostat was always comfortable. Although it resembled a regular cafeteria, it looked a lot nicer than most public schools—another perk of attending a school in an upper-class part of the state. Lots of tax dollars are put back into the schools.

Some students of the school's athletic teams always sat together. But for the most part, the cafeteria was a mixture of students sitting together: first-year students, sophomores, juniors, seniors, athletes, non-athletics, artistic, non-artistic, short, tall, etc.

Carrie sat at the very end of the cafeteria, facing the entrance. She wore an oversized red sweatshirt and light crew fleece gym shorts, again exposing her strongly built athletic legs and her hair in a messy bun. She had purposely sat alone, waiting for Kelvin's arrival. Kelvin knew it as soon as he walked in. The two made eye contact instantly, and whatever appetite Kelvin had quickly vanished.

Without saying a word, Kelvin slid into the table and sat directly across from Carrie.

"So, how was your trip back home?" She didn't waste any time. "I heard it was interesting."

Kelvin's expression momentarily remained stoic and then showed guilt. "It's not what you think."

"Don't give me that," Carrie snapped back. Her tone was sharp and low, although there was no way another student could hear what they were talking about. But she knew news traveled fast throughout these hallways.

"How do you explain having a connection with another girl?"

Kelvin's guilt quickly turned to anger. *Connection.* That was the word Ryan used. Carrie stared into Kelvin's narrowed look. He wasn't present. His mind was elsewhere. The rage in Kelvin's eyes erased whatever anger or feeling of betrayal Carrie had on her expression. Her eyes now looked a bit bigger–softer, her face flushed, and there might have been a slight quiver on her bottom lip.

"It wasn't-" Kelvin picked up on Carrie's sudden feeling of betrayal. His voice turned softer. The last thing he wanted to do was to hurt Carrie. "It wasn't a connection, babe."

"How do you explain getting to know some girl during a long trip?"

*Shit. She's right. How do I explain this? Why did Ryan tell Carrie? I thought he was my boy.* Kelvin's mind was spiraling.

"Who is she, Kelvin?" Carrie asked with a plea in her tone.

"Nobody," he answered, looking Carrie square in the eyes. She's just someone who sat next to me during the trip home. Her sister put her in an uncomfortable situation, and she just wanted to pass the time until she got home."

"And you had to be the knight in shining armor?" Carrie's tone was now stern.

Like Kelvin, Carrie looked Kelvin squared in the eyes. She squinted for a few seconds before rising off the lunch table.

"I gotta go," Carrie said in a disgusted low tone.

Kelvin must have blinked about a thousand times. He started to stutter his words.

"Wait, what? Are we - are we - are we… good?"

Carrie kept her stare at Kelvin. She slowly shook her head before replying.

"No, Kelvin… We're not good."

Kelvin swallowed hard. He didn't want to make a production of this in front of the student body in the cafeteria, so he remained seated, gazing up at Carrie.

"What does that mean?"

"You'll figure it out," Carrie coldly replied.

She didn't bother giving Kelvin another second of eye contact, quickly turning around and walking out of the cafeteria.

# THE BREAKUP



Were we together? Were we broken up? The only way Carrie could have found out about Analis was through Ryan. Why? Why would he tell her? What was his angle?

I purposely avoided Ryan for the rest of the day. I didn't want to get into it with him, especially with this headache that didn't get any better. Luckily for me, he didn't stay after school to watch the girl's soccer team take on Toll Gate High.

I sat by myself at the end of the bottom bleachers, facing West's bench. The May afternoon sun was in full effect, and for the first time this season, the Western Cranston breeze wasn't a problem. For the first time this season, all the girls on the team didn't wear long-sleeve shirts under their jerseys or gloves, nor did they have to bounce around on the sideline to stay warm.

As a CM (Central midfielder), Carrie gracefully flowed through the pitch–her ponytail bouncing and rocking side to side with every jog and sprint. Because of her strong legs, she could efficiently run by defenders and shred tackles. Whenever the home team turned the ball over, she got back on defense without a problem. Today, it felt like she was playing on another gear. It looked like Carrie was a Ferrari, and the rest of the girls were Fords. Learning about Analis had a noticeable effect.

After the game, I remained seated on the bleachers until Carrie's coach finished talking to the team. Then, everyone stepped onto the turf field to congratulate the players.

When I stepped onto the field, I couldn't help but notice that more people were in attendance than I realized. I dodged and weaved my way through people, saying hellos to parents and students who had said hi to me first.

Damn, this headache is killing me.

I finally spotted Carrie hugging her sister at midfield and stepped closer. She must have felt my presence because she quickly glared at me. Still, with her arms wrapped around her sister's neck, her eyes pierced through mine from fifteen yards away, and she shook her head at me.

She didn't have to say it. We were done.

After not hearing or getting word from Carrie the following day, I woke up to a few text messages.

I can't believe you did this. - Carrie

I heard what happened. - Amanda.

Is it true? - George.

I can't look at you the same anymore. - Carrie

When I stepped out of my room, my dad had already left for work. I showered and got dressed in sweatpants, a hoodie, and a fitted baseball hat. My father must have gotten up earlier than usual because, on top of our stove, there was a takeout breakfast container of Mangu (Mashed plantains with Dominican fried salami, two fried eggs, and onions.)

*Today wasn't going to completely suck.*

After devouring my breakfast, I slipped on my backpack and headed out the front door. The sky was gloomy, and the temperature had dropped about ten degrees from yesterday. Classic New England spring.

The text messages from Carrie continued throughout my walk to school.

It's the fact that I had to hear it from someone else that bugs me even more.

I thought I meant something to you.

*Will it make a difference if I reply? She seems angrier today than yesterday.*

> You really fucked up, Kelvin.

*Yup. She's clearly angrier today.*

I still had that headache from yesterday. Maybe it wasn't entirely the same, but it was close enough to not even engage in a back-and-forth through a phone screen. My father always said if it's going to stress you out, it isn't worth it.

> I heard what happened. Are you good? Where are you? - Ryan

*Fuck him. He's the last person I wanna see right now.*

I needed to talk to Carrie face-to-face. She was definitely worth it. I wasn't about to leave things like this.

As I walked into school, I felt the eyeballs on me. It wasn't unusual. I was the star shortstop whose older brother broke up the Golden couple who happened to be with the most desirable girl in school. But the stares felt different. There was satisfaction behind those glares as I walked through the halls.

> Get your shit out of my locker after homeroom. - Carrie

> Don't call or text me after this. - Carrie

I stopped in the middle of the hallway and stared at my phone.

*Damn. It wasn't a guess anymore. It was confirmed. We were OVER over.*

# CHAPTER SIX

The Boys

"So, it's a wrap for you too?" Jason asked. Jason had been sitting on the top step of Jonathan's front porch on this mid-sixties-degree evening. Jason was eighteen years old, turning nineteen in a couple of months. The URI basketball player had just completed his first year and had just gotten back home to enjoy his summer vacation.

Jason was Damian's cousin. He was good-looking, African American, tall and lean, standing at six feet six inches with a low haircut. His facial hair was finally starting to come in. What once was a light shade on his chin and the area between the nose and upper lip turned into a mustache and goatee. He wore a pair of diamond stud earrings, dark-colored fleece shorts, basketball sneakers, and a light hoodie.

"I don't know," Jonathan replied.

Jonathan was dressed similarly to Jason, accessorized with a baseball cap. Then it hit him. The wording almost went over his head. Sitting on the middle step of his front porch, Jonathan looked up, puzzled.

"Too?… You said too."

"What?" Jason asked.

"You asked, so It's a wrap for you too."

"Ohhhhh. Yeah. Kelvin. I was talking about Kelvin. His girl broke up with him."

"Carrie? For real?"

"Yeah. Then it looked like he had a panic attack because he went to the hospital, blaming it on some headache."

Before Jonathan could ask, Damian, who had been sitting on a chair on the porch, inches away from the front door, spoke up.

"It WAS a headache, Jason. He always gets headaches."

Damian was Jonathan and Kelvin's eighteen-year-old stepbrother. Damian's father, Michael, had married Kelvin and Jonathan's mother two years after their parents divorced when they were just seven. Damian was African American, clean-cut, handsome, and tall, standing at six feet five inches. The Providence College commit shooting guard already had an NBA-ready body, weighing two hundred and fifteen pounds. His voice matched his appearance. It was strong and deep, like a true basketball team leader. Since their mother and father's marriage, the three young men shared a little sister, Junelie, a pretty twelve-year-old girl.

Jonathan stood up on his feet, worried and perplexed. "When was this?"

"Like three hours ago," Damian replied. "You were hitting with Anthony at the institute. Your mom took him."

The front porch light shined directly above Damian, making him appear sage as his long frame sat on the chair above the others seated on the steps.

Gregory, a fast-talking Dominican who had just turned seventeen and one of Kelvin's childhood best friends, had been sitting next to Jason the entire time. Gregory was on the lighter shade of the Caribbean Islander skin tone. He sported a "Temp haircut" that one could describe as a relaxed taper that fades around the temples, creating a unique and stylish look. In Gregory's case, he styled his temp with perfect medium-trimmed curls. He was averagely built, standing around five foot ten. Weighing around a hundred and eighty-five pounds, Gregory carried lots of power on the baseball field and looked the part, often wearing fitted enough shirts to show muscles in his biceps and forearms.

There was no confusion about where Gregory came from. Like Damian, Jason, Jonathan, and Kelvin, he often eloquently mixed slang with proper speech. In contrast to Damian's commanding tone, Jason's deep yet relaxed voice, Jonathan's hint of confrontation in his smooth voice, and Kelvin's even-keeled tone, Gregory's voice was a bit high-pitched.

"I keep telling him to get his head checked out. My mom's cousin had an aneurysm a few years back. Come to think of it, yo, Jonathan, you be getting headaches too. Why don't you both get your heads checked out?" Gregory asked.

"I did before… I was diagnosed with migraines."

Suddenly, Betsy's white SUV pulled into the driveway of the two-storied home, which sat on the border of Providence and Cranston, Rhode Island.

Jonathan shifted his body, directing his gaze at the well-illuminated driveway while the rest of the boys' eyes darted at Betsy's SUV.

"There goes your mom right there," Jason said.

Betsy and Kelvin got out of the car. Both were wearing sweatpants. Betsy wore a crewneck sweatshirt with her hair tied in a ponytail. Kelvin wore a fitted, long-sleeved, plain shirt and a baseball cap.

Betsy was a young mother at thirty-six years of age. Like many Dominican women in their mid-thirties, Betsey didn't look a day older than twenty-seven despite having three children. She was short, standing at five foot one, and that's being generous. Her dark, wavy hair reached down to the middle of her back. Her brown skin always appeared to be healthier than most women. Despite experiencing hardships early in her life, she still had a certain twinkle in her eyes that most young people have, making it hard for others to believe that she could be a mother of two young men in their late teens.

"Yooooo. What's up with you? What they say?" Damian asked, rising off his chair.

"A waste of time, bro," Kelvin replied as he made his way to the front porch. "They gave me an IV but couldn't do anything else because they said the neurologists on call were all tied up."

Betsy walked ahead of Kelvin. "Junelie and Michael aren't back yet?" She asked Jonathan.

"No."

"Betsy, Tashia made dinner. We didn't know what time you'd be back." Damian said.

Betsy exhaustedly smirked. Her body was tired from sitting around in a crowded emergency room only to leave without a single answer.

"That sounds great," Betsy replied.

"Mash potatoes and salmon," Damian added.

"Even better," Betsy said before entering the front door.

Jonathan sat back down on the bottom step. Kelvin walked up the stairs and sat on the empty chair beside Damian.

"How you feeling?" Damian asked.

"I'm okay."

"If he wasn't okay, he'd still be in the hospital, admitted, waiting for those neurologists," Gregory added. "Anyway, what you gonna do now that you're good?"

"Do about what?" Kelvin asked. He felt drowsy since walking up from the morphine medication through his IV. He sagged in the chair more than sat in it.

"He's talking about school. You staying at West or coming to Central after your brother leaves?" Jason asked.

"Ohh. I don't know."

"Carrie broke up with you. You think your boy Ryan told her what happened between you and that girl on the train, and you've got nothing left at West. Why stay?" Jason added.

"He's right," Jonathan chimed in.

"Facts," Damian added.

"I see the logic, but don't go to Central," Gregory said. "You got this whole identity crisis thing going on. You got like a handful of Spanish kids and another handful of black kids in your school, and all these white boys surround you. Then you come here on the weekends and off days from baseball and chill with us because we're your people, but you also like your classmates and teammates, but you wanna stay true to the culture too. But then your right-hand man in school is that Ryan kid. So, you feel like he played you, and you got nobody left, and I get it. But don't use that as an excuse to leave a good school and come to the hood."

"West is a public school just like Central," Jonathan said.

"Yeah, but West is way better in terms of education. It's probably even better than mine," Gregory replied.

"That's cap, bro," Jonathan said. His voice rose. Not in anger, but in a way, one does when a debate is about to start after hearing something one doesn't like.

"Nah. I ain't capping. Look what's going on with the teacher shortage. Especially the schools in the hood. Then ones that are left act like they don't care or they actually don't care." Now, Greogory's voice rose, matching Jonathan's tone. "Not everyone is you, Jonathan, Damian, or Jason, where you get a D-1 scholarship out of an inner city public school. People like me, we gotta go to a better high school to get a scholarship to a good college," Gregory explained.

"And West provides that?" Jonathan asked in a passive-aggressive way.

"YES. Yo, that school has special classes and programs to get you ahead and prepped for college. They even got law classes and go to mock trials."

"Mock trials?" Damian asked, confused.

"Yeah," Gregory replied

"What's a mock trial?" Damian asked.

"A mock trial is a competition when the kids taking law classes in their school compete against other high school kids from other schools who study the same thing. They go to a real courthouse and present their case and everything before a real judge, too."

"Damn." Damian was shocked. "I didn't know schools do that."

"That's because you go to Central. These schools—Central, Hope, Mount—are forgotten about. The private schools get the advantages. The public schools located in the rich part of the State get those perks. Kelvin goes to one of those schools that gets those perks. Why would he want to leave all that to come to a school in the hood?"

"You go to a school in Cranston, too, Greg. Does your school have those advantages?" Jonathan asked.

"Some of them, yeah. East is kind of on the poor side of Cranston, but we got more perks than any public school in Providence. And we're way more diverse than West."

Jonathan smirked, feeling where Gregory was getting to. Damian started to laugh, and Jason started to shake his head before bursting out with a loud laugh. Gregory locked eyes with Kelvin, who was now standing upright. Seconds later, Kelvin joined the guys laughing, leaving Gregory clueless.

*What the hell is so funny?* Gregory thought to himself. The laughter went on almost a full minute before the boys composed themselves.

"Yo, you didn't have to go so hard in the paint. Just say you want Kelvin to go to East with you," Jason said.

"I'm saying, yo. All you had to do was say that," Jonathan added.

"I think Park East is a good choice." The voice came from behind Kelvin and Damian. The boys laughed so much that neither noticed Betsy standing at the doorway. Betsy had a smirk on her face. Like the actual neighborhood cool mom to the teens on her street, it warmed her heart when the boys talked intellectually. "Park East is a good school. They have classes that keep you engaged in the classroom. So the drop off from West to East won't be much. And you get to be on the same baseball team as Gregory... I don't know what your father told you, but Jonathan's reason for going to Central is because your father lived in Providence, too, at the time. But now, since he lives in Cranston, you only have two choices. East or stay at West."

"There's another question after that," Jonathan added.

"What's that?" Betsy asked.

"Gregory and Alex are also shortstops who rotate from second base to short every other inning. If Kelvin goes to East, between him, Alex, and Gregory, who's gonna play short, and who's gonna play second base?... Finally, who's gonna ride the bench or kick the third baseman to the bench?"

# CHAPTER SEVEN

Senior Night

K elvin had been upset with Ryan for recklessly telling his girlfriend about Analis because he knew news traveled fast through the high school hallways.

It's been two weeks since the breakup, and Kelvin hadn't seen Carrie much. Purposely, of course. The two knew how to detour their routes to their classrooms despite agreeing to stay friends. *Friends.* As if that could happen when at least one broken heart hadn't been mended. Kelvin didn't give it too much thought. Baseball and deciding where he'd attend school come September preoccupied his mind.

The Friday and Saturday nights that were once meant to be with Carrie were substituted with hitting and fielding sessions with Sandy, Jonathan, and their friend Alex at Sandy's indoor complex. Sandy always played the Hip-Hop music he liked growing up, often rapping lyrics as he showed his sons that he still had it as he fielded ground balls and hit baseballs off the 90+ mile-per-hour pitching machine.

"Dad, what old man song is this now?" Jonathan asked, putting on his batting gloves.

"What's the matter with you? You never heard of the Wu-Tang Clan? Method Man?"

"It's super old."

"Way better than the garbage that you all listen to now."

"That beat is trash."

"At least we can understand what he's saying, unlike that mixture of crying and mumbling that's in now."

This was the norm. Sandy proceeded to teach his kids what he felt was real music, on top of polishing their baseball skills.

---

When Jonathan's senior night came around, Kelvin had done enough to preoccupy his mind. Summer break was right around the corner, so his email inbox was flooded with messages from his summer travel team. School finals were approaching, and seeing Carrie in the hallways was a bit easier now. He and Ryan resolved their issues.

Ryan had taken full responsibility for telling his long-term girlfriend about what transpired between Kelvin and Analis. In a sense, Kelvin understood. Had he still been with Carrie, the hypothetical possibility of sharing what happened with Carrie between Ryan and another girl wouldn't be outside the realm of reality. But the guy code in him knew he'd never do such a thing. Instead of holding that against his friend, he completely forgave him. The two have been friends since the seventh grade when they first met as rivals in Little League when West Cranston squared up again at Kelvin's Washington Park before becoming teammates in their freshman year when Kelvin attended West.

When Kelvin and his father decided West was the school he needed to play for, he wasn't well received. Clicks and strong friendships had already been formed by the kids who grew up in the Western Part of Cranston. Bonds formed over sleepovers, camps, Little League baseball, middle school alliances, and vows to play together throughout high school were formed and agreed upon before Kelvin's arrival. So when Kelvin outshined everyone, including every single varsity player during tryouts, winning the coveted shortstop position as a freshman, it was as though the outsider had broken a code and a sacred bond. This wasn't supposed to happen. A senior wasn't supposed to lose his starting shortstop position to a freshman, and a junior varsity player wasn't supposed to miss out on a roster spot because a varsity player was bumped down to make room for Kelvin. Although not a single word of malice was uttered toward Kelvin, most of the guys on the team made him feel like an outsider during his freshman and sophomore years before finally warming up to him during his junior year.

Kelvin's quiet yet standoffish attitude didn't help

the situation, but he never lost sight of what was most important: baseball. He never let the cold shoulders affect his play. His lone-wolf demeanor, keeping most of his teammates at bay, prevented the team from perfectly gelling off the field. But to the naked eye, when he stepped onto the field, the team appeared to have the best chemistry in the state. The only guys who welcomed him with open arms from day one were Ryan and Darius.

He needed to let bygones be bygones because tonight was the big night. May 25th, Metropolitan West versus Central High School. Kelvin Machado versus Jonathan Machado.

Being the younger brother of the senior star short-stop, Kelvin participated in his brother's ceremony, posing for pictures alongside Betsy, Sandy, his younger brother, six-year-old Amir, his younger sister, twelve-year-old Junelie, and step-brother Damian.

Despite being members of the same family, Sandy, Betsy, Junelie, and Damian wore Jonathan's team's colors, black and gold. Kelvin understood you only get one senior night, so he didn't mind. It fueled his competitiveness, knowing none of his family members rooted for him. That wasn't true. This was something Kelvin created in his head to give him more motivation.

The stage was set after every senior presented his parents with flowers, and all the family pictures were taken. The night was a comfortable 74 degrees; the base-ball field lights shined bright, and the outfield fence was decorated with poster-like pictures of each senior on the team.

While Central High School neighbored an academically gifted high school in Classical, both schools were in a *shady* area on the corner of Fricker and Cranston Street. The two schools were smacked between two of the most dangerous streets in Providence, the other being Broad Street. When you walked East onto Broad Street, there was a 711 gas station and a Burger King beside it. Homeless people, drunks, and drug addicts almost always preoccupied the front lots. It was just a taste of the everyday life of the average kid living in a broken city.

Central High School's baseball field wasn't any different. It was across the street from one of Providence's housing projects. Despite the location, this senior night was a packed house. Both the home and away bleachers were full. Those who weren't lucky enough to find a bleacher seat brought their travel chairs, while the rest in attendance stood and watched behind the outfield, first base, and third base fences.

Just before the start of the game, Kelvin sat quietly inside the dugout, wearing his batting helmet while slipping on his batting gloves. As he watched Jonathan and the rest of his teammates take the field in their white uniforms with yellow pinstripes, Kelvin couldn't help but notice coaches and players from Park East in attendance posted behind the left-field fence. When he shifted his gaze to the right, he saw one of the State's top private college prep schools, La Salle's head coach, and some of its players, including his cousin Anthony, wearing their team's burgundy hats, standing behind the right field fence. That's when it hit him. This was much more than just a baseball game. This was an event. In Kelvin's case, this was an audition.

Whoever said baseball was a dying sport was probably right. Kelvin wondered if fans from more popular sports like football and basketball now crossed over to baseball due to those leagues' political stances, hence the growing popularity of baseball. The lack of speed of the sport and how the sport's biggest fans were past forty years old may be accurate, but baseball was alive on the night of May 25th, watching the Machado brothers go head-on.

———

To Kelvin's surprise, he was batting leadoff (1ˢᵗ). Ever since he stepped foot on the baseball field on the Varsity team in ninth grade, he consistently batted second. *Why did coach switch me and Tommy in the lineup?*

The field lights appeared brighter than usual as Kelvin walked toward the batter's box, and there was a rare sense of anticipation within the crowd. Kelvin and his team wore their away uniforms, which consisted of grey pants and a red jersey with the world West across the chest in black. Kelvin accessorized his away jersey with red batting gloves and his red elbow guard.

When Kelvin finally stepped into the batter's box, he quickly directed his gaze at Jonathan. Jonathan wore gold cleats for his special night, black wrist tape, and his trusted all-black infielder's glove on his left hand. Jonathan made eye contact with Kelvin and gave him a head nod. Kelvin felt his shoulders slightly sag with relief and resisted the urge to smirk. *Oh, it's on.* He welcomed the attention this game was getting. He felt excited about what he and his brother were about to do.

When Jonathan's teammate, pitcher Pugsy, threw the first pitch, Kelvin wasted no time. With one bat swing, he hit the ball a hard line drive to shallow center field. Knowing he secured the base hit, Kelvin half-sprinted toward the first base with his eyes on the center fielder, securing the baseball off the grass.

The Metropolitan West fans clapped and cheered, momentarily drawing Kelvin's attention. When Kelvin directed his look toward his team's supporters, he saw *her*. Carrie was sitting next to Vanity on the top bleacher seats. For the first time in a long time, Carrie wasn't in sweatpants and a sweat sweatshirt. She wore her hair in a bun, light blue jeans, and a white top.

Vanity and Jonathan had worked things out, which showed in her pricey and preppy wardrobe. It's funny when you really know someone; you can almost tell how someone feels based on their attire. For an entire week after Vanity learned about Jonathan's Miami plans, she wore T-shirts, sneakers, and jeans and didn't wear any makeup.

Carrie's jeans fit her athletic body like a glove, and her blouse—not a T-shirt, but a blouse—exposed her feminine shape in her strong core.

*Focus, Kelvin. Focus.*

Kelvin redirected his attention back to the game. Bugsy shook off a few pitches before settling on the pitch he wanted to throw Kelvin's teammate, Tommy. During that process, Kelvin took some steps to his right to get a good lead off first base. In a mid-squat stance, his eyes were pierced at Pugsy, anticipating a throw over to first base or a pitch.

Kelvin knew Pugsy had trouble throwing over to the

first base and had committed a few errors throughout the season. His heart would race in normal circumstances, fearing getting picked off, but he knew Pugsy didn't want to risk making an error on senior night. So, as Pugsy's leg rose for his windup, Kelvin took off in a full sprint toward second base to steal second base. His cleats kicked up dirt with every forceful stride, and his arms swung back and forth. He noticed Jonathan quickly make his way to cover second base, anticipating the throwover from his catcher. While keeping his stride, Kelvin quickly peaked at Central's catcher, who was getting ready to throw the ball over to Jonathan.

*Just two more steps.*

Kelvin quickly and internally counted to two and slid into second base. He felt his hands land and grab onto second base just a split second before feeling Jonathan's glove on his left bicep. When Kelvin glanced up, Jonathan held his glove up with the baseball inside for the middle-aged umpire to see.

The umpire spread his hands while yelling, "SAFE."

Still lying on the infield dirt at second base, Kelvin heard the cheers from the West crowd. He watched his brother throw the ball to Pugsy before rising off the dirt onto his feet. His confidence before the game intensified after he got his base hit and stole second on the next pitch. He couldn't help but smirk as he began to dust off the dirt from his jersey.

"You know you were out, right?" Jonathan said, inching closer to Kelvin.

Kelvin continued to dust and wipe away the dirt off his jersey and pants. There was a happy and warm feeling growing inside him. It was the feeling of belonging. Jonathan was the star recruit. Jonathan appeared in the Little League World Series when he was twelve. Jonathan was the one who had the *Major League All-Star* trajectory. It was hard enough getting a base hit off the hard-throwing two-hundred pound, Pugsy. It was harder stealing a base, beating the throw off Notre Dame's recruit and the State's top catcher. Kelvin was on top of the world, and this was only the top of the first inning.

"You wish," Jonathan replied with a smirk.

"This inning is gonna be your only highlight."

"Over-under, I hit for the cycle."

"Ha," Jonathan laughed out loud."Did you cop some weed from someone across the street before the game started?"

"I'm at least going three for four tonight," Kelvin confidently stated.

"You're going two for four. Your second hit is gonna be a cheap blooper into the outfield."

"Oh, the blooper will be over your head for my third hit."

The two brothers chuckled briefly as Jonathan backpedaled into his shortstop position.

———

Bottom of the 1$^{st}$ with two outs with the bases empty.

———

Jonathan had managed to work a 3-2 count against none other than Jackson. Their feud over Vanity had ended long ago, but Jackson still hated Jonathan's guts. Jackson had struck out the first two batters with just six pitches. He didn't have to throw the next pitch in the strike zone. He could have easily thrown a splitter out of the strike zone to make Jonathan chase.

*He's throwing it inside.*

Kelvin knew Jackson wanted to challenge and beat Jonathan. Anticipating the next pitch, Kelvin took two steps toward his left. Kelvin knew Jackson wanted to throw his favorite pitch, the circle change-up that landed right on the bottom of the strike zone. It was an impossible pitch to barrel up. However, because of Jonathan's bat speed and the strength of his forearms, he could pull his hands inside and hit the ball the opposite way.

Once Jackson started his delivery, Kelvin got light, standing on the ball of his feet in a slight squat. When Jackson's pitch made contact with Jonathan's bat, the sound of the crack of the bat echoed. The ball was hit hard. Jonathan took off running on contact. Kelvin quickly reacted and took two more steps to his left. The ball skipped off the grass just past the pitcher's mound. Jonathan had a base hit for sure. The ball would take another hard bounce just by second base before rolling into the outfield. Jonathan was sure of it. That was until Kelvin got to the ball by stretching his arm as far as he could. Instead of stopping when he felt the ball in his glove, he went forward with his momentum, making him take another step. And in a swift motion, he spun around as he transferred the ball out of his glove into his throwing hand. Finally, Kelvin threw the ball to his first baseman milliseconds before Jonathan could reach first base.

The first base umpire balled up his fist and threw a downward air punch, singling Jonathan out. The *oohs* and *ahhs* coming from the crowd were deafening, making it hard for Jonathan to hear the umpire say out. It wasn't until Jonathan saw Kelvin and the rest of his teammates start to jog off the field that it hit him that his little brother just made a highlight play against him.

"Yeah! There you go, baby!" Ryan yelled out, continuing his jog toward the dugout.

When Kelvin reached the dugout and saw the smirk on his coach's face, it finally hit him. His coach wanted Kelvin to hit lead-off so he could get more at-bats. He wanted Kelvin to shine when the lights shined brightest. He truly believed in Kelvin. It made him feel important. He instantly felt more than just a player. Coach had his back.

When Kelvin entered the dugout, his teammates were more than excited. They were electrified at what transpired on the field.

"LETS GOOOOO!"

"Let's keep it going!"

"HELL YEAH!"

"Let's go West!"

The exhilarated teens due up to bat quickly grabbed their bats and put on their helmets. Kelvin quietly sat on the bench, trying to soak in this high.

When Ryan entered the dugout, he reached out toward Kelvin. Smirking, Kelvin reached out, and the two performed a classic teammate handshake that ended with a slight man hug.

"Hey, that's what I'm talking about," Ryan said, sitting beside Kelvin. "That was smooth. It was like watching Jeremy Peña."

Kelvin quietly smirked, keeping his gaze on the field and watching his brother take the field. Oddly enough, his energy wasn't matching his teams. Like a true friend and teammate, Ryan picked up on it.

"Hey, what's up with you?" Ryan asked.

*Oh, you're the best teammate I ever had and a great friend, but I think I'm leaving the school. So that means I'm leaving you to play with my best friends at our rival Park East.*

Kelvin took his eyes off the field, rotated his head left, looked the excited Ryan in the eyes, and lied.

"Nothing. Just focused on the game."

# CHAPTER EIGHT

Senior Night

I t was now the bottom of the seventh inning, and Metropolitan West had a 5-2 lead. Kelvin had the game of his life, going four for four with a double and three RBIs, including a monster home run over the center field wall. The stat line didn't stop there. On defense, he assisted on ten outs, including five double plays. However, the job wasn't done. Central had runners on first and second base, and Jonathan was up to bat with two outs.

Despite having a bad game, going 0 for three, Kelvin knew his brother could change the score and the game's momentum with one swing of the bat.

Darius, the closer, one of three minorities, and the only black kid on the team, had faced Jonathan half a dozen times over his high school and travel ball career.

The senior was a big kid, standing at six feet one and weighing almost two hundred pounds, and dominated most batters. Jonathan wasn't one of them. He was perfect, six for six, including two home runs off Darius, causing Kelvin to panic as he silently shifted around at his shortstop spot.

Kelvin felt his heart race as he watched his brother enter the batter's box. Suddenly, he felt hotter than usual, and the sweat caused his jersey to stick to his chest and back. Once again, Kelvin got ready as Darius threw a pitch at Jonathan.

Ball one.

*Damn.*

Kelvin lightly kicked around some dirt while Darius tried to settle down on the pitcher's mound.

*Come on, Darius. You got this.*

Kelvin got into his ready position again, watching Darius throw another pitch.

Ball two.

There was a loud murmur in the home crowd. Kelvin heard the moans and groans from his crowd.

Kelvin kept his eyes on Jonathan as he kicked around some more dirt. This time, he was more animated about it. He could see Junelie and his youngest sibling, Amir, standing directly behind the fence behind the home plate.

*When did Amir get here? Did his mom bring him? Or did he ride with Dad?*

Amir wore a red T-shirt and a red baseball cap. Like many other times, he was present for his brother's games. People often joked about how Amir was born on the baseball field. Ever since he was a year and a half old, he carried a light baseball bat around during games. Six-year-old Amir was a young phenom. With a father like Sandy and two oldest brothers who always took him to practice, he was far more advanced than even eight- and nine-year-olds.

Kelvin noticed the joy on Amir's face. So many times, Kelvin and Jonathan trained Amir on where to be on the infield, how to track the ball, and what angles to take on a hard and soft hit ball.

Kelvin knew Darius had to throw his next pitch in the strike zone, and Jonathan would put a good swing on it. He had already made a spectacular defensive play against his brother. His gut told him he'd have to make another if Jonathan didn't hit a home run.

Darius got into his wind-up and threw his pitch. Jonathan was ready and put a good swing on the ball. The ball jumped off Jonathan at an exit velocity well over a hundred miles and an hour. It was a line drive traveling three feet above Kelvin's head. In a quick reaction, Kelvin jumped up as high as he could and caught the ball in the air.

The ball was caught before Jonathan could complete his fourth step in his sprint. The crowd's oohs and ahhs were louder this time, and Kelvin's teammates' roar quickly followed.

When Kelvin landed on both feet, he glanced at Jonathan, who was already taking off his batting gloves and hanging his head, clearly disappointed. Would Kelvin have reacted differently if he had been in Jonathan's shoes? Being senior night, the state's top player, facing your younger brother on your night, and you lose? Of course, he'd react the same way. This was supposed to be Jonathan's night, and Kelvin had a part in ruining it for him.

Before his thrilled teammates could reach him, Kelvin jogged over to Jonathan, who had been slowly walking toward his dugout on the first base side of the field.

"Yo. Yo!" Kelvin said, trying to get Jonathan's attention.

During this bittersweet moment, Kelvin's heart broke for his brother. Jonathan took off his helmet, glancing over at Kelvin. Before he could say anything, Kelvin hugged him.

What was once the cheers, screams, and claps from the Metropolitan West crowd soon became defining sounds of claps, cheers, people whistling, and awws from everyone in attendance.

"Yo, good shit, bro," Jonathan said to Kelvin, embracing his brother's hug.

"You too," Kelvin replied.

"You balled out tonight."

"I got it from you."

Jonathan lightly tapped Kelvin on his chest. "Go celebrate with your team. We'll catch up later."

———

After the ten-minute post-game talk from the coach, the team was dismissed, and Kelvin walked out with the game ball to greet his family. Vanity was standing with them, and Carrie had gone home. No surprise there. Betsy smiled from ear to ear; Sandy had a proud smirk;

Damian and Gregory were grinning, and Junelie and Amir walked toward Kelvin to greet him with hugs.

Upon arrival, Amir's head crashed into Kelvin's stomach, making him grunt with a laugh. The front of Kelvin's jersey and pants now looked like he'd been doing army crawls throughout the evening. His right elbow had minor scratches, and his hat looked like it needed to be dumped into his laundry. That didn't matter to Junelie, who hugged her big brother.

"How did I do?" Kelvin asked.

"I wasn't surprised," Junelie replied.

Kelvin glanced past Jueline toward his family, but something else caught his eye.

*No. It couldn't be. Could it? Nahh. My mind is playing tricks on me.*

Kelvin was just about to redirect his gaze at his family when Analis walked toward an SUV with friends fifty yards away near the parking lot.

Vanity had picked up on Kelvin's apparent stare. To Vanity, it looked like Kelvin had just seen a ghost. She quickly turned her head and tried to figure out what had grabbed Kelvin's attention. All she could see was a group of girls walking toward an SUV. That's when it hit her. The girl on the train was here. She quickly reached into her back pocket, took out her cell phone, and sent a text message to Carrie.

> I think the girl Kelvin met on the train was at the game.

# CHAPTER NINE

Who is she?

"S he's dope," Kelvin said, softly tossing a tennis ball near the ceiling and catching it bear-handed as he lay in bed.

After the game, Jonathan informed his mother that he'd be staying at Sandy's for the weekend. The boys had spent the night scrubbing the grass and dirt stains off their uniforms and putting them to wash, engaging in conversations throughout the night. They mainly talked about the game, key plays, each at-bat, turning points of the game, and their relationship status, which led to talking about Analis.

Kelvin's room was spacious, with a walk-in closet where he stored his trophies. His computer desk was next to his window, and his forty-two-inch television faced his bed. However, there was an enormous gap between his bed and the walk-in closet, so a queen-sized air bed was blown up and placed in that space for Jonathan to sleep in.

While Kelvin tossed the ball to himself, Jonathan raised both his legs in the air, one at a time, grabbed the heel of his foot, and pulled it back, stretching his hamstrings.

"The way she is, her style, the way she talks—it's just different," Kelvin added.

"She is dope... So, Analis, huh? Who woulda thought?... So, it's a wrap for sure between you and Carrie, then?"

"That's what she wanted. How do you know Analis?"

"I don't really know her. I know who she is. We bumped into each other here and there, like at the mall and the movies. Things like that."

"Who does she chill with? Anyone I know?" Kelvin asked.

"I don't know. I don't think so. She's got a couple of cousins at Central. Other than that, you know how it is. She knows someone who knows someone who knows me."

"She got a boyfriend?"

"I don't know. I don't think so."

"Oh."

"So, you gonna holla at Analis?"

"I don't even have her number. She's straight with me too when she found out I was with Carrie."

Jonathan sat up on the air bed. His head peeked over Kelvin's mattress.

"But nothing happened between you and her. How

could she get mad about Carrie? I still don't understand how Carrie got mad at you, anyway. "

*Maybe because Carrie knows me so much, she saw the guilt in my eyes, meaning she knew somehow I liked Analis. There might be a chance that I like Analis much more than I like Carrie, which is crazy because I've been going out with Carrie for a whole year.*

"I don't know. I guess I'll never figure it out. Why do you think Analise was at the game tonight?" Kelvin asked.

Jonathan began to chuckle. Suddenly, Kelvin held onto the ball instead of tossing it back up. He pressed his palms on his mattress, and using his triceps, he pushed himself up and sat up.

"What's so funny?" Kelvin asked, confused.

"You got it bad, huh?" Jonathan replied with a grin.

Kelvin sucked his teeth, narrowing his eyebrows at his brother.

"She came to see Jacob."

"Who?"

"Her cousin Jacob. The freshman who made the team. He's our center fielder. I think next year he'll play short. He's good. Anyway, that's her cousin. She came to see him. At least, I think."

"Oh."

"You should come with me to Christina's graduation party?"

"Christina? The Christina that runs track for your school, Christina?"

"Yeah. What else are you going to be doing? The regular season is over, and travel ball doesn't start until mid-June."

"Who's gonna be there?" Kelvin asked.

" I don't know. But, hey, you never know who you might run into."

# CHAPTER TEN

<u>New Count</u>

Proms and graduations came and went. Cross-town rivals Park East, led by Gregory and Kelvin's best friend, Alex, eliminated Metropolitan West in the playoffs. Central had gotten eliminated by private school powerhouse Lasalle, led by Kelvin's travel ball teammate and cousin, Anthony. Finally, just completing finals a week before the summer ball season gave Kelvin a rare break from baseball.

Between the time of senior night and the weekend after graduation weekend, Kelvin's and Carrie's so-called friends status turned bitter. Carrie accused him of lying about the girl on the train because she was watching him play on Senior night. Kelvin didn't know how Carrie knew Analise was there, nor did he know

Carrie knew what Analise looked like. Despite his efforts to prove his innocence, he didn't try too hard. They were broken up. What was the point in trying? Whatever lingering feelings he still felt for Carrie, he positively dealt with them—their movie nights turned into extra training sessions or hanging with the boys. Whenever he and Carrie crossed paths, he smiled at her instead of ignoring or frowning. He was genuinely sorry about hurting her and realized he didn't owe her anything else.

*If I chose to come back to West, am I gonna be dealing with this bull-s*** All the time?*

Since becoming a single guy again, Kelvin grew closer to his already close inner circle. It was perfect timing but bittersweet. The guys had the entire summer for a last hurrah filled with long nights, and stories they'd tell their future kids about before Jonathan flew out to Miami and Damian started basketball training camp in late August for Providence College.

Tonight wouldn't be one of those nights. Damian had taken off to New York City with his father for his last travel ball basketball tournament before becoming a full-time collegian ball player. Alex and Anthony were on a flight to the Dominican Republic for the summer, where they would spend time with their fathers' side of the family and play professional baseball as sixteen-year-olds and seventeen-year-olds. Finally, Gregory was attending the Park East graduation party. Tonight, it was only Kelvin and Jonathan with Vanity in hand, who was weirdly quiet on the ride to Christina's party.

Once Jonathan parked his car half a block from the house party on Wheeler Avenue on the Cranston side of the Providence and Cranston border, outside Washington Park, Vanity pulled down the mirrored visor. Like always, she used the mirror to double-check that she looked more than presentable. And like countless times, she did. She looked immaculate. Her light makeup boosted her elegant face. She wore her long hair down, making her soft brown skin shine healthier. She wore a light-shaded yellow button-up short-sleeve shirt with light blue jeans. Both Jonathan and Kelvin wore nice jeans. Jonathan wore a black pair, while Kelvin's was blue. Both brothers wore a nice pair of sneakers. Jonathan wore the all-white low-top sneakers that complimented his shirt, and Kelvin wore the popular *cool greys* that complimented his shirt. Jonathan wore a medium-broad gold chain with his attire, while Kelvin kept it simple, wearing his smartwatch.

As the three walked up the quiet block, they heard the music grow louder as they approached the house.

"It sounds like the party is outside," Vanity said, wrapping her arm around Jonthan's elbow.

"It is," Jonathan replied.

"I thought this was a central party? I think we're in Cranston," Kelvin added.

"It is a Central party. The location was changed about three hours ago. I got the text from Adonis."

"Why?" Vanity asked, watching her steps on the dimply light street.

"It's quieter over here, I guess. Christina lives on Sacket Street. Whoever has a house party there is just asking for some unwanted people to walk in. You know how that goes. Shady stuff goes down; then the cops shut the party down if a fight doesn't. So the party got moved here to her uncle's place."

Kelvin and Vanity understood. Just as they approached the house, they spotted numerous teens and adults walking carefully beside two cars parked in a driveway leading to a wooden fence.

The music grew louder, and Jonathan, Kelvin, and Vanity could hear loud chatter. It was a mixture of Spanish, English, slang English, and slang Spanish.

As Jonathan, Vanity, and Kelvin carefully walked around the two BMW cars parked in the driveway, Vanity felt the first feeling of sweat on her hairline due to the humidity.

When the trio entered the backyard, to the right, a large pavilion covered an outdoor couch-like seating area that happened to be on top of outdoor hardwood flooring immediately caught their attention. To their left, a spacious outdoor deck accessorized with a stainless steel grill and a medium-sized outdoor dining table was preoccupied with numerous people, and in the middle between all of that, teens and adults conversed with one another in small groups.

Jonathan, Vanity, and Kelvin said their hellos and small-talked to the people they knew and were familiar with. Throughout the night, the DJ varied his music from Latin to the English music teens listen to today. Grown-ups drank alcohol and gave a pass to those who had just graduated and wanted a taste of alcohol. Some in attendance danced, while others stood in the background, nodding and singing.

About an hour after arriving, Kelvin sat on the couch under the pavilion. The pavilion had yellowish, dim, intimate lighting. Sitting there and watching, he noticed the dark concrete space between the pavilion and the deck. Those who engaged in conversation and danced used the bright lighting from the deck and the pavilion to be able to see. Suddenly, Analis appeared out of the crowd and into the pavilion lighting.

Kelvin felt his heart doing the funny thing again, skipping a beat. Analis was as beautiful as ever. She wore her curly hair out, falling a couple of inches past her shoulders. She wore light blue ripped jeans, a peach-colored haltered crop top, and a thin gold necklace that rested perfectly just under her collarbone.

Kelvin's heart accelerated. He expected Analis to scowl at him as she approached whoever she would speak to in the pavilion seating area. Instead, Analis looked at Kelvin and smiled, surprisingly inching closer to him.

"Machado," Analis said with a grin.

Kelvin was taken aback. What happened to *you're for everybody?* What happened to the cold look? He blinked a couple of times, shaking off this surprising turn of events.

"Future sports doctor," Kelvin replied, returning a grin.

Analis sat next to Kelvin.

*Damn, she smells good.*

"So you're Jonathan's brother," Analis's question was more of a confirmation statement.

"Yea… So, you know my brother?"

"I know of him, but my cousin knows him better."

"Who's your cousin?"

"Christina. This is her party."

Kelvin fought back a laugh.

"What? What's so funny?"

*Oh, that my brother always has my back. He knew you'd be here. Maybe he didn't trick me into coming here, but he sure as hell convinced me, probably for this reason.*

"Nothing," Kelvin replied. "So, how you been?"

"I've been good. I saw you play when you played against your brother."

"What did you think?"

"You're good. You're very good. I was actually surprised."

Analis momentarily looked away. Kelvin's eyes darted back onto the crowd. He wondered why Analis was speaking to him, let alone sitting beside him. Once again, the DJ put on a Latin song, causing the adults to dance with one another.

"I heard you and your girlfriend broke up," Analis said, turning her head back toward Kelvin's direction.

"Yeah. Yeah, we did. How's your *situationship*?"

Analis smirked. The dark spot between the pavilion and the deck grew more crowded, the music volume grew louder, and the intensity of the conversations around them was deafening. Despite that, it felt like Kelvin and Analis were the only two people there.

"There isn't a *situationship* anymore. It was never gonna work out... Why did you break up with your girlfriend?"

"... She broke it off with me."

"Oh," Analis sounded and appeared disappointed.

"Can I tell you something?"

"Go ahead," Analis replied, suddenly appearing disinterested.

Kelvin picked up on the sudden mood change. *What's wrong with this girl? Should I really tell her why Carrie dumped me? What if she thinks I'm a weirdo? But what do I have to lose?...*

Before Kelvin could speak, the DJ played a song that shifted Analis's mood again.

"*De que te quiero es verdad,*" Analis sang out loud with her eyes closed, full of passion. "You dance salsa?" She asked Kelvin.

Kelvin smirked and nodded. Analis quickly rose to her feet, grabbed Kelvin's hand, and guided him off the pavilion and onto the unlit area used as the dance floor. The two teens started to dance to Chiquito Team Band's *Si Quieres,* with Analis singing the lyrics the entire time.

"*Enamorado!*" She sang out loud in the climax of the song.

The passion on her face while singing the song and her smile was mesmerizing. She was authentic, witty, funny, direct, passionate, honest, and sexy. Kelvin cared about Carrie. He believed they had something special. But in reality, he has never felt the jolt in his heart he was now feeling with Analis throughout his relationship with Carrie, as the lyrics said, *Estoy the de ti. Enamorado.*

---

After Kelvin and Analis finished dancing, they slipped out of the backyard and sat on the house's front steps, where they could talk alone without raising their voices. The front of the house was dark. The only lighting on the front porch was a small light bulb above the front door. The limited street lighting gave Kelvin and Analise some added illumination.

During their talk, Kelvin learned that Analis would attend the University of Rhode Island (URI) in the fall. Kelvin filled in Analis on his indecisiveness about what school he'd attend for his senior year. Yet something didn't sit right with Analis. Why the sudden need to change location? Kelvin was at a good school with a good baseball team. Why leave? After she pressed Kelvin a bit, he finally gave him.

"Okay. Can I tell you something without you thinking I'm some weirdo?" Kelvin asked.

"There's something you should know about me, Machado. I like honesty. It doesn't matter if the truth is hard. I'll respect you instead of resenting you."

"Okay," Kelvin said, nodding. "Carrie broke up with me because of you."

Analis was caught entirely off guard. Her skin flushed, her eyebrows narrowed, and her eyes blinked about a thousand times.

Anticipating a barrage of questions, Kelvin quickly started to explain. He went into detail about how Carrie found out he and Analis had met on the train and how he had mentioned it to Ryan, causing the trail into Carrie's finding out. Then, after hearing about Kelvin and Ryan's strained relationship, Analis was left speechless, but a question tugged at her.

"Why didn't you fight for her?"

"What?" Now, it was Kelvin who was blindsided.

"I know we're all young, and we're not supposed to settle down because we still have our whole lives ahead of us. That's one of the reasons why my situationship didn't work out. He wanted me to be his girlfriend, and I don't want a boyfriend right now, especially right before I head to college. But you've been with this girl for a while. Why didn't you fight for her?"

Kelvin stared at Analis. He didn't know her well, but there was something there. He felt it. And for the first time, the cool and confident Analis seemed a bit vulnerable.

*Maybe she was drinking, too?*

Kelvin decided to go for it.

"I might sound real corny."

"You will, but go on."

Kelvin cleared his throat before getting into it. "I didn't fight for Carrie because…" He stopped short, remembering what Analis had just told him. With his eyes gazing into hers, he did the only thing he felt he could. He lied. "I feel the same way you feel about this relationship stuff."

Confusion consumed Analis. She squinted her eyes at Kelvin, trying to read his, hiding her disappointment.

"What?" Analis asked.

"Yeah. I know we have another year left, but I don't even know if I'll be in that school next year. She plays soccer, and I play baseball. Chances are, we're gonna go to different colleges. We're young. Why prolong the inevitable? Why not just cut it off right now? She broke it off, and I let it be."

"Okay then," Analis replied.

Analis opened her mouth to say something but was interrupted by a female voice calling out to her from the driveway.

"I gotta go."

"Okay," Kelvin replied.

Analis rose to her feet. Kelvin remained seated.

"It was nice catching up with you, Kelvin Machado."

"It was nice catching up with you, Analis Ruiz."

"I'll be right there," Analis yelled to the female, expecting another cry out for her.

Analis gave Kelvin one last smile before walking off the front steps. Kelvin watched her the entire way.

*Stop her. Stop her, you idiot. Ask her for her number. What's the worst that can happen? A lot. You're already feeling her a lot more than you felt Carrie, but she doesn't want a boyfriend, and she's heading off to college. You'll be wasting your time.*

Kelvin watched Analis start to turn the corner and head back into the party. He thought to himself, *I'll look her up on Facebook or IG. I'll find her tomorrow, and I'll make it right.*

The thing is, he was wrong…

# CHAPTER ELEVEN

<u>Postponed game.</u>

The following morning was strange. Kelvin woke up with a headache. There was nothing unusual there. What was off was the feeling of sore shoulders, neck pain, and lethargy. The feelings were instant when Kelvin opened his eyes. Today, Kelvin planned to join Jonathan, Ryan, and Gregory for conditioning work at Sandy's Institute.

After Christina's party, Jonathan decided to sleep over again instead of driving back home into Providence after dropping off Vanity less than half a mile from Sandy's house. Sitting up in bed, trying to shake off this feeling, Kelvin could hear some music.

Jonathan was awake, playing Joey Badass's music while showering. The sun was shining bright, illuminating Kelvin's bedroom. He often questioned why he hadn't purchased darker curtains.

Kelvin hopped off his bed and walked over to his bedroom's doorway. The music grew louder since the bathroom faced Kelvin's bedroom. He pressed his palms on each side of the edge of the door and leaned his upper body forward at a ninety-degree angle, pushing his body toward his palms, trying to stretch out the pain in his shoulders.

*Damn, what is this pain?*

Suddenly, the music stopped, and Jonathan, only wearing boxer briefs, gripping his towel in his left hand, emerged from the bathroom. His upper body was still semi-wet from the shower, which had somewhat straightened the minimal curly hair on his chest. A deep vertical line formed between Jonathan's eyebrows as he stared at Kelvin.

"What are you doing?" Jonathan asked.

"My head, my neck, and my shoulders hurt."

Jonathan moved closer to Kelvin and stared into his brother's eyes. "Your eyes look like you drank something last night. Are you sure you're not just hungover? Did Dad see you like this?"

Kelvin stopped his stretching and stood up straight. He wasn't sure, but his eyes looked foggy. He felt it. The back left side of his head felt like a sharp needle was being dug into it, and the shoulder pain had spread into his rear deltoids.

"Take me to the hospital, please," Kelvin said through a wince.

This wasn't an excuse to get out of today's workout. This wasn't because he was tired from last night. This wasn't because he wanted two baseball-free days before summer ball started. And finally, this wasn't because he didn't want to hear Sandy's constant criticism. This was real, and Jonathan saw it in his brother's eyes.

"You can't take something for it and go back to bed?"

"This one feels different."

Jonathan arched an eyebrow. "How?"

Kelvin backpedaled into the bedroom. His legs felt like they weren't entirely under him, and Jonathan picked on this.

"Okay," Jonathan said, walking into the bedroom. "I'll take you. Let's go."

---

After forcing Kelvin to eat something, the brothers changed into comfortable attire: basketball shorts and a T-shirt. Jonathan drove Kelvin to the emergency room at Rhode Island Hospital. On the ride over, Kelvin had alerted his parents. Betsy had already been at work and informed Kelvin that she'd walk over if anything serious arose, but she assured him that he was experiencing one of those migraine headaches.

The large and spacious emergency room was surprisingly empty. Having opened in 2005, Rhode Island Hospital's Emergency room looked much newer than most. The lobby floor was carpet, the waiting chairs were leather, the tan paint on the walls appeared to have been retouched, and a large flat-screen TV was mounted to the rear wall, so those experiencing long waiting times had some entertainment.

Check-in was routine. Kelvin was greeted by the slightly older triage nurse with a surprisingly British accent. The triage section of the emergency room was behind the check-in station, and there were ten small rooms with a curtain in the entryway for privacy. The British nurse took Kelvin's blood pressure and temperature with a state-of-the-art electronic device, requiring one swipe of the forehead to read his temperature accurately. After completing the small task, the British nurse walked Kelvin and Jonathan out of the triage station and into the enormous yet busy emergency room hallways en route to his actual room, where he'd be attended to.

Kelvin's emergency room was surprisingly more extensive than expected. It had a sink to the left of the entrance, a small drawer on the rear right side, and monitor screens on the left wall. A stretcher with a white sheet was positioned in the center of the brightly lit room. Kelvin's eyes darted directly at the stretcher through a squint, wondering how comfortable he'd be.

Upon entering, Kelvin felt the sudden temperature change. Goosebumps immediately arose on his arms, and his body tensed up like when he first stepped outdoors on cold January mornings.

"This is you. Lay down on the stretcher. I'll bring an extra chair for your brother and a warm blanket," the British nurse said, noticing Kelvin almost shivering.

"Damn, why is it so cold in here?" Jonathan asked.

"Keeping cold temperatures helps slow down bacteria and viral growth because bacteria and viruses thrive in warm temperatures."

"Oh."

"I'll be right back," The British nurse said with a smile.

After a few minutes, Kelvin was lying on the stretcher under the warm blanket the British triage nurse had brought for him, and Jonathan was seated in a chair to the left of Kelvin. After learning how bad Kelvin's headache was, the British nurse turned the lights off and closed the curtain separating Kelvin's room from the walkway between the nurses' station.

Suddenly, a younger nurse in her late twenties slid open the curtain and walked into Kelvin's room.

"Hi, I'm Katie. I'll be your nurse for today."

Katie was blonde, slim, and of average height. The lighting outside Kelvin's room illuminated Katie, exposing her blemishless face and pretty smile. She wore powdered blue hospital scrubs, an athletic pair of sneakers, a smartwatch, and her hair in a ponytail. She held a small plastic cup in her right hand with two pills in it and a small plastic cup with water in her left hand.

"What's your name?"

"Kelvin Machado," Kelvin replied, sitting up on the stretcher.

Katie made her way to Kelvin's right, slightly bent over, and closely examined his hospital bracelet.

"Can you tell me your birthday, please?"

"Yeah. It's 11-11-2005."

"Okay, good," Katie said, standing upright. "I understand you have a bad headache."

"Yeah."

"Do you usually get headaches?"

"Yeah, this one is just different." Kelvin started to shrug his shoulders while explaining to Ketie exactly how he felt. "I got this weird pain in my shoulders and neck, too."

"I see. Well, I saw your blood pressure results were normal. I'll give you a choice. Do you want to take these? They're slightly stronger than Tylenol. Or do you want an IV before getting a brain cat scan?"

Kelvin quickly glanced at Jonathan, who was preoccupied with his cell phone. He was probably texting with Vanity or was on social media.

"I'll take the pills."

"Okay."

Katie handed Kelvin both cups. He tilted his head back and put the pills cup to his mouth, allowing the tablets to slide onto his tongue. Then he took a big swig of the water and swallowed the pills before handing both cups back to Katie.

"Okay. They should be here shortly to take you to cat scan. Do you need anything else?"

"Um, I don't think so."

Katie reached under Kelvin's stretcher and located a remote between the mattress and the base. She grabbed it and handed it to Kelvin.

"If you need anything, just press the red button, and I'll be right in."

Five minutes after Katie left Kelvin's room, a large man wearing black hospital scrubs slid open the curtain and walked in, holding a folded-up white piece of paper. The man was darker than Kelvin, wore eyeglasses, had shaggy black hair, and his five o'clock shadow grew into full stubble.

"Hi, Kelvin?"

Once again, Kelvin sat up on the stretcher. Jonathan barely glanced at the man.

"I'm Tony. I'm here to take you to cat scan."

"Okay."

Tony quickly walked behind the stretcher and unlocked it, like one does a stroller. Kelvin laid back down, staring at the ceiling, as Tony navigated the stretcher through the emergency room. Although the lights in the hallways were bright, and the sounds of monitors, call bells, painful screams, and hospital personnel chatting were loud, this didn't bother Kelvin. His headache had worn off a bit.

*Damn. What a waste of time.*

When Tony wheeled Kelvin into the emergency room's cat scan room, two Caucasian female cat scan techs, wearing hospital scrubs, awaited him, standing before the cat scan bed. The room was large, with a wall-sized tinted window and door facing the cat scan machine.

After receiving quick instructions from the techs, Kelvin laid on the slim cat scan bed. The female techs opened and walked through the window door, closing it behind them.

Kelvin was informed the test wouldn't take more than five to ten minutes. When the cat scan machine was turned on, Kelvin could see the tiny red and yellow lighting within the large ring in the device itself as it spun in circles.

Right after the cat scan test, Tony wheeled Kelvin back to his room, where Jonathan was still engaged in his phone.

"Mom stopped by," Jonathan said, watching Tony walk out.

Kelvin tried to re-adjust himself on the stretcher, trying to find some comfort on the thin mattress. "What did you tell her?"

"That you were at cat scan, but you looked like you were feeling better."

"I am. It just sucks that they're gonna have us waiting here forever before they tell me I'm all good."

"Well, since you wasted our day, I'm picking what we eating for takeout," Jonathan said, digging his phone into his pocket.

Kelvin squinted his eyes and narrowed his eyebrows at his brother. "What? No Vanity tonight?"

Jonathan let out a long sigh. He was always sure of himself. He often portrayed himself as being the one with the unbreakable armor. Kelvin could see the glitch in his armor now. His shoulders slumped, and he couldn't stop his heel from tapping the floor.

"Yo, John, what is it?"

"If I tell you, you better go to your grave with this." Something was menacing in his tone. "I'm serious, Kelvin."

His brother took Kelvin aback. The narrow stare turned into worry. "What's up?"

Jonathan opened his mouth but was quickly cut off by how fast and brash the curtains opened. Both Kelvin and Jonathan stared at Katie rushing in. The cool, calm, and collective Katie was now tensed, trying to mask the fear in her eyes. That's when it hit Kelvin. Although Katie was clearly in her late twenties, she couldn't have been too far removed from nursing school, or something seriously scared her. What was it?

Katie locked eyes with Kelvin. Her expression was unsure. She looked at him as if she were watching something outside the realm of possibility.

"You have to lay down. I have to put an IV in you right now," Katie said urgently.

Kelvin and Jonathan looked at one another, equally confused. Jonathan rose off his chair while Katie walked over to the small drawer at the room's rear and pulled out an IV kit and bag.

"Kelvin, you need to lie down now," Katie repeated more urgently.

*What the hell is going on?*

Kelvin did what he was told, allowing Katie to put an IV in his right arm. She then connected the IV line to a bag and hung it behind Kelvin before rushing out. Jonathan edged over to Kelvin's left side.

"That was weird," Jonathan said with his arms crossed. "Someone else probably came in shot or something that she came in that crazy."

Kelvin stared down at his arm. The initial pain had disappeared from the syringe, but the discomfort of the IV tubing taped onto his skin remained.

Suddenly, a set of Caucasian men wearing white hospital jackets entered Kelvin's room. One man was tall, clean-shaven, had short brown hair, and wore eyeglasses. The other was a heavyset man around Kelvin's height. What was once a clean-shaven head was a stubble mess, and his black beard was oddly well-kept.

The men's demeanor was calm and collected, but

their eyes told a different story. Neither of them could realize it, but their eyes widened. They were *astonished*. The heavyset man stepped forward.

"Kelvin, I'm Dr. Bob Saugy. This is Dr. Dennis Sousa. Where are your parents?"

"My mother is upstairs," Jonathan said before Kelvin could answer. "What's up? Is my brother good to go?"

Kelvin could almost make out a frown on Saugy's face.

"No. I need you to call your mother immediately."

# CHAPTER TWELVE

<u>The bleed</u>

After receiving Jonathan's call, Betsy rushed downstairs to the emergency room. The walk wasn't far. Her unit secretarial post was on the fifth floor of the bridge building, which happened to be directly on top of the Emergency Department. With a quick elevator ride down to the first floor, a swipe of her employee ID through the double doors, and a short walk, passing the fast-track and chest pain pods, she reached Kelvin's room in four minutes.

Betsy wore hospital scrub bottoms, accessorized with a short-sleeve plain black T-shirt. She wore golden hoop earrings, and her hair was in a bun.

It was a miracle her legs didn't completely give out from under her after hearing the news. Her facial expressions went through a series of changes: squinting, narrowing of the eyebrows, blinking uncontrollably, quivering lips, face paling, and bulging of the eyes. Suddenly, everything became almost entirely deafening to her. The sounds of hospital monitors seemed distant, the sight of the nurses and secretaries sitting at the nurses' station appeared blurry, and Dr. Dennis Sousa's voice sounded muffled.

*"Mrs. Machado!"*

When Sousa's voice finally got to Betsy, she found herself leaning against the emergency room wall, half a foot away from Kelvin's room.

"It's Perkins. Mrs. Perkins," Betsy replied.

She didn't know why she needed to correct Sousa, but it helped her escape her stagnant state.

"I don't - I don't understand. How is this possible?" Betsy asked.

"We won't know until we do an MRI on him after we admit him."

"I see."

"Do you want to tell him the news? Or should we?" Saugy asked.

"I can't," Betsy replied, almost breaking into tears.

"Okay. We'll tell him."

---

Kelvin hadn't relaxed since being told his mother needed to be present. Something was wrong, and he knew it when Sousa and Saugy ushered Betsy out of his room so they could talk privately.

*It's been twenty minutes. What is it?*

Jonathan hadn't sat back down and paced around

the room. Kelvin wondered if Jonathan was worried about him or what was happening between Jonathan and Vanity.

When the curtain opened again, Kelvin could see his mother standing behind Dr. Sousa and Saugy but could not see her face.

"Kelvin," Sousa said, stepping forward. " We're admitting you to the Neuro ICU.

Kelvin felt a cold chill run through him. Surprisingly, he was expressionless. Jonathan stopped his pacing and froze, glaring at Sousa.

"I'm afraid you have a significant brain bleed. So, we need to get you upstairs right now to stop the bleeding and run more tests on you." Sousa added.

The room fell silent. Like Kelvin, Jonathan was expressionless. Truthfully, they didn't know what to say. This news blindsided Kelvin. This was the last thing anyone expected.

"But - but I feel fine now," Kelvin said in disbelief.

"That's the meds. We'll know more tomorrow after your MRI. Transport will be here shortly to take you upstairs."

*This doesn't make sense. I feel fine. I swear. I was just at a party yesterday. I even feel good enough to go hitting after I leave here. How could I be bleeding inside my brain?*

# CHAPTER THIRTEEN

<u>The AVM</u>

I t didn't matter that Kelvin's Neuro ICU room was more prominent than some hotel rooms and that his bed was probably more comfortable than some of the hotel room beds. It didn't matter that Kelvin had a single room instead of sharing his with another patient. And it didn't matter that he had cable TV and a wall-sized window looking out the city. What mattered was that Kelvin was supposed to be discharged today with particular medications to control the bleeding and return in two weeks for surgery. However, here he was, in the hospital indefinitely. Yesterday was the worst day of Kelvin's life, and he couldn't remember what happened after one in the afternoon.

It had now been the third day since Kelvin's Emergency Room visit. The first night went awkwardly smoothly since arriving at the Neuro ICU from the Emergency Room. He didn't have a headache or any other pain but was treated by his Neuro ICU nurse as if he would break if he did anything on his own. He wasn't allowed to climb out of bed and go to the bathroom alone, even though the bathroom was two feet away from his bed. He was given a sizeable plastic urinal and instructed to do his business there. If he needed to do the good old number two, he needed to ask a nurse or a CNA to wait by his bathroom door.

On the morning of the second day, Kelvin was wheeled down to the MRI department in a wheelchair. Throughout the ride, Kelvin experienced a series of temperature changes. The older part of the hospital still had a dull tan-like yellow paint on the walls and felt humid. Whenever Kelvin crossed over to the newer part of the hospital, the hallways were painted white and blue, the lights were brightly lit in white LED lights, and Kelvin shivered from his body feeling cold.

*This isn't anything like it is on TV.*

Unlike what Kelvin saw on movies and TV shows, no hospital employee smiled his way; no one stopped and asked what his deal was, let alone looked his way. Everyone, from doctors in white coats to surgeons in scrubs with cloth-paper-like shoe covers, nurses, housekeeping employees, and transporters wheeling patients on stretchers, just went about their business. It was as if these people were taken over by the people in downtown Manhattan en route to work, disregarding what horrors were happening in the streets of New York City.

It didn't take long for Kelvin to be prepped for his

MRI. His earplugs were inserted into his ears, a small panic device shaped like a rubber ball was handed to him, and another warm blanket was placed over him before the slim MRI bed slid him into the machine.

After the hour-long MRI, Kelvin waited in his wheelchair for a half hour for the transport department worker to wheel him back up to his room. When Kelvin finally reached his room in the wheelchair, a familiar face was seated on the window ledge, staring out the window.

"Carrie?" Kelvin asked. Although he knew it was Carrie, his question was more of a reassurance.

Carrie quickly turned and locked eyes with Kelvin from across the room. Like typical Carrie, she wore long black gym tights and a yellow t-shirt with the words *Yellowjackets* in blue lettering across the breast. She wore her hair down and her glasses, which she hardly wore because she preferred contacts.

Whatever resentment Carrie had for Kelvin was gone in an instant. She didn't know if it was because she still had feelings for him, or if it was the sight of him wearing a hospital gown that tied from behind his neck, exposing his tight black boxer briefs and a white muscle shirt, or because she watched him rise out of a wheelchair, but her eyes watered up with tears.

"Your dad went home to get you clothes, your mom is in the cafeteria getting breakfast, and Jonathan is on his way here," Carrie said, looking away, turning her attention back to the window, fighting back the tears.

When Kelvin stood tall, the young transport pulled the wheelchair away and exited the room. While watching Carrie stare out the window, Kelvin couldn't help but notice how beautiful she looked. It was a gloomy day out. Kelvin remembered seeing guests and visitors in hallways wearing long pants, light sweat-shirts, and jackets. But here she was, looking like home. Despite the grey sky darkening Kelvin's room, Carrie's blonde hair still shined as bright as ever. It could have been his imagination, but he could still make out the green in her eyes.

Kelvin walked across his room, passed his bed, and sat on the recliner next to the window ledge. When Carrie turned her head to face Kelvin, the tears were gone, but Kelvin could still decipher Carrie's worry. The widened eyes, arched eyebrows, and awkward silence weren't hard to disguise.

"Who told you?" Kelvin asked.

"Vanity."

"Oh."

"How are you feeling?"

"Despite being told I'm bleeding in my brain, I feel fine."

There was a hint of sarcasm in Kelvin's tone, not in a malicious delivery but in a light-hearted way to shed some light on his unfortunate mishap. Picking up on Kelvin's wit, Carrie cracked a smile. Kelvin did, too. This was the first time he smiled in over twenty-four hours.

"They say I might be going home tomorrow on medication, depending on what they find in the MRI," Kelvin said as he stared at his right arm. His IV line catheter wasn't attached to a longer line with an IV bag.

Carrie couldn't help but stare at the beginning stages of bulging veins in Kelvin's forearms and calves.

His calves had more muscle tone, and his biceps appeared slightly larger than Carrie had remembered. He didn't let the breakup hamper his discipline in the gym.

Of course, he felt fine, Carrie thought to herself.

"That's good. I'm just at a loss for words. When I heard what happened, I uh…"

"I'm glad you came," Kelvin said, sensing Carrie's struggle to express her feelings.

Carrie smiled. It was the first time she had smiled in a while. "Ryan is here too. He's downstairs."

*My boy Ryan. Of course, he's here. Gregory, Alex, Damian, Anthony, Jason, Jonathan. They're my day 1s, but Ryan is my boy. Carrie is here. She's actually here. How can I leave West? Why are Carrie and I even broken up? This is a mistake.*

"Carrie, I'm sorry."

Carrie's eyes grew a bit larger. Her dark green eyes appeared softer through a crooked smile. Kelvin readjusted himself on the recliner to sit up straight.

"I shoulda told you. I shoulda tried harder to make you understand that nothing happened between me and that girl on the train, and I shoulda never let you break up with me. I didn't wanna break up… I'm sorry."

Carrie's crooked smile turned into a happy one, and her cheeks blushed. Suddenly, the sun appeared to be breaking through the gloomy skies, and what seemed to be a gloomy June day felt like it was going to be a beautiful one where people would be out barbecuing, playing pick-up basketball games, and riding around in their cars with their windows down.

Something strange started to happen. While Kelvin looked at Carrie, his vision began to come and go. It was as if he was blinking uncontrollably. The image of Carrie quickly became a foggy one, like a baby first coming into this world. He could hear Carrie say his name, but her voice sounded distant. The blinking image slowed with extended periods of a black image between Carrie's beautiful but worried, foggy face.

Seconds later, Kelvin's vision turned entirely black. "Kelvin! Kelvin!" He heard Carrie's distant voice cry out to him.

———

A few hours after Kelvin's scary episode, Betsy and Sandy were somewhat calm enough to comprehend the information Neurologist DR. Apple had given them. Just two hours ago, this calm and collected doctor had looked Betsy and Sandy in the face and told them that he would die if they didn't agree to let him plant a stent into Kelvin's brain.

The situation was dire, and for the first time, Betsy, who had seen countless times the thirty-nine-year-old Dr. Apple stroll the hallways in his white doctor's jacket with his perfect white teeth, his perfectly shaved bald head, and his perfectly groomed black beard, look in disarray. The doctor, who never seemed to sweat, looked like he had just walked out of a sauna, and his perfectly ironed scrubs were a wrinkled mess.

Now, the three sat in the doctor's station, just behind the unit secretaries in the Neuro ICU. Betsy and Sandy sat beside each other with their chairs close. Dr. Apple sat in front of them, resting his work laptop on his lap.

"A ruptured brain AVM?" Sandy asked, narrowing his eyebrows.

"A brain arteriovenous malformation is what it's called," Dr. Apple said. "The short term is AVM. This is a tangle of blood vessels that connect arteries and veins in the brain."

Betsy gasped as Sandy quietly tried to make sense of all this. With a quick glance at Sandy and Betsy, Dr. Apple saw that Betsy was familiar with the condition, while Sandy needed further explanation.

"So it's a knot of tangled blood vessels, arteries in your son's brain."

Sandy's face grew pale. Although he wasn't familiar with much medical terminology, he knew any internal knot in anyone's body was severe.

"But um… How? How did this happen?" Sandy asked.

Dr. Apple opened his work laptop and said, "He was born with this condition."

Dr. Apple rose off his chair with his laptop in hand and sat on the vacant seat next to Betsy, letting Betsy and Sandy see the image of Kelvin's brain MRI. On the right side, the image was clear and appeared normal. But Betsy's tired eyes rested on the imaging of the left side of Kelvin's brain. Given that the left part was dark grey with a black spot, she understood it was abnormal.

"See, this condition is rare," Dr. Apple said. "Last time I checked, about one percent of Americans are born with this. Do you see the dark black spot here?"

Betsy had already spotted it, and it only took Sandy a second to locate it.

"That's the source. This is the initial AVM. All the dark grey is the AVM tangled up with more vessels, veins, and arteries."

"Meaning the knot got bigger," Sandy added, now understanding.

"But how? How did this go undetected?" Betsey asked. The question was more directed toward her. As far as she could remember, Kelvin always had headaches. Why did she settle on the migraine diagnosis from incompetent doctors in Miami? Her baby boy could have died earlier, and she could have prevented this by pushing the headache issues.

Dr. Apple's eyes appeared heavy and droopy. There were rumors that he was expecting his first child in a few months, and he didn't appear robotic for the first time since he was a resident. It could be because although the chances are slim to none, this could happen to his unborn child, and he was living the horror in real time with Betsy and Sandy.

Dr. Apple cleared his throat, fighting through this potential horror. "It happens when there are no prior imagining tests, which happens often... We have to focus on surgery now, which won't happen until we drain all the spilled fluid in his brain."

Sandy's eyes started to well up with tears, but somehow, he refrained from crying, while Betsy didn't bother drying her wet face.

"How - how long until you drain everything out?" Sandy asked.

The aisle between the secretary and the doctors'

station was busy. Transporters wheeled patients in and out of the Neuro ICU in stretchers, and visitors visiting loved ones checked in with the secretaries, but to Sandy and Betsy, it felt like they were all alone with Dr. Apple.

"He has a lot of fluid. We're looking at anywhere from five to seven days, maybe more."

"Save my son. Please, Dr. Apple," Betsy quietly pleaded.

"I'll try my best."

# CHAPTER FOURTEEN

*While in the darkness.*

I don't remember what happened after I blacked out. The last thing I remembered was looking at Carrie's face. Everything was black for a while. I don't remember hearing anything. I was just in darkness.

Three things immediately ran through my mind. One, was I dead? Two, I couldn't be. If I were, I'd like to believe I'd be appearing for my judgment day. The third one was that I needed to pray more. Not just pray but believe more. I mean, I believe, but I need to be closer to God.

Something strange started to happen within the darkness. The sounds of fingers snapping hallowly rang in my ears... Then, after a few snaps, I began to hear the beat of a song, followed by lyrics. It was the song, Stalking You from A Boogie With The Hoodie.

I wasn't in darkness anymore and was suddenly standing at home plate at an unlit and empty baseball field. It was a summer evening when the sky twilight lighted. I played some games when the sky was like that, and I wouldn't say I liked it. The ball was hard to track coming off the opponent's bat. My out-fielding teammates would say it was the worst time in the outfield.

The baseball field was enormous. I wasn't just at a field; I was at a stadium. As I looked straight ahead to center field, I noticed an entire section in the center field bleacher covered in black and buildings peaking and towering over the stadium facade. This was just any facade; this was the famous "frieze." That's when I realized I wasn't at just any stadium. I was at Yankee Stadium, Old Yankee Stadium. Why was I here? I've never been to old Yankee Stadium. I've heard the tales from my dad about how there was no place like it. Every time I watched an old video of Derek Jeter making a miraculous play, David Juctice's three-run home run in to take the lead over Seattle in game six, and, of course, Aaron Boone's walk-off homerun in game seven of the ALCS, the roar, happiness, and enthusiasm of the crowd looked like they were going to collapse Yankee Stadium.

I was days away from turning four when the Yankees won their twenty-seventh championship in 2009, so I don't remember much. However, the crowd doesn't seem as engaged when I watch old videos of the fans in the current Yankees Stadium as it did pre-2009. But my question wasn't asked: Why was I standing in Old Yankee Stadium?

I glanced down to check out what I was wearing. Oddly enough, I wasn't wearing a baseball uniform—I wasn't even wearing baseball attire. I was wearing light blue jeans, popular wheat boots, and a fitted crew-neck Lacoste sweater.

When I looked back up toward center field, I started to walk toward first base. As I rounded second base, a Latin song began playing in the stadium's speakers, making me stop. I looked up, trying to locate the speakers, but rested my stare at the famous frieze.

There was something magical about how the frieze looked in the twilight sky. I stood in probably the most famous baseball stadium before its demolition, under the most beautiful sky. Was I dead?

Suddenly, Bad Bunny's voice became clearer as he sang his lyrics from La Canción. I've never heard this song before. In translation, the artist talked about how he thought he had forgotten about this woman until a particular song started playing. He says he remembers how he and the woman sang, danced, and kissed while they were drunk. Why was this song playing?

As the song's hook repeated, I started to hear distant voices. Then, suddenly, I woke up.

# CHAPTER FIFTEEN

<u>"You weren't here."</u>

Jonathan hadn't checked on Vanity since they last saw one another in the Neuro ICU waiting room the day Kelvin almost died. After thirteen days, Kelvin was finally discharged from the hospital. Eleven days had passed since he'd last physically seen Vanity. Like the average teenager, they texted daily with the nightly Facetime before either was ready for bed.

After Vanity's younger brother, Sterling, let Jonathan inside, it didn't take long for Jonathan to walk through the house and out to the backyard, finding Vanity lounging on the family's pool chair a few feet away from their inground pool.

Despite having that one humid night two weeks ago, the weather wasn't hot enough to be inside the pool. The noon sun shined brightly, and the weather was warm with a slight breeze. Vanity's family's pool was something you'd see out of a catalog. The feet ranged from three to nine feet; marbled flooring inside the pool, colorful LED lights that were used for night swims and outdoor cocktail parties, a gazebo on the opposite side of the poolside tables, and a stainless steel pool fountain resting on the center ledge on the nine feet side of the pool.

Vanity had on a plain black bikini top and a pair of blue ripped jean shorts and wore her hair in a messy bun. A book rested on her lap since she enjoyed daytime summer reading. However, to Jonathan, the book appeared to be more of a prop than anything else.

"Hey, babe," Jonathan said as he approached Vanity.

When Jonathan reached Vanity, she was already sitting up straight. Jonathan leaned in for a tap kiss, but Vanity had other plans, slightly moving her face, resulting in Jonathan's kiss landing on her cheek.

"So, Kelvin is coming home soon."

"That's good," Vanity replied, watching Jonathan pull up a chair beside hers. Her tone was dry, and she did not want to force anything fake. Deep down, Jonathan knew she wasn't happy with him at the moment. He knew she felt terrible about what Kelvin was going through and wouldn't put any unwarranted disagreements or problems on him.

Vanity closely watched Jonathan. The way he dragged one poolside chair to hers, making the legs scratch the ground, irritated her. His quiet, confident demeanor now appeared like arrogance, and those once cute, deep dimples could have just been two stupid holes in his face. For the first time since she could remember, she viewed him as a dumb jock as he placed his poolside chair next to hers and sat down, facing her.

"Look, I'm sorry. I'm sorry that I didn't react the way you wanted. I was doing some thinking and-"

"Before you say anything, I want you to know that I bailed you out," Vanity sternly interjected.

Jonathan tilted his head in confusion. "What do you mean you bailed me out?"

"I took care of it."

"What?"

"I took care of it," Vanity said, piercing her eyes through Jonathan's.

Jonathan started to speak slowly, choosing her words carefully. "Vanity… What are you talking about? We haven't talked much about it since you told me you were pregnant."

Vanity finally closed her book and placed it beside her. She sat up on the chair, swung her legs around, and positioned herself to face Jonathan.

"Jonathan, I got an abortion."

Jonathan remained seated. Despite being motionless, his skin suddenly became pale, his forehead wrinkled, and the size of his eyes doubled while his pupils flickered back and forth like black flies trapped in a jar.

"I got an abortion, and you weren't there. When I found out I was pregnant, I was scared to death. There were a couple of nights when I called you because I needed to be with you, and I didn't get your call until the next day. I get it. Your brother is in the hospital. And what he's going through is crazy. I'm sorry for that. I am. But I needed you. I was carrying your baby, and you weren't here for me."

Jonathan felt his stomach turn with every word from Vanity's mouth. He opened his mouth to speak, but nothing came out.

"Plus, you're going to Miami, and I'm staying up north. This could never work out. Even without a baby, this wasn't going to work out. We were fooling ourselves, thinking this could ever work. We were prolonging the inevitable by staying together throughout the summer. So, like I said, you're off the hook."

Vanity's world was crumbling by the second, but she remained stoic. She was expressionless, although Jonathan could see the fierceness in her eyes.

"Babe, what I wanted to say was that I reached out to Miami and-"

"I don't care what you did or didn't do anymore," Vanity interjected. "I've determined that I won't be someone who derails your dreams… I won't make the mistake your parents did, causing us to resent each other." Vanity now had tears in her eyes. She swore to herself that she wouldn't cry. She needed to hold it together. "You need to leave."

Jonathan slowly rose off the chair without a single protest, silently shattering Vanity's already broken heart into a million pieces. Jonathan glanced down at Vanity, trying to make eye contact with her, but she kept her gaze straight, staring into space. It was over. There wasn't anything he could do about it.

Jonathan decided not to return through the house and left through the backyard. As Jonathan reached the fenced-in door, Vanity said, "Take care of yourself, Jonathan."

"Yeah. You too," Jonathan replied.

# JOURNAL ENTRY

**Jonathan**

My pops is obsessed with me and my brother writing down our thoughts and feelings in a journal. He says it's because Kelvin and I are like him–guys who bottle their emotions and pretend like everything is fine. I'm not like that, though–Kelvin is. I'm like my father when it comes to girls. *Womanizer, player, he ain't shit* are the terms associated with him. Although we share the same traits when it comes to girls, a good-hearted asshole would be the correct assessment for me.

I knew Vanity had a man when we met, but I never pursued her out of respect. I also never asked Vanity to diss Jackson and get with me. Things just happened. Truthfully, Vanity is my first girlfriend. I mean, I've messed around and talked with girls, but I never liked anyone or, dare to say, loved any of them the way I feel about Vanity.

Vanity is great, but she's a lot. Not in a bad way–but

a lot. She's constantly planning things for us: weekend breakfast spots to hit, movies to watch, which social parties to attend, what to wear, itineraries after I'm done with my games when she travels to Massachusetts and Up-State New York with her older cousins when I'm playing travel ball. Lately, it's been colleges.

Why couldn't I tell her about Miami? Why couldn't I just be honest with her? Fear. The truth is, I do love Vanity. At least, I think I do. What does a seventeen-year-old guy know about love anyway? I want her with me, and I know for a fact that she hates the excessive heat, the south, and especially hates Florida. Her plans were always to stay in the northeast, attend URI, and not go anywhere further down than Rutgers for an out-of-state experience. I knew there was no way she would agree to go down south.

But why did I hide my Miami aspersions? Again, it was simple: I was afraid of her breaking things off with me because we'd have a definite expiration date. As corny as it sounds, that's the truth.

She wasn't even supposed to find out that URI, Rutgers, and Boston College offered me full rides. I was going to keep that shit private and lie to her if and when Miami gave me an offer. I know that's the cowardly way of doing things, but I wanted to prolong whatever time we had left. How was I supposed to know that Kelvin was going to get sick at the same time she found she was pregnant? Like, how am I supposed to handle that shit?

I wanted to be there for her, but how could I leave my brother? Kelvin was already borderline antisocial, and I made shit harder for him at his school. I was one of the few people he opened up to and wasn't afraid to be vulnerable with. I mean, Vanity could have handled being a few weeks pregnant on her own, right?

Is this what life must have been like for my father? Choices? Priorities? I heard how life was great in Miami. It was the happiest my mom had been. Then everything changed when my father was traded, and we had to come up north. I figured she'd be happier being closer to her hometown. What was back home that my mother didn't want to return? And why do I feel like I have to escape home?

These damn journal entries. I thought the way my father made Kelvin and me do them was stupid. I honestly just scribbled a few words here and there in it. I thought it was the writer in him trying to make us more like him when, for the first time, I saw the pros in this. I wasn't a hundred percent honest with Vanity and truthfully myself, just like he wasn't honest with my mother and himself, and journaling kept his sanity. I am actually more like him than I thought.

My pops is making sure that we aren't too alone with our thoughts as we navigate life in a more complex world than before. I know what I have to do now.

# CHAPTER SIXTEEN

<u>26 outs</u>

Kelvin still hadn't remembered much from the day he coded. All he remembered was when he woke up, he had a drain attached to his skull, a few centimeters above the front right side of his hairline, and about a quarter of the right side of his head had been shaven off. Hours turned into days, and days turned into a couple of weeks. The sun rose and set, his hospital food had been barely touched, and his room TV channel hadn't moved from ESPN, although the games had been watching him instead of being watched.

On the tenth day, Kelvin's stent (drain) was removed from his head. Five stitches were used to stitch up the incision where the stent was placed, just above his hairline. Kelvin's shades had been up. Ironically, the sky was identical to the last time he saw Carrie: dark and gloomy but with less rain.

Kelvin felt relieved to have the stent removed. It was as if shackles had been removed from his ankles. Suddenly, he could walk to his bathroom to relieve himself without using a urinal. It was a day to celebrate a minor milestone. With Damian, Gregory, and Ryan keeping Kelvin company, Betsy felt secure enough to drive home and bring Kelvin comfortable clothing. When she returned, the nursing staff helped Kelvin wash up and get out of bed.

To Kelvin, it was as if he were an infant taking his first steps. His toes gingerly touched the floor, sending an unfamiliar feeling through his sense of touch. His legs felt oddly heavy, making his first step more of a slide as he clutched the nurses' hands to his left and right.

"It's okay. Take your time. It's completely normal. Think of it as an older car being turned on for the first time in months," The younger nurse to his left said, sensing Kelvin's urge to panic.

With the help of the two nurses, the tingling sensation escaped Kelvin's feet with every tentative step. Once Kelvin entered the bathroom, most of his muscle memory was back in his legs. No more in-bed washcloths and no more cat baths. He was finally able to take that well-deserved hot shower.

Later that day, Kelvin received many visitors, from relatives to current teammates. However, Carrie was the only person he hadn't seen since being conscious. Even Vanity showed up after strangely texting Kelvin to make sure that Jonathan wouldn't be present. The two talked for half an hour, where she shared she was the one who told Carrie about the girl on the train being at the homecoming game and expressed remorse after learning about the possibility of Carrie and Kelvin getting back together after learning about Carrie's visiting Kelvin at the hospital.

*Where was Carrie?*

After Sandy, Michael, and Junelie said their good-byes for the day, Kelvin and Betsy found themselves alone in the room. The television was on but left on mute. With a five-foot-even frame, Betsy curled up into the recliner beside Kelvin's hospital bed and closed her eyes for much-needed rest.

Kelvin glanced at his bedside table and reached for his cell phone. He hadn't checked his social media accounts for two weeks and decided now was the time. When he opened Facebook, he noticed over fifty messages posted on his page.

<u>The messages read:</u>

"Get well soon."

"God got you."

"🙏"

"Thinking of you."

"💪"

"🤍"

"You got this!"

Most of the messages posted on his page were repetitive. In contrast, others posted songs, and teammates from both West High and his travel ball team posted pictures of Kelvin alongside his teammates with positive messages.

Suddenly, the barrage of messages became too much for Kelvin. He decided to close down Facebook and open his Instagram app, where he could enjoy pictures and videos. To his disappointment, he was greeted with more of the same. Direct messages flooded his inbox, followed by numerous requests to be followed by strangers he'd never met.

*Bad idea.*

Kelvin still couldn't comprehend what he was going through. He knew he was born with this rare brain condition that caused an aneurysm and understood that he needed surgery. What he couldn't comprehend was how he was still functioning. He wasn't dumb. He knew people. Visitors and his nurses looked at him in awe. He wasn't supposed to be awake, let alone go to the bathroom with the help of stool softeners, and he wasn't supposed to have the power to shower on his own. So, how could he possibly know how to respond to people's messages? He may have appeared like a walking miracle to the average eye, but deep down, he knew something was wrong. He felt it in his gut.

There was a light knock on his door before Kelvin could put his phone on his bedside table. When Kelvin glanced up, the tall, light-skinned man with messy blonde hair was already walking in. He didn't wear a white doctor's jacket or scrubs, although he wore his hospital badge on the left breast, displaying his job title. His dark brown suit was a wrinkled mess; thick reading glasses and the light wrinkles on his cheeks and eyes gave away his mid-fifties years of age.

"Kelvin Machado?... I'm Dr. Noran," he said through an accent.

Kelvin couldn't pinpoint the accent. It wasn't American. And given Dr. Noran's complexion, he assumed it was European.

"Hi."

Betsy quickly opened her eyes and sat up on the recliner. Dr. Noran noticed Betsy rising off the recliner. "Oh, hi. You must be his big sister?"

"Mother," Betsy corrected, walking towards Dr. Noran and holding her hand out for a handshake.

"Oh, my apologies. I'm the neurosurgeon. I'm here to discuss your son's surgery."

Betsy backpedaled two steps and sat beside Kelvin on the edge of his bed. She rested her nervous hands on her lap, waiting for Dr. Noran to speak.

Like everyone else, Dr. Noran looked mesmerized at the sight of Kelvin awake and normally functioning. But there was something else there. He looked admiringly at Kelvin.

"Outstanding," Dr. Noran said more to himself than directed at Kelvin.

"What?" Betsy asked, confused.

Dr. Noran smiled, exposing his tan-colored teeth for the first time. An indication of too much coffee. But what doctor doesn't drink much coffee when they have to be awake to tend to their patients?

"Kelvin, you are an extraordinary young man. You know, every time I walk onto this unit, all of the patients aren't awake. The brain is such a delicate organ. One of the main symptoms of having an AVM is being tired and sleepy. But yet, here you are, awake."

Betsy remained expressionless. She didn't care for the theatrics.

"After seeing that all the fluid from your brain bleed has been drained out, you are cleared for surgery tomorrow morning."

"Tomorrow morning?" Betsy nervously asked.

"Yes. The sooner, the better. The thing is, we cannot operate you, meaning cut you open. Your AVM is located deep in the left side of your brain. It's too dangerous to operate on. You run the chance of dying or having severe brain damage."

"If you can't operate, what's going to happen then?" Betsy asked. This time, there was desperation in her voice.

Kelvin remained calm, mainly because he still couldn't comprehend the information. It was as if his nervous system was taking its time adjusting to something brand new. He didn't say a word or nod. He just sat on his bed without breaking eye contact with Dr. Noran.

Noran replied, "Gamma Knife Surgery."

Kelvin squinted, making a facial expression for the first time. Betsy did the same, rising to her feet.

Before either Kelvin or Betsy could get a word out, Dr. Noran continued. "Gamma Knife Surgery is radiation surgery. What we do is we attach a special helmet to your head. The helmet has-"

"I've seen those," Betsy interjected in awe. "I've seen a couple of patients with those things on their heads in the hallways."

"You work here?"

"Yes. I'm a unit secretary."

"Okay, that's good. I'm glad you've seen them. Do you see how they have visors?"

"Yes. And small little holes, too, right?"

"Correct." Dr. Noran flashed another smile, more enthused. "So we use the visors to cover up the parts of the brain that don't need radiation. Those small holes are meant for the radiation to go through. So, we zap the direct radiation to the exact location of the source."

"Have you done this type of surgery before?" Betsy asked.

"It's all we do. We do them every week. It's a rare surgery. I believe we're one of four states that do it. We were the first. That's why most people do not know this procedure exists. It's not invasive, and as a result, it significantly lowers the chances of brain damage."

For the first time in two weeks, Kelvin flashed a smile. Suddenly, the unbearable weight he'd been feeling on his shoulders disappeared. This nightmare was going to be short-lived.

"But I have to warn you about the recovery process. One, I'm legally obligated to, and two, I feel it's morally right."

Kelvin's smile quickly became slanted.

"The recovery period is two years. I know for a fact that this procedure is going to zap away your AVM. I question how many times we have to do it... See, you have the biggest AVM I have ever seen. So, as long as you have an AVM in your brain, you risk it growing again, no matter how tiny it is. So after two years have passed, and if you still have an AVM in your brain, we have to do another round of the Gamma Knife Surgery… I also want to stress to you that you have suffered significant trauma to your brain. Whatever residual side effects you may have, Gamma Knife doesn't cure that."

"Side effects?" Kelvin asked, breaking his silence for the first time.

"Yes. The brain is an unpredictable thing. For example, you can get edema, headaches, and temporary memory loss. What I do know for sure is that you cannot afford to take more trauma to your brain. I understand that you're a baseball player, right?"

"Yeah."

"There's a good chance you may not be able to play baseball ever again."

Kelvin must have blinked a thousand times in a femtosecond. "What?"

"I've watched baseball a few times. I saw a player get hit in the head. Yes, this rarely happens, and yes, you all wear helmets, but you cannot afford to take any hits to the head. It can be diving for a ball or accidentally running into someone impeding your path to the base. It's too dangerous. Despite having the Gammer Knife Surgery, you are considered a walking critical condition patient. Kelvin, I cannot stress this enough. Without the Gammer Knife, you are going to die. With it, you need to make changes that may change you forever if you hope to have a normal life."

"Don't tell me that, Doc," Kelvin barked back.

Slanting his head, Dr. Noran replied, "I have to, Kelvin–"

Before Dr. Noran could finish, Kelvin interrupted

with more base in his voice. "No. No, you don't. Fuck outta here. You're telling me that I can't play baseball anymore. You're telling me I can't live my normal life anymore?"

Betsy placed a firm hand on Kelvin's leg, almost reminding him to be respectful.

"Kelvin, *calmate*," Betsy directed.

"Calm down? Ma, really? I feel fine. All the blood is drained out of my brain. I'm good."

"Do you want to die, Kelvin?" Dr. Noran firmly asked without changing his facial expression. It's a yes or no question. You don't have to do this. But if you want to live, you need to do this... So, what's it going to be?"

For the first time in two weeks, despite almost dying, Kelvin suddenly started to feel his world crumble. The realization of never playing baseball again had never crossed his mind. His eyes began tearing up as he broke eye contact with Dr. Noran as he lowered his head, hiding the tears running down his face.

"Are you sure this is our only option, doc?" Betsy asked, holding in her tears, feeling her son's sudden pain.

"I am one thousand percent sure."

# JOURNAL ENTRY

*I'm a ballplayer...*
*At least, I used to be...*

*Baseball is in my DNA. It's who I am. As sons of a ball player, my brother and I spent time in professional locker rooms, from the minor leagues to my dad's short stint in the pros. It was as if we were practically born and raised on a baseball field.*

*T-ball, coach pitch, Little League AAA division, Little League Majors, All-Stars, middle school, AAU travel ball, high school ball. Baseball is what I identified with. It wasn't forced on me by a father trying to live his dream through me.*

*I love it. It's the thing that I love the most. Sitting in the dugout chewing and spitting out sunflower seeds while talking or joking with teammates, timing the opposing pitcher from the on-deck circle, and playing my own mind games with the pitcher during my at-bats are my personal favorites. But how can I forget about the pre-game stretches* and warm-ups, where you know whether it is going to be a good day or not? Or how about knowing what you did wrong after a swing and miss and correcting yourself on the very next pitch?

See, I'm more than just a student of the game. This is my life. I make sure to run enough miles during the off-season, get more than enough batting and fielding reps in at my dad's indoor institute, and I make sure to watch what I eat while trying to bulk up more size and muscle.

Tomorrow is the most important day of my life. I go in for surgery. According to these specialists, I won't be able to play baseball anymore, or I run a high risk of dying. This AVM, this fucking disease, is stripping my identity.

What life will I have if it doesn't involve baseball?

For the first time, I can't hide how scared I am. I am afraid of losing the life that I have, scared of dying during surgery, scared of dying shortly after or at any time during this process, scared of never playing again, and scared of the unknown.

This whole brain bleed thing happened so quickly. I didn't even have a chance to sit back and let it sink in. Every time my brain starts to wander into that place, I get interrupted by a nurse coming in for blood work, I'm being transported across the hospital for more testing, or I have visitors. But now that my mother is curled up in the recliner next to the bed, under some blankets, and all I can hear is the beeping of the hospital monitor in my room during this silent night, I'm afraid to let my brain go there—to that place where I can really think about this brain bleed.

My surgery is supposed to be at 7:00 AM, and it's a quarter past one, and I can't sleep. Right now would be a good time for one last distraction.

# CHAPTER SEVENTEEN

<u>New Count</u>

After his Gamma Knife Surgery, Kelvin was instructed to stay inside his home for at least a week. The four screws of the Gamma Knife helmet created four incisions in Kelvin's head—two in the front, just above each eyebrow, and two in the back. The incision on the back left side was where all the radiation was inserted, already causing the area to experience hair loss. It's only been a day since Kelvin left the hospital, and he had forgotten the technical explanation for staying indoors. All he remembered was that it had something to do with the combination of the radiation and the minor open wounds; he needed to avoid direct sunlight until the wounds closed.

Since returning home, Betsy and Sandy have

secretly and constantly debated where Kelvin should stay during his recovery. Betsy didn't want Kelvin out of her sight. She was his mother and the primary caregiver while Kelvin was growing up. She only allowed Kelvin to live with Sandy so he could attend a better school. She was the primary reason Kelvin was the starting short stop at Metropolitan West High School since his freshman year. She had the rightful say on where Kelvin should be staying.

On this particular evening, Kelvin was surprisingly comfortable. Maybe because the barrage of visitors had lightened up, and he didn't feel claustrophobic for the first time in weeks. Staring out the window while seated on his bed, he couldn't help but notice the twilight sky. It was the same color as the *dream* or vision he had while he was dying. Sitting by the window, staring at the sky, alone with his thoughts, would have been perfect. But he wasn't alone. Junelie and Amir were keeping him company.

It wasn't out of the realm of possibility that Junelie and Amir would be inside his home at the same time, but it was strange. Deep down, Kelvin knew something was off. As Kelvin lounged in bed in his basketball shorts and a T-shirt, Junelie constantly talked and told him how she had made the all-star team in her softball league and had requested his jersey number.

Amir took the liberty to play the best baseball video game on Kelvin's PlayStation Five. It was as though this was somehow orchestrated.

Sandy stared at Betsy from behind his kitchen island. Although it's been over twenty years since they met, to Sandy, deep down, Betsy was still the same girl he met in Home Room during their high school sophomore year. Like Sandy, the petite, thirty-seven-year-old mother of three with soft eyes looks much younger than her age. Right now, Sandy recognized the look in Betsy's eyes. It's the same look he received when she'd given him ultimatums as she sat across the kitchen island.

Sandy's kitchen was a chef's dream, with big windows, the latest black and stainless steel appliances, and a small three-piece chandelier that added an intimate mood.

Betsy's big gold hoop earrings, her light makeup, her hair tied up in a bun, and her fitted blue jeans with the white crop top tank top reminded Sandy of the girl he'd fallen in love with. At times, he'd catch himself fantasizing about *what if? What could have been if I wasn't so selfish? Wouldn't life be complete if we were back together?* But with one look at Jonathan and Kelvin, those thoughts are quickly wiped away. All the sacrifices he's made, making his relationship unique as co-parents with Betsy and Mike, has made this family dynamic extraordinary.

Everything went smoothly. It worked effortlessly. Everyone understood their role. All the hard sacrifices were made. At least, that's what Sandy thought before Betsy asked for a favor.

"But... But Kelvin has a place to stay," Kelvin replied after a long pause.

"But we both agreed this would only be temporary," Betsy insisted more than reminded.

It was as if Betsy had pulled the rug from under Sandy. It felt like a counter punch one never sees the coming. Those are the ones that stun you. Betsy's eyebrows were straight, and her mouth was closed tightly. A look Sandy thought he'd never seen again.

"Okay, let's just think this through-"

"There's nothing to think about, Sandy. This was temporary. I'm his mother and need to take care of him."

Another punch. This time, a sucker punch to the gut. Sandy almost winced at Betsy's statement. Kelvin was fragile, a walking patient set free to roam the world in critical condition, and Betsy wanted to take care of her baby boy. What was the harm in that? None. Everyone understands the moment a mother gives birth, she will undoubtedly protect her child at all costs, so there was no surprise at Betsy's eagerness to bring Kelvin back home. She failed to realize the impact of her words and the message they send when you can no longer settle for being cordial.

Sandy deeply inhaled before leaning back against his stainless steel dishwasher counter, allowing Betsy to notice the weight of her words. The two locked eyes, and Sandy could see the enlarged pupils and the glistening in her eyes. Without realizing it, Sandy had a frown on his face.

"I'm sorry. I didn't mean-"

"It's all good," Sandy replied, waving off Betsy's attempted apology.

"No, Sandy. I'm serious. I didn't mean it like that," Betsy said more adamantly.

Sandy let out a long sigh. He sighed because she did mean it like that.

"I can take care of him too, Betsy."

"I never said that you can't."

"Have you thought this through?"

"What do you mean?"

Sandy stepped forward, pressed his palms down on the kitchen island counter, and leaned over.

"Where's Kelvin going to sleep? You have Junelie, Damian, and Jonathan? Where's Kelvin going to sleep? Or are you guys just going to stick him on a couch or an airbed?"

"What? Of course not."

"So which kid are you going to up and move out of their bed?"

Betsy's eyebrows went from straight to arched. She expected Sandy to be laid back and go along with what she proposed. It's what Sandy always did when it came to the kids. Baseball was his priority. After baseball, his new profession was the top priority. Regarding living arrangements, who had what weekends and holidays with the kids, Betsy was in charge while Sandy just went along. The last thing she'd expect was a defiant Sandy.

"Look, Betsy. You heard the doctor. Kelvin may never play baseball again, which means we have to realize that Kelvin may be changing into someone new. Baseball is all he knew. Who knows who he will be if that's taken away from him? So, I think keeping his surroundings as normal as possible is important. More importantly, we should treat him like we always do. I don't think it'll be good for him if he sees us treating him differently because we're silently panicking."

Betsy's eyes burned angrily as though Sandy was attacking her, but the soft and emotional shine in her eyes appeared.

"How about you take a copy of my keys? Give Mike a copy, too.?"

Betsy's forehead wrinkled.

Reading her mind, Sandy continued. "So you can physically check up on him whenever you want. It's okay."

Betsy cocked her head to the side and gave Sandy a crooked smile.

"I can't accept that."

"Sure you can," Sandy insisted. "Like you said, you're his mother. You want to take care of him. I want you to know that he's going to be okay here too."

Betsy smiled, shaking her head, and accepted Sandy's kindness. Going along with it made her feel like she was giving in—to what? She wasn't sure. All she knew was that, for the first time, she felt a sense of security in Sandy's words.

Sandy was a terrible husband, not because he was a bad guy, but because he put baseball above everything and everyone else. He was so consumed with being the best that he didn't have time for anything else. This was why he was heavily recruited, why he could have gone pro straight out of high school despite having all the top baseball college programs at the palm of his hands, and why he started as a freshman for Boston College over the senior.

When Sandy was drafted, he was labeled *The Latin natural*. His young wife took a back seat. His two young sons followed suit. It didn't take long for Sandy and Betsy's marriage to fall apart. He chose baseball over Betsy despite having been together since high school. Baseball over the girl was his choice. In the end, the joke was on him. He thought prioritizing the game he loved as a kid would lead him into a hall-of-fame career. Instead, the constant reminder of his sons growing up daily without their father around left him unfocused. He knew all too well what it was like only seeing his father during winter holidays and every other summer and not having him around when he most needed him.

It didn't take long for the first-round pick, a potential hall of famer, to be released without the interest of many teams. Luckily for him, Sandy wasn't just a jock. He was intelligent and put his record-setting rookie deal to good use by returning to school and getting his degree. Again, the road to succession wouldn't come without a price. His sons retook a back seat. Studying, deadlines, projects, and internships en route to his master's and that professor career trumped his ex-girl-friend, Ruth, Amir's mother.

Betsy was now staring at the result of Sandy's growth—a man who had spent the last few years internally punishing himself, trying to make up for his mistakes. She opened her mouth to speak but was interrupted by Kelvin's voice from a distance.

"I'ma be okay here, ma."

Sandy rotated his head to the left while Betsy

quickly turned her entire body towards Kelvin's voice. There he was, standing barefoot in a plain white T-shirt and navy blue basketball shorts that exposed the bottom of his quads. It could have been Betsy's imagination, but she thought the helmet's incisions in Kelvin's forehead were closed and began its scabbing stages.

Kelvin's demeanor gave nothing away. He stood up straight and remained stoic, but his eyes were those of a wounded puppy. Feeling the pang in her chest, Betsy couldn't bear to see Kelvin like this. She quickly glared at Sandy, fighting back tears.

"Everything is already different. Everyone is treating me differently. Dad is right. This is the only place where I feel normal."

Like Kelvin, Sandy stood up straight, crossing his arms, further exposing the size of his forearms and biceps.

"Who's treating you differently."

"Everyone is." Kelvin's voice cracked. "It's like everyone is walking on eggshells around me. I don't like it."

*I fucking hate it.*

"How much of this conversation did you hear?" Betsy asked, now dry-eyed.

Kelvin could have confessed to finding Amir and Junelie under Sandy's roof together being strange. He could have mentioned that knowing he had a long recovery ahead of him, he felt fine and wished everyone would stop treating him like an antique piece. He could have touched up between relatives driving from New

York and his grandmother flying in from the Dominican Republic; being attentive to his every move was exhausting, and now overhearing the talk about the possibility of not being able to play baseball again felt like a stab in the back, because instead of talking amongst themselves, they should just be transparent with him. Instead, he lied.

"Just the part where Dad was offering his keys to the house so you can come any time you want, and he wants you to know that I'm okay here. I'm assuming you want me to come back with you."

Kelvin's phone made a loud ding noise before his parents could say anything. He quickly broke eye contact with them, focusing on his hand digging into his pocket. When he felt the cold steel of the rectangular phone, he pulled out and quickly saw that Carrie had sent him a text message.

*Finally.*

It was like a magic genie had cast a happy spell on him. His stoic demeanor had disappeared as his lips curled a bit, exposing a smirk. Almost forgetting he'd been standing before his parents, Kelvin quickly glanced up, hiding his excitement.

"I'm fine. I really am," Kelvin said before turning around and heading back to his bedroom.

---

Kelvin waited until Betsy and Junelie went home before responding to Carrie's text. Sandy was in the living room with Ruth, summarizing Amir's day since she always needed debriefing.

> Took you long enough to reach out
> to me.

Kelvin put one hand behind his head. He lay on his bed, watching the three small dots form in the grey bubble on the text message screen, anticipating Carrie's response.

> Sorry.

> ...

> It's been a weird time.

> What's going on?

> It'll be too much to type. It's a long story.

> I'm literally not doing anything. I can't do anything. All I have is time right now.

> ...

Kelvin watched as the three dots appeared and disappeared before appearing again. Carrie was thinking about what to say. Kelvin felt a pang in his chest.

*Not her, too. Don't tell me she's going to treat me weird like everyone else.*

> You really don't remember anything
> about that day?

Kelvin grinned as he slid his hand out from behind his head, allowing his head to rest on his pillow softly. He used both his hands to type quickly.

> I remember you coming to see me. I remember our talk; your face was the last thing I saw before I woke up again.

Kelvin stared at his phone, waiting for the dots to appear again. After a full minute and no reply from Carrie, Kelvin sat up in bed, eyes glued to the screen as if magically forcing the dots on the screen himself. Suddenly, his heart rate intensified with every silent passing second. Then, finally, the dots appeared again. He didn't know why he suddenly felt anxious. All he knew was something was wrong, *AGAIN*.

> I can't do this, Kelvin. I can't take on a sick person. Sorry

There it was. It was a sucker punch to the gut. Kelvin felt it all: wet eyes, hot flashes, eyebrows scrunching, the feeling of being submerged under water.

*Take on a sick person? What do you mean take on? I'm a sick person? That's how you see me? Is that how everyone sees me?*

> I've just been through a lot the past couple of weeks. I'm sorry.

*You have been through a lot? What about me?*

Kelvin wanted to say so much. Instead, he just settled for

Okay.

Kelvin tossed his cell phone across his bed before lying flat on his bed. Staring up at his ceiling, trying to fight back tears, for the first time in his life, he asked God, *why me?*

# CHAPTER EIGHTEEN

<u>Sixth Inning</u>

They say we bounce back when we take losses. You're forced to question who you were when you're stripped of your identity. *What good am I? What am I really worth? Who am I?* It's like you're playing in a nine-inning game, which is rare for us teens, and you're in the sixth inning. You're down by two or three runs. The game is far from done, but it's not simultaneously. The opposing pitcher has been dominant, and your strengths have failed you miserably.

Picture this being a ninety-degree, humid, sunny summer game, and you have to face this workhorse of a pitcher again, who had been getting stronger as the game went on. He's struck you out twice, and the embarrassment is engraved in your brain. You step into the batter's box, and your team needs you like your life depends on it. What kind of player will you be? The same one from the previous two at-bats, or will you lay down a bunt, or maybe slap a cheap base hit the opposite way to get a base and start a rally?

You quietly transform into something else without noticing when you're alone with your thoughts for an extended time.

Three weeks have passed since Kelvin's surgery, and besides church, he hardly left the house. He thought about it all: the morning he woke up with the abnormal headache, the trip to the emergency room, the initial CT Scan, the surprising brain bleed news, being admitted to the Neuro ICU, being treated like fine China, Carrie's face, the dream, learning he very well may never play baseball again, and Carrie calling him a *sick* person.

Two days ago, Kelvin's uncle (Sandy's younger brother), Jualian, came over to visit for an extended period, staying in the guest room. Julian was thirty years old, although he looked twenty-five. Although he was a couple of inches shorter than Sandy, his dark complexion was identical to Sandy's. Like his big brother, his shoulders were broad and toned, his biceps and forearms were muscular, and his legs were almost as strong as a soccer player's. He always kept a low-even haircut, and a perfectly groomed goatee coincided with his million-dollar smile, exposing his dimples. All of his features attracted many women to him.

Kelvin suspected Julian volunteered to or was asked to stay and check on him, as his parents suspected he'd been slowly falling into depression. Any normal kid would run out of the house once medical freedom had been granted, but not Kelvin. Gregory, Damian, Jonathan, Jason, and Ryan had visited daily. However, as the days passed, Ryan's visits became less frequent.

Just yesterday, Kelvin spent the day in his room texting with Carrie, who had reached out to him after calling him that awful word. His television and his computer remained off the entire day. He hadn't even bothered putting up his window blinds. Although it was summertime, his room was dark and felt cold. The sun peaked from the edges of the window blinds, making his room appear like he was a prisoner in solitary confinement with minimal sunlight. All that was missing was for Sandy to slide in Kelvin's meals from a small door slide.

> I'm sorry about what I said, Kelvin.

Kelvin could hear Sandy, Julian, and his Godfather, Francelin's voices coming from the kitchen. Amir had made the eight-year-old all-star team as a six-year-old, and today was his first game. The legend of the young phenom was growing, and his father and uncles were gearing up for Amir's big day.

> Why'd you say it?

Kelvin kept his eyes glued on the phone screen as he gripped his cell phone in his hands, lying face up in bed. He watched as the three dots appeared but was suddenly interrupted by Julian storming into his bedroom.

Julian wore ripped blue jeans shorts and a fitted white plain V-neck shirt, which exposed a gold chain.

"I'ma let you know something right now," Julian stated in his deep, raspy voice, starting Kelvin. "I'll let you sulk and mope around here for one more day. Don't be soft. You ain't a bitch. Let's go. Get up, and face this shit like a soldier." Julian added.

Kelvin sat up in bed, staring at his uncle. The brightness behind Julian in the hallway suddenly made Kelvin realize it was nearly noon.

"I don't know what happened yesterday at your neurologist appointment. I don't know what you told your parents, but I know you ain't being real. I'ma give you two choices for tomorrow. You get up early, make your bed, and come with me to the barbershop so you can look good. When you look good, you feel good. Then you're going to your Amir's second game tomorrow. Choice number two is, I'll drag your ass out of your bed, throw you in the shower, I take you to get a haircut, and we go to your brother's game," Julian added. His glare darted through Kelvin's from across the room. His full lips were tight, and his jaw was rigid and tense as if he were a drill sergeant.

Julian's eyes wandered around Kelvin's room before making eye contact briefly with Kelvin. "One more day," he said before turning around and closing the door, leaving Kelvin staring at a closed bedroom door.

If everyone thought Sandy was tough, Julian doubled his intensity. Growing up, Julian was the one who constantly tested the waters, the one who continually got into trouble and kept questionable company. His behavior had gotten so bad when he reached his teenage years that his mother sent him away to military school. After being hardened in the confines of cold military school for four years, Julian transformed himself into a no-excuses, self-driven man, and now a successful personal trainer and nationally known cycling coach, known for his intensity.

Kelvin's phone chimed again from another text message from Carrie, snapping him out of the momentary shock his uncle had just given him.

???

Kelvin had given Julian his undivided attention, and he hadn't noticed Carrie's answer. He reached behind him, grabbed his phone off his bed, and started to scroll back to catch up, pupils bouncing back and forth like two bugs trapped in a mason jar.

I don't know. I was just scared. What I saw that day was scary. You understand? It was traumatic. How can I get over that?

???

I don't know how to respond to that.

I just want you to understand that seeing what happened to you up close and personal is still hard on me.

Why couldn't you just tell me that in person?

> Because it's easier just texting it.

Of course, telling someone something hard behind a screen was easier. Teens and young adults today hide behind screens more often than not. Kelvin just sat back and stared into his cellphone screen, suddenly remembering the times Carrie did this.

After Carrie broke up with Kelvin and learned about Analis (the girl on the train), she texted to explain her reasoning and express her feelings about everything. Similarly, after learning about Analis' presence at Central's senior night, Carrie shared her feelings again through text messages.

Kelvin wasn't like that. Neither was Jonathan. Sandy and Betsy raised their boys *old school*. They were taught that if you had something to say, you should say it to that person's face. *Never choose the cop-out. They'll respect you a lot more for it*, Betsy would say.

*Why hadn't I picked up these behavior traits before? Why is it easier through a text?*

Kelvin shook it off. It wouldn't do him any good speculating if Carrie wouldn't flat-out say it. What bothered Kelvin was that he thought no matter how bad it was, he believed Carrie was someone who wouldn't waiver from him. Yes, watching someone pass out in front of you, requiring immediate medical attention, can be traumatizing. But to distance yourself from that person because you feel traumatized is selfish. If you're scared because of this, imagine the person going through this.

*I get it. You got scared, but what about me? I'm the one living with this, not you.*

Instead of typing that, Kelvin hardened his jaw. There weren't any more tears and no more glassy eyes. Something changed in Kelvin during his appointment with his neurologist yesterday. His time was now more limited than most, and he wasn't going to waste it on nonsense. Suddenly, Julian's words echoed in his brain. *Don't be soft. You ain't a bitch. Let's go. Get up, and face this shit like a soldier.*

Kelvin quickly texted Carrie back.

> I get it. I understand. TTYL gotta go to Amir's game.

He tossed his cell phone behind him on his bed, hopped out, walked toward his door, and opened it.

"Yo, Uncle Julian! Dad! Can you make me a haircut appointment in the next hour so I can go to the game with ya?"

---

Mendon, Massachusetts, was fifty minutes from Sandy's house, where the 8U Nipmuc All-Star tournament was held. The Little League complex looked like any other well-maintained one with three different fields, with the main field positioned in front of the concession stand. The concession stand was a green-painted, two-storied brick hut where a teenager occupied the second floor to announce each pitcher and batter. The length of the field was the standard size, with bleachers positioned on both the first base and third base side with plenty of grass space after the bleachers and behind the outfield fence, where parents set up canopies with travel chairs to watch the game comfortably while protecting themselves from the scorching July sun.

Kelvin and Jonathan found a vacant spot directly behind the center field fence, where they stood, resting their folded forearms on top of it. Both brothers were dressed similarly; Jonathan was in gym shorts, a teal Florida Marlins hat, and a light grey dry-fit material t-shirt, and Kelvin was in basketball shorts, a navy blue Yankee hat, and a white t-shirt.

Sandy, Julian, and Francelin stood under a canopy on the first base side. There was no surprise there. Sandy always wanted a closer look at the game for several reasons: one, to get a better view of his son, two, to see what he did right, and three, to see what he did wrong. Even though Amir was only six and should have been exempt from harsh criticism, his advanced play and understanding of the game permitted Sandy to voice specific suggestions to his young son.

Kelvin had just told Jonathan what exactly occurred during his appointment with his neurologist, which left Jonathan shell-shocked.

"How-How am I supposed to respond to some shit like that?" Jonathan asked, keeping his gaze on Amir's game, trying hard not to break down.

The truth is, Neurologist Dr. Woo had informed Kelvin that people with his condition usually do not live to see the age of twenty-eight, let alone live long enough to see thirty. If they do, they live with brain damage. Kelvin begged his mother to wait out in the waiting room while he met with his neurologist because Betsy tended to make Kelvin anxious. Promising he'd tell her everything, Betsy complied. But Kelvin kept to himself what Dr. Woo said about his expected lifetime.

"Respond the same way I did when you told me Vanity got an abortion."

Sucking his teeth, Jonathan replied. "That shit ain't the same."

"Sure it is. It's surprising."

Jonathan now gave Kelvin his undivided attention, shifting his body to face his brother.

"You know it's not the same… What are you going to do? Tell Mami and Papi?"

"No," Kelvin replied. "How do I tell them if I don't even know if it's true?"

Jonathan raised an eyebrow, which made a sweat drop trickle down the edge of his left eye. "What do you do mean?" Jonathan asked.

"I don't know if it's true. It's weird. The dude was loud. It was like he was yelling but wasn't. Everything he kept saying was you can't do this, or you're gonna die. Everything led to I'm gonna die. So something clicked in me." Kelvin stopped short, trying to put his words together, leaving Jonathan with anticipation. The urgency was displayed on Jonathan's face through his bulging eyes.

"What? What clicked in you?"

"Everything. Like yeah, it scares the shit out of me that some specialist who specializes in the brain and knows about my condition says that I'ma die, but I don't feel like I am. I don't believe it."

"Like being in denial?"

"Nah, I really don't believe it. It lingers in my brain, but I don't think I'll ever believe it. At least, I hope not."

Jonathan wiped the sweat off his forehead before squinting his eyes. He stared at Kelvin. He stared at him, observing his little brother. Suddenly, Kelvin was a different person. The cheers from parents when their team scored were drowned out. Jonathan couldn't hear anything else other than Kelvin.

"So, what clicked in me was that nothing else mattered. Just my life and what I wanna do. And if I die doing what I wanna do, so be it. But Jonathan, nothing else matters."

As Amir stepped up to bat, Jonathan shifted his body again, resting his forearms on top of the outfield fence. He was wearing the Cranston West Little League All-Stars white and teal uniform. Six-year-old Amir looked tiny compared to all the eight-year-olds on the field.

"You know, they say Amir is gonna be better than both of us," Jonathan said, watching his little brother getting into his batting stance.

"He is… So, you gonna be good by yourself down in Miami after knowing about Vanity?"

Jonathan shrugged his shoulders. "I guess."

Kelvin kept his gaze on Amir, as he was up two balls and had no strikes on the opposing eight-year-old pitcher with the blond curly hair peeking out of his baseball cap. However, he felt the sudden change of mood in his brother.

"You just told me that Vanity got an abortion, but you didn't tell me what happened—like what led her to do that."

Kelvin watched as Amir chose not to swing at a ball near the strike zone, which was once again called a ball. He felt that deep down, had it been him, he would have swung at the pitch. Jonathan opened his mouth several times to answer the question but hesitated, trying to find the words. To the naked eye, both brothers stood expressionless, watching a game, but so much was being said through their nonverbal behavior. The roles were even now. No more big brother to little brother, no more big brother knows best. Kelvin had matured overnight. Honestly, he had no choice since his life depended on it.

"Remember the day we walked into the E.R.?"

"How could I forget?" Kelvin replied, watching Amir walk toward first base after taking ball four.

"Well, remember in your waiting room when I told you I had something to tell you and made you swear that you wouldn't tell anybody before the doctors came in and told you that you were bleeding in your brain?… Well, I was gonna tell you that I had just found out that same morning that Vanity was pregnant."

"How, though? We went to that—" Kelvin suddenly stopped himself, remembering *her*, remembering Analis. Everything of that night came back to him—how she looked, how she smelled, how they danced, the undeniable chemistry before she threw the curveball at him by saying, *I don't want a boyfriend right now.*

"Yo, yo, you good?" Jonathan asked, snapping his fingers at Kelvin, snapping him out of his trance.

"Yeah, yeah, I'm good," Kelvin replied with a minor shake of his head. "But yeah, how'd you find out that morning since we went to that graduation party the night before? She knew the whole time?"

"No. She said her period was late and didn't notice until she went through her app."

"Her app?" Kelvin asked, confused, raising both eyebrows.

"Yeah, some period app. She said something about doing something on her phone and remembered she hadn't checked her app. So when she found out she was late, she went to the pharmacy and bought a test that came in two. They both came out positive. She texted me and told me. She said she couldn't blow off a family thing and for me to just go play ball with you and the boys like we planned later. But you know we didn't do that since we went to the hospital."

"Oh shit."

"Yeah."

"Why'd she get the abortion, though?"

"She said because I wasn't there for her..."

Kelvin felt a pang in his chest. It was the same feeling when Carrie initially broke up with him, the same one he felt when she said I can't take on a sick person.

"I was the reason she got an abortion?"

"She said she understood why. She knew you were sick. She didn't blame you. She blamed me. I guess it makes sense. If I can't multitask, being there for my sick brother, how can I take on having a baby and playing college ball?" Jonathan had a smirk on his face. It was hard to tell if it was a relieved or sad one. "But... I feel like I made the wrong choice."

"So you were gonna choose the girl?" Kelvin asked with a chuckle.

"Yeah. What Vanity didn't know was that I was reaching out to both Rutgers and URI since the offers were still on the table. I wanted to explain the situation to them. I was more in contact with URI because I assumed she'd stay closer to home, being pregnant and all. But in the end, she took the choice away from me."

"Wow. You really were gonna choose the girl. I never expected that from you."

"There's always baseball and a girl," Jonathan said, mimicking Sandy. "But anyway, back to you... What do you wanna do? You said nothing matters other than what you wanna do."

"When do you leave for Miami?"

"In four or five weeks."

"I wanna play baseball. I know I can't, at least right now. But I gotta get back on the field to at least run drills, and I wanna hit, at least off a tee. I know I can't tell Mami, but can you help me train to get back into baseball shape?"

"What if Mami finds out?"

"We'll just have to make sure that she doesn't."

# JOURNAL ENTRY

*What I hate*

*Kelvin*

You wanna know what I hate? The *I know how you feel* comments. No, you don't. The comparisons of your past traumas that somehow make our conversation into something you went through annoy the shit out of me. Although I'm reserved, I consider myself an empathetic and sympathetic person. So, saying *I know how you feel* and comparing my life-threatening issue to something that <u>YOU</u> got over doesn't sit well with me.

You know what else I despise? Feeling like this–angry. But I can't help it. Although I'm not physically constrained, I feel like it. My mother doesn't want me to lift anything, and my pops barges into my room every hour or so to make sure that I'm okay. I can't drive, but no one wants me to let myself go for walks.

Don't they know that the more time I spend alone

with my thoughts, the more I think about not currently playing in a baseball game? I need to be active and do stuff before I go insane. And I don't want to be treated like some toddler who just learned how to walk. I haven't had training wheels since I was four years old. It'll be better for my mental state of mind if everyone just backed off and put their training wheels back where they found them.

# CHAPTER NINETEEN

Hot and Cold

Jonathan followed in the footsteps of Providence's own *Jeremy Peña* by outshining every single player during the perfect-game tournament in Atlanta. It's what landed him that elusive offer from Miami University. Having participated in the tournament for three consecutive years and showing scouts that he was one of a kind landed him offers from Boston College, URI, and Central Connection going into his junior year of high school.

With his fielding glove in his left hand, dirt on his left shin, dirtying his calf-high white sock, kicked-up dirt on his light grey baseball cap, and his sweaty red t-shirt stuck to his chest, the sudden realization that he'd be missing this year's tournament crept into Kelvin.

The last week has been a difficult one with sudden

mood changes. At any given moment, those around Kelvin couldn't predict which Kelvin was present. One moment, he'd be his usual self; the next, he'd be quiet and distant; lately, he'd been short, direct, and border-line mad at the world. Even something as innocent as fielding ground balls from Jonathan, who was once full of life while blasting music from their portable speaker, had turned into silent sessions where Kelvin's demeanor acted like he was playing in game seven of the World Series. It was as if he was punishing himself for what had happened to him.

Jonathan stood at home plate with a baseball in his left hand and a trainer bat in his right, staring at his brother, lost in a trance, in the shortstop position.

"Yo!… What's up with you?" Jonathan shouted. "I almost hit you with that ball."

"Again. Let's go. Hit it harder," Kelvin replied, shaking himself out of the trance. He kicked back some dirt with his cleat and readied himself, anticipating the next ground ball.

Jonathan tossed the ball to himself, quickly grabbed the bat with both hands while the ball was in the air, and hit the ball when it came back into his swing zone. The ball rocketed toward Kelvin's right. Kelvin quickly moved his feet to his right to field the ball. The ball skipped off the dirt half a food before reaching Kelvin, making an awkward bounce that would typically result in an error or a base hit, but Kelvin anticipated it. He got down on a backward-sideways, one-legged kneeling position with his shin touching the dirt, his right palm pressed against the dirt; he rotated his glove backward, brought his glove up from the ground into the air, grabbing the ball into his glove.

"Ohh, good shit," Jonathan shouted.

Kelvin stood up and tossed the ball away from him toward first base. "Again," He yelled. This time, his voice had a lot more base to it.

Jonathan's sweaty eyebrows curved as he wiped away a sweat drop with his thumb before it could sting his eye. Noticing the sudden angry change in his little brother's posture, he knew it was time to end this session.

"You had enough," Jonathan said in a direct tone that one would describe as a coach.

Kelvin's nostrils flared as he shot a Mike *Tyson-esk* look toward his brother from nearly a hundred feet away. "I'll tell you when I've had enough," he hollered back.

Jonathan turned his back to Kelvin, tightly gripping his bat in his right hand, and started to walk toward the dugout. Without bothering to look at Kelvin, he said, "I'm not doing this with you, Kelvin."

"What?"

Jonathan headed into the dugout. Kelvin watched his brother place his baseball bat on the bench and start to stuff his glove into his baseball bag.

The sun felt like it got hotter by the femtosecond, and Kelvin's sweat was starting to make his shirt transparent.

"Yo!" Kelvin called out to his brother. This time, his tone was apologetic.

It was too late. Jonathan made his way out of the dugout, wearing rubber slippers, carrying his baseball bag like a backpack, gripping his bat in his left hand while using his index and middle fingers in his right hand to hold his turf cleats by the heel.

"No, Kelvin. I ain't doing this shit with you," Jonathan reiterated, now standing a foot away from first base, scowling at Kelvin. "When I agreed to help you, I thought you were gonna have fun. You're not having fun anymore. Since you're not having fun, you don't love this anymore."

The words landed like blows to Kelvin, causing him to silently wince.

"I mean, look at you," Jonathan started to raise his voice in a lecture and pleading mixture. "You're standing in the baking sun after Mami told you you shouldn't be in the sun for too long because you'll get a headache. It's like you're doing this shit on purpose. Why? You couldn't wait until like six? Why does it have to be now?"

"Come on, you know that too much sun shit is all lies."

"It doesn't matter," Jonathan exploded, throwing his arms out and holding them out, currently looking like a T. "You can't compromise? I know you're mad at that Dr. Woo guy. I know you're mad that this shit happened to you. I know you are. I'd be, too. I get it. Yo, trust me, I get it. But you can't do a complete 180 on us. If you wanna be mad at the world, fine. You gotta blow off steam somehow. But don't punish yourself in front of the people who are trying to help you. You're killing Mami and Papi when you do that."

"Jonathan-"

"I'm telling them what that neurologist said to you."

Kelvin's eyes budged so big they looked like they had physically burst out of their sockets. Before Kelvin protested, Jonathan said, "It's time to be real. Come on. Let's go."

"I'm not going anywhere with you."

Jonathan shrugged his shoulders. "Fine. Walk back home. Maybe it'll give you time to think about everything I said."

Jonathan turned around and headed toward the field's exit. Kelvin kept his eyes on Jonathan the entire time. He stood there in the sun, watching his brother open the trunk and place his baseball gear in it. He watched him as Jonathan walked back to the driver's door and exchanged a glance with him before climbing into the car and driving away.

Kelvin wanted to kill Jonathan. Not literally but figuratively because he was about to drop a bombshell on his parents; he was about to do the one thing Kelvin pleaded with him not to do. He looked up at the sun. Usually, the sun makes people wince, shut their eyes, and look away, but Kelvin kept his open. Surprisingly, his eyes didn't burn. He just stood there, looking at the sun with tears in his eyes.

Oh, how he wanted to kill Jonathan, mainly because he was right. He was absolutely right. When you're transitioning and trying to find yourself, you're juggling new emotions. It could be nerve-wracking accepting this new you who you don't even know yet. And the last thing you want is someone calling you out on your own bullshit.

# CHAPTER TWENTY

<u>Two Outs</u>

"Okay. What we need is a second opinion," Betsy said.

Surprisingly, she took Kelvin's eminent fait calmly. At least, that's what it appeared like to Jonathan. Sandy had invited Betsy and Michael over, along with Damian and Junelie, for a small barbecue, anticipating that Jonathan and Kelvin wouldn't be out long enough to make Betsy worry about Kelvin's well-being.

*Dad, we're only gonna be an hour. We'll be here and showered before Mom gets here.*

Sandy should have known better. Kelvin had been on edge and was very unpredictable. So it was almost predictable when Jonathan walked through the door an hour late without Kelvin.

"That man isn't God. He can't determine someone's fait," Betsy added, tying her hair up in a ponytail. She didn't know if it was the humidity or the fact that Kelvin withheld life-altering information about his health that made her hotter. Still, Betsy imagined her powered blue tank top starting to show a sweat-wet mark on the abdomen section. She wore mid-leg thigh-high blue cut-off jean shorts and a thin gold necklace, which now stuck to her collarbone. She embarrassedly felt her underarms starting to feel a bit moist and figured retying her curly hair in the ponytail could add some fresh air.

Sandy, Jonathan, and Michael knew what was happening too well. Kelvin lied. He wasn't himself, and they all feared he may never be the same again. But there comes a point in these sensitive situations when one asks oneself, how do I find the balance between a support system and a disciplinary parent?

"Maybe he's going through the stages of grief," Michael said, trying not to sound dumb as he attempted to give Kelvin some leeway.

Betsy snapped her head left, staring at Michael, who sat beside her at the glassed, round deck table. He wore khaki shorts, a red shirt with a gold lightning bolt logo in the center, and a pair of all-black sneakers.

Michael felt the blank stares of Sandy and Jonathan, mixed in with Betsy's " *explain yourself* stare, and started to elaborate. "You know, denial, sadness, anger, acceptance. I forget the others. But it's clear what's going on with him."

"But he isn't dead." Betsy felt her voice rising and stopped herself short. Taking a deep breath as she looked up at the blue sky, blinking away tears, she changed her tone. "No one is dead for him to feel this way."

"Are you sure about that?"

Everyone turned their direction toward the voice coming from inside the house. The back door had been open with the screen closed to prevent bugs from entering the house. The lights were turned off, but the open windows had let the sunlight illuminate the entire house. The way the kitchen was set up with its Island, the refrigerator positioned on the opposite wall of the stove, and the walking space directly behind the kitchen wall made it difficult to see who had walked into the house.

"The kid thinks his dreams are dead," Julian continued, stepping into the kitchen, holding a fresh bowl of fruit he had purchased at Whole Foods. He was dressed in light blue fitted jean shorts, designer sneakers, a stylish tanned tank top, and his gold chain. "Of course, he's going to be going through it, especially as he's learning to accept his new self," Julian concluded.

Betsy pressed her lips so tight they almost disappeared. She watched her ex-brother-in-law, with whom she has a love-hate relationship, step onto the back deck.

"How long have you been listening?" Sandy asked.

"I've been here the whole time," Julian replied, placing the bowl of fruit on the center of the table.

"*Tio*, you shoulda seen him today. I never seen him like that," Jonathan said, grabbing a piece of pineapple.

"I bet. Has he answered any of your phone calls?"

"He said he's on his way back home," Sandy replied.

"Nephew, Ima tell you a quick story before Kelvin comes back home. This can be beneficial to you, too, Damian." Julian quickly made eye contact with Michael. "I don't mean to step on anyone's shoes here."

Waving him off, Michael replied, "It's all good. Go ahead."

Damian nodded with an expressionless look on his face.

"Back when I was taken to military school."

"You were in military school?" Damian quickly asked, suddenly interested.

"Yeah. I spent my sophomore, junior, and senior years there. Even though my mother was amazing, I was a bad kid, running around with the wrong crowd. I was dumb. My big brother was a baseball stud. He'd already laid out the blueprint for me, and I could have taken it further. Anyway, that's neither here nor there… What I want to say is that when I arrived at military school, I felt like my family didn't love me anymore. It was like I was dead to them."

Betsy softened her eyes as she watched Julian tell his story. She'd known Julian for most of his life and saw the transformation in him, but never knew the specifics of his transformation.

"To me, life was done. My mother didn't want me. My brother didn't love me. I was away from the life that I knew… I want you young men to know that don't get comfortable with being comfortable. You're going to PC to play ball, and you're about to leave for Miami to play ball, and that's all great. But I need you guys to expect uncomfortable. Why? Because we evolve. We're not a finished product. And to be an amazing person, you must constantly evolve, killing bad habits and toxic traits. See it as killing versions of your old self."

Ironically, everyone at the table nodded silently. Julian sat a little taller in his chair.

"Damian, you wouldn't be the ball player you were if you were content with your ball-handling skills. You knew you needed to work on your jump shot, right? Now that you are entering your college career, you have to bulk up because these aren't high school kids you're playing with—these are men, right?"

"Right," Damian replied.

"You have to treat every aspect of life that way. The thing is, we usually have time. But there are cases where we're forced to do so before we want to."

"Kelvin," Betsy said softly.

"Right. See, Kelvin was already making another transition into his new self. But this AVM derailed all that. So now he's struggling to find a replacement, and I get it. I felt like I wasn't supposed to be shipped to military school, so I had to become this new person I didn't want to be. I felt it all. Betrayal, anger, depression. It's what Kelvin is feeling now. He's asking himself why he is going through all these emotions. He's literally killing two versions of himself while trying to figure out who he needs to be instead of who he wants to be. That's a lot for a seventeen-year-old kid to take."

"He can't lie to us or hide important information about his health, either," Betsy said.

Julian slowly threw his hands in the air. "I know. I'm not absolving him of his actions. I'm just giving you an example of his mindset... Look, you and Sandy are amazing parents, but you're tough, and rightfully so. Maybe right now isn't the time to be tough because you're the parent, and he's the kid."

"We gotta show him another way," Sandy said, looking at Betsy.

"He's so closed off. You know he's always been. He's just like you. He never talked about his feelings. *El es seco.*"

"I know. So show him. I think the second opinion is a good idea. We show him we don't believe what Dr. Woo said. He's scared. I am, too, but we can't show him that we're more scared than he is."

"There's something else," Julian said.

"What?" Betsy asked, wiping her tears away.

"Whatever he's trying to hold in, he's gonna have to let it out sometime."

# CHAPTER TWENTY-ONE

<u>Dr. Johnson</u>

"And how are the headaches?" Dr. Johnson asked.

Dr. Johnson's office was comfortably large. Despite Kelvin being seated on the paper-sheet-covered examination table, there was significant walking space between the table and the door, and the same went for the distance between the table and the window. Despite the size, Dr. Johnson's office was like any other doctor's: bright lights, tiled flooring, a small sink by the wall, informational posters on serious health risks, and a rolling chair to roll around at will.

"Consistent, I guess."

"How many times a day or week?"

Dr. Johnson's voice matched his appearance: Strong and direct but had an endearing sooth. His warm eyes and welcoming face put an ease to Kelvin, unlike the last previous specialists. It could have been the fact that Dr. Johnson was the first man of color he encountered as a doctor and immediately felt seen; maybe it was because the six foot four neurologist opened up talking about basketball instead of talking down to him with instructions on things not to do, or perhaps it could have been because he didn't raise his voice predicting his fate the way Dr. Woo did. Whatever the reason, Kelvin's heart rate was at ease as Dr. Johnson examined and questioned him.

"About twice a week."

"I think they're getting worse," Betsy said accusingly, reminding Kelvin to speak the whole truth as she sat by the window, clutching her purse.

"They were worse; now they're just the same, or I got used to the pain," Kelvin replied.

Dr. Johnson maintained eye contact with Kelvin and smirked.

"We can do something about that. I can put you on headache-prevention medication. I don't know how your body will react. Some medications make you lose your appetite, and some have no effects."

"I'd rather not play the trial game."

Dr. Johnson smirked again. "I didn't think so."

"What are we going to do about what Dr. Woo told my son? Are there any other tests we can do?" Betsy asked, being the only one in the room who was not at ease.

Dr. Johnson cleared his throat, stepped back, and positioned his body at an angle, simultaneously facing Kelvin and Betsy.

"Kelvin just went through an intensive radiation surgery not long after getting an MRI. It isn't ideal for getting another MRI so close to being exposed to radiation, especially being so young. See, the brain is a sensitive and unpredictable thing. Expect the unexpected."

"So, what Dr. Woo said is a lie?" Betsy asked.

"No," Dr. Johnson said, shaking his head. "But it isn't true either. Truthfully, nobody knows, and I think you should take comfort in that because your son is extraordinary. I've seen exactly nineteen patients with ruptured AVMs."

"How many survivors?" Betsy asked, edging off her seat so much it looked like she would take off sprinting at the sound of go.

"Nine. Kelvin here is part of those nine. Ask me how many came out of it normal?"

"How many?" Kelvin asked.

Dr. Johnson held up his index finger. He locked eyes with Kelvin. "Just one… You."

Betsy covered her mouth, covering her gasp.

"Kelvin, it's never a good thing to experience a ruptured brain AVM that big. I haven't seen one as big as yours in my entire career, and I've been at this for twenty-one years. Those survivors I mentioned all have some brain damage where they can't talk right, have memory problems, and body function impediments. You are the only one I have ever seen walk into my office without help and function perfectly fine. It's incredible. I'm not here to discredit Dr. Woo, but I assume he was cautioning you because he was blown away and didn't know how to react. I can't say that for sure, but wow. You're something else." The way Dr.

Johnson spoke was powerful and mesmerizing at the same time. It was as if Denzel Washington had been lecturing on brain conditions.

"So, I'm good?" Kelvin asked, sounding hopeful for the first time in a long time. His eyes widened with innocence, the way a young kid would after holding in his cries after a shot because they would get a lollipop afterward.

"No," Dr. Johnson replied. "Far from it. "As I said, I don't know where Dr. Woo got those assumptions from. Age twenty-eight, age thirty. If I could elaborate better on his behalf, I assume he was referring to the life expectancy after someone suffers a massive hemorrhage the way you did. Very seldom do people your age experience something like that. So I think most, if not all, of his patients were A, a lot older, and B, had severe brain damage. So yes, ten to thirteen years is a proper estimate, given the complications said patients will endure."

All the hope Kelvin had shown was quickly wiped away.

"But you have youth on your side. That's the only reason why you look like nothing ever happened to you."

"Give it to me straight, doc. Can I play baseball?"

"Kelvin? Really?" Betsy embarrassedly asked. "I'm so sorry, Dr. Johnson."

Dr. Johnson laughed. Kelvin didn't let up.

"Can I at least go lift weights? I have an uncle staying with us who can train me."

"Kelvin, *ya coño*." Betsy's embarrassment had reached annoyance. All she wanted was for her son to be healthy, and she was wary of him putting himself in harm's way.

Kelvin rotated his head to look at his mother in a lighthearted way. It was his first physical movement since shaking Dr. Johnson's hand.

"I'll tell you what, Kelvin. I'm not going to clear you to play baseball just yet."

'I've been taking ground balls with my brother," Kelvin quickly added, making Dr. Johnson chuckle again.

"Okay. You can stick to that. Nothing too hard. If you want to take swings off a T, that's okay, too. But no live games, not even pick-up games. I'm not a big baseball guy. I love basketball. But I do watch SportsCenter, and I see players diving on the floor, sliding into bases, and occasionally getting drilled by a pitch. Your surgery is too fresh, and Dr. Woo is right. Any trauma to your head can result in death. You understand?"

Kelvin nodded.

"As for weights, as long as you're breathing right, inhaling and exhaling, not holding your breath, you should be fine. So getting stronger, polishing up your swing, and working on your defense on the field is fine by me. Just pace yourself. You're not always going to feel great. Some days, your head is going to hurt. Trust your body and listen to it."

"Yes, sir," Kelvin said, trying to contain his genuine smile, which he hadn't shown in a long time.

"Okay. I'll see you back here soon, a month after your next MRI. I'll see how your brain looks then, and we'll take it from there, okay?"

"Okay."

"And if you need one of those headache prevention medications, just call my office, and I'll send a slip in. How does that sound?"

"Good."

"That sounds great," Betsy said, rising off the chair. "Thank you so much, Dr. Johnson. I feel so much better now."

"I'm happy to hear that." Dr. Johnson turned his attention back to Kelvin and held his hand for a handshake. "See you soon, young man."

Kelvin firmly shook Dr. Johnson's hand. "Yes, sir."

Dr. Johnson waved goodbye to Betsy and left his office, giving Kelvin and Betsy time to walk out alone. Kelvin quickly grinned at his mother, who wanted nothing to do with what came next.

"Kelvin, not so fast."

"Ma, you heard him," Kelvin replied with a big smile that looked like he was seconds away from splitting his cheeks open. He hopped off the table and dug his hand into his pocket. "I gotta call the guys."

"Kelvin?"

Kelvin stared into his mother's worried eyes and quietly understood. "I promise I won't do more than what I'm allowed to."

Betsy's lips curled into a slight smirk. "Come on. Let's go."

---

The University of Rhode Island's TD summer success program allows those selected to reside on campus from early July until early August. Students can take classes and must maintain at least a cumulative average of 2.5 GPA or higher to be eligible for the need-based Hardge/Forleo Grant. (TD) Talent Development recruits and serves Rhode Island high school graduates with college potential who come from historically disadvantaged backgrounds, most of whom are Scholars of color.

TD scholarships for Community Leadership recipients receive up to $70,000 for tuition and living expenses and opportunities for paid summer employment, peer networking, and mentorship. Up to twenty scholarships are available to be awarded.

Analis was ready for the next stage of her life, entering adulthood. It was Friday, the day to go home for the weekend, and Analis found herself at a nearby *Subway* at the Emporium, a walking distance plaza from the URI campus. She could have chosen to wait to eat once she got home since beach traffic was heading towards her direction, not towards Providence, but the growl in her stomach told her otherwise.

Analis stood in the crowded line, waiting to order her six-inch tuna sandwich, dressed in grey spandex shorts, a teal T-shirt, and a pair of low-top white sneakers, exposing her gold anklet. She wore her curly hair out for the first time in a week, excited for a fun weekend. Her eyes were glued to the menu, trying to decide whether to add chips and a soda or settle for a bottle of water, when she heard a female voice call out, "Professor Machado!"

Analis swiftly rotated her head toward the entrance and spotted a dark-skinned man stop short of the front door to wave at the young woman, calling out to him before heading out. He wore a navy blue polo-style shirt, exposing his muscular biceps. His knee-high tan golf shorts displayed the muscle tone in his lower quads and calves, which put doubt in the average person who questioned if this person was a college professor or a collegian strength and conditioning coach. She couldn't help but notice the resemblance.

*"My father is a creative writing professor at URI."*

She didn't know why and couldn't explain it, but Analis quickly stepped out of the line and headed toward the exit. She pushed the door out and spotted the man halfway into the parking lot.

*Damn, this guy walks fast.*

Time was running out. She decided to go for it since any of the cars nearby could be his.

"Professor Machado," Analis yelled out, speed-walking toward the man.

The man stopped and quickly turned around. Now, the resemblance was confirmed. This had to be Kelvin's father.

"Excuse me, sir, but do you happen to be Kelvin's father?"

Sandy had a puzzled look on his face, watching Analis step closer to him.

"Yes. How do you know my son? I don't mean to stereotype, but you don't look like you went to West."

"I went to Classical, sir. I met your son on a ride back from New York a couple of months ago."

Sandy's eyebrows arched in sudden realization, and his eyes widened. "Please, call me Sandy... You're the girl from the train?"

She couldn't see it, but Analis felt her cheeks blush.

She suddenly found herself at a loss for words when she discovered Kelvin had told his father about her.

"Um, yeah. Yes, that's me... Hey, I sent him a friend request on Facebook last month. He hasn't accepted me, which is fine if he doesn't want to be my friend, but I noticed a lot of people writing get-well messages on his page. Is he okay?"

Sandy squinted his eyes at Analis. "So, you don't know?"

"No, sir."

"Wow," Sandy said, realizing that Kelvin had not just been closed off to his family and friends but also to the entire world. "I don't remember seeing him on social media since it happened. He suffered a massive brain aneurysm due to a brain condition we didn't know he was born with."

Taking a step back, Analis brought both her hands up to her mouth and covered her gasp. Sandy stepped forward and reached out to Analis with a single hand. "He's okay. He is okay."

Analis took her hands off her mouth and slanted her head to the side, looking more puzzled by the second.

"What? Really?"

"Yes. Physically, at least. He's walking and talking perfectly fine. He's just going through some changes."

Analis didn't know how to respond. She nodded without saying a word.

"You're here in the TD program, right?"

"Yes. I was getting something to eat before I went home."

"Good. How are you liking TD?"

"It's good," Analis replied with a grin.

"You should stop by the house and go see him."

Analis raised her eyebrows. Suddenly, she couldn't feel her stomach growling, and the humidity had cooled off.

"If you like… I think he'd appreciate the surprise," Sandy added.

"Um, yeah. Sure."

"Let me give you my address and his phone number. No pressure. I don't want you to feel like you have to see him."

"Professor Machado, I mean, Sandy, I don't do anything I don't want to do."

Sandy smirked. It warmed his heart that this girl was interested in his son's well-being. Sandy knew how much Kelvin had cared for Carrie. They weren't inseparable, making their relationship work better than the rest. They weren't the cliché couple. They had their independence, and when they brought their worlds together, everything fit perfectly like the right pair of batting gloves. It had to take someone special to get Kelvin's attention.

Sandy didn't know the dynamics of Kelvin and Analis's connection or friendship. All he knew was that this girl had left an impact on him. After a couple of months of not being in contact, she knew something was wrong with him, and she cared.

*That must have been one hell of a train ride.*

Analis readied her phone, waiting for Sandy to give her Kelvin's phone number.

"Here's his."

# CHAPTER TWENTY-TWO

Jonathan

One could never go wrong with Sundaes, especially on a hot and humid summer evening. Jonathan pulled into the crowded parking lot on Oaklawn Avenue, and Jason rode in the passenger seat. The sun had begun to set. Although it was still pretty light enough outside to enjoy your ice cream without your vision being interrupted, the parking lot and street lights had turned on.

Sundaes' exterior was relatively small, with only two windows, one for ordering and the other for picking up. The wall was painted white-black in a cow's pattern, and the overhead sign was painted pink with the Sundaes lettering in white.

Tonight, Sundaes was rocking with small and large

families, young and old couples, and groups of teenage boys and girls enjoying an evening out.

After finding the last vacant parking space, Jonathan and Jason approached the long line to order, dodging kids running around the pavement and waving hellos at people who recognized the two local star athletes.

"You really just getting a chocolate shake? You can make that at your house," Jonathan said to Jason.

"Yeah. I don't eat ice cream like that. You really gonna wear that chain," Jason replied, tapping Jonathan's new medium-sized and length gold chain. "Just cause you're going to Miami, you ain't gotta be all Miami Vice." Jason was referring to Jonathan's tank top. He wore a colored tank top with dark palm trees looking over buildings designed all over the shirt, light blue fitted cut-off jeans, and comfortable low-top sneakers.

"I ain't gonna front. The way you bulked up, that chain fits you like it fit MJ when he wore it in that dunk contest," Jason added.

"This is my pop's old chain. He gave it to me."

"I can tell. You never wore that in the hood. You'd probably get robbed."

"That's why I wore it here," Jonathan replied as they got to the back of the line.

"Yeah, now the problem is you look like a drug dealer to these white people."

"Not when people here know my pops and my brother. Plus, some of them know who we are."

"Fact," Jason said, nodding his head. "So, if anything, you do all the talking then. I'm putting my trust in you… But yo, where do you see yourself living when you make it to the league? Some place like this or in a city?"

Jonathan rubbed his chin. "Maybe a place like this where I can have the big house but still be close enough to people. I lived in the hood my whole life, and I can't live anywhere near it if I make it to the league…"

"I said city, not the hood," Jason corrected.

"Ohhh. Okay. If I get drafted to say to Boston, which I hope I don't, I'll live in a place like this, a small town. If I get drafted to Miami, I'll have a crib by Coconut Grove. If I get drafted to New York, I'll for sure live in the city. You?"

"With my luck, I'll get drafted to some place like Oklahoma, San Antonio, or Milwaukee. I'll have no choice."

Jonathan looked away from Jason. His focus was elsewhere, with his eyes glued to the pickup window. There she was, grabbing her double-scooped ice cream in a cone, enjoying her evening with her group of friends. Why wouldn't she? It was a summer night. Soon enough, she'd start her first chapter of adulthood on a college campus.

When Vanity turned around, she did a double-take when she spotted Jonathan standing at the back of the line. Whatever her friends were talking about suddenly became mute to her. Jonathan stepped to the side, out of the line, to impede her walkway since she was heading in his direction.

When Jason finally noticed what was happening, he told Jonathan, "I'll get you that chocolate chip cookie dough. Go do your thing."

Vanity realized she was parked across the street, and

to get to her car, she had to cross paths with Jonathan, who was now purposely standing outside the line. She tried to walk straight alongside her friends and not look at him, but it was too late.

"Vanity," Jonathan called out to her.

She wanted so badly to keep walking, but deep down, she couldn't resist. She immediately locked eyes with Jonathan.

"We need to talk."

"We did talk," Vanity replied.

"No. You talked, and I listened. Just hear me out, please."

Vanity turned to her friends, who were all standing behind her, piercing death glares through Jonathan's soul. "I'll be right back," Vanity said to her friends before turning back to face Jonathan. "I'm parked across the street. You got ten minutes."

"Okay… Look, you're right. I wasn't there for you. I wasn't, and I'm sorry."

Jonathan's eyes were round and warm. His voice wasn't the usual deep and dominant tone.

"The thing is, I was scared. I was scared for my brother. I know us guys act like life in general isn't a big deal, but this shit is scary. Plus, add the fact that I didn't know exactly where we stood after I told you about Miami, and it was just a lot. I thought you needed space because you acted like it. I mean, how can I know how much space to give?" He was rambling now. He could tell by the way Vanity squinted her eyes and titled her head at him. "I just want you to know how sorry I am. I was going through a lot and should have been around a lot more. But I'm only eighteen. We both are. You've always been mature beyond your years. Not everyone is like you, especially guys."

Vanity rolled her eyes. She was done with Jonathan's rambling. Just before she sucked her teeth and was able to step around Jonathan, Jonathan finally found the correct words.

"You didn't give me a chance to choose."

Vanity's nose flared so much she could have been a Brahma bull.

"I'm sorry I didn't react the way you wanted me to on the spot, Vanity. And I did come around, just not as timely as you wanted me to, but you didn't give me a chance to switch schools. I reached out to Miami and told them about our situation. Not yours, but our situation, and even though I committed there, they gave me the freedom to reach out to the schools that I hadn't turned down yet. The schools that you've been deciding whether to go to or not. I was going to go play at whatever school you chose."

Vanity's perfect face wrinkled. Her eyes glossed, trying to hold her tears in, glancing around at the happy people enjoying their ice creams so she wouldn't look into Jonathan's eyes.

"I was choosing you and the baby, Vanity. I just needed to get my thoughts together. I didn't know you were going to get rid of it because of me."

"I didn't do it because of you," Vanity protested, snapping her gaze back at Jonathan. "I did it for me."

"What does that mean?"

"Take it how you want to, Jonathan."

It was flight or fight time. Stay and go back and forth with Jonathan or walk away, maybe forever holding her peace. She chose flight, side-stepping away from Jonathan, leaving him with his words in his mouth.

"Vanity, I'm sorry," Jonathan semi-shouted as Vanity reached the sidewalk.

Without turning around, her drowning eyes filled with tears, and staring at her friends, she said, "I know."

# CHAPTER TWENTY-THREE

Seventh Inning Stretch

Teenage house parties rarely got out of control in the western part of Cranston, Rhode Island. Kelvin rarely went to parties. But as long as he could remember, there was always a chaperone, a parent, or a significantly older sibling, and the police were never called. He often wondered where were these house parties had alcohol around, which always ended with some girl in the hospital with alcohol poisoning, like his Calculus classmate, Cheryl, who was rushed to Rhode Island Hospital on Memorial Day Weekend. Or like Kirsten, who slipped and fell into Jonny's pool, causing her friends to jump after her. In both instances, Kelvin was away at a travel ball baseball tournament.

Gregory was at work at his part-time job, Damian had been out with his mother's side of the family, and

Jonathan and Jason were out, leaving Kelvin alone without any plans. The last thing he wanted to do, feeling rejuvenated, was be alone with his thoughts. So Kelvin finally took Ryan on his offer to attend a class-mate's party.

The late afternoon sun had finally set into the evening, decreasing the humidity by two percent. Kelvin wore blue jean ripped shorts, a Forrest green T-shirt, and a pair of all-white low-top sneakers and hung around the back patio all evening.

The party was full of people he knew–Ryan and his girlfriend were conversing with recent graduate Jackson. David, the baseball team's senior catcher, was across the crowded backyard with his girlfriend, Jules, his best friend, Sean, and Stacy, another girl from his class. Even Carrie's crew was there: Carrie, Amanda, Eve, Marilin, and a girl named Daenerys, whose name made her more appealing to the boys at school because of the *Game Of Thrones* television show.

*Why did I even come?*

Ryan was his boy, but he mingled with everyone else but Kelvin, oblivious to what had happened to Kelvin. Maybe it was the mere image of witnessing Kelvin physically able to do things in the flesh. People, especially teens, have a short attention span to under-lying issues when the exterior appears normal.

Everywhere Kelvin glanced around in the half-grass-concreted backyard with the back patio over-looking the yard, he watched classmates, current team-mates, and ex-teammates drink from the red cups of what most likely was spiked drinks, socializing with one another. But he couldn't bring himself to join any of them, so he just stood awkwardly against the patio railing until someone tapped him on the shoulder.

"Did you get kicked off your baseball team or something?

Kelvin turned to see Carrie in a short, summer-red halter dress and a red cup in her hand. "I was at my cousin's bridal shower lunch earlier, and I did feel like changing," She added, explaining the overdressed attire.

"What do you mean if I got kicked off the team?" Kelvin asked, slightly pushing himself off the patio railing.

"I mean, you're just standing here all alone in a trance. You didn't even see me come out of Jared's house and call out your name. I thought you got bad news or something."

"Oh."

Suddenly, Kelvin realized that was the first time he was standing face-to-face with Carrie since the day he almost died at the hospital. Carrie saw the blank expression on Kelvin's face quickly transform. Even with the darkness of the night, the lighting from the interior of the house illuminating the back door through the glassed sliding doors made it easy for her to see Kelvin's eyes round, slightly dilated.

"Here," Carrie said, holding out her red cup, hoping Kelvin could let loose. Maybe it was guilt for coming off harsh the last time she communicated with Kelvin; perhaps it was the gut-wrenching knot she felt in her stomach that she made a massive mistake in breaking with him in the first place, but she desperately wanted him to take a sip of her drink.

"No, I'm good. I can't drink," Kelvin said, shaking his head.

"You can't, or you won't?" She asked, internally kicking herself for sounding flirtatious.

"I mean, I can't. I never drank before, and I'm not going to start now while recovering from brain surgery."

Kelvin was back to almost expressionless. Whatever Carrie saw in his eyes was suddenly gone. He stood taller and straighter than she could remember, with confidence that would command the entire yard if everyone weren't busy socializing.

Carrie didn't have a good rebuttal or response, so she guzzled her drink in embarrassment, looking away, anywhere but into Kelvin's eyes, but she felt his eyes on her. She thought to herself, *this Kelvin is different. When did this happen? How does he suddenly have complete control over my feelings? Does he still have feelings for me? Why do I feel so guilty?*

"Carrie, what did you really mean when you said if I got kicked off the team?"

Carries eyes darted back and forth, glancing back up at Kelvin.

"I overheard Jackson tell some of your teammates that he told your coach that because of your condition, you can never play baseball again and that your coach will have your position up for grabs next season." Carrie blurted out. "I don't know how Jackson found out."

Kelvin knew. Ryan. The trail started with his mother. Worried Betsy must have said something to Ryan's parents, the word was then spread to Ryan, who undoubtedly blurted the news out to the team. Jackson, who was still upset over Vanity breaking things for him for Jonathan, took the opportunity to hurt Jonathan by derailing Kelvin's plans to be the starting shortstop next season.

"I'm so sorry, Kelvin. I thought you were here sulking, then I realized you didn't know, and I didn't know how to tell you." She was rambling now and didn't know how to stop. "I mean, I should have told you right away. I didn't know if you were still mad at me over the last time we texted. The truth is, I'm sorry about how my texts came out. This is all brand new to me, and I can't imagine how you're feeling." Her words were coming out almost a hundred miles an hour, her eyes watered with tears, and her hands flared up and down, and it was surprising she didn't spill her drink.

"Hey," Kelvin said calmly, touching her forearm. "I know. And it's okay… I should go."

Carrie furrowed her eyebrows. "Why?"

"Let me ask you a question before I go… Did Ryan know about Jackson telling coach?"

Kelvin could see Carrie's throat moving as she swallowed. It was all the confirmation he needed. "Thank you for telling me," he added, giving Carrie a quick smile and sidestepping away from her toward the sliding glass doors.

Neither Carrie nor Kelvin noticed how crowded the deck was until Carrie saw Kelvin dodge and weave through kids before reaching the sliding doors. She could see a group of girls lounging around in the house's interior. When Kelvin opened the sliding doors and stepped into the kitchen, Carrie heard the group of girls' laughs.

She decided to go after him, something she should have done long ago. She quickly navigated her way through the tipsy teens on the deck into the kitchen, with her eyes glued on Kelvin as he made his way through the living room, where girls occupied the couches. Carrie thought to herself, *if I threw a party and let people inside my house, my parents would kill me.*

She reached and opened the front door seconds after Kelvin walked out and spotted Kelvin halfway down the front steps.

"Hey," Carrie called out, stopping Kelvin in his tracks.

Kelvin turned around without saying a word, landing his eyes on Carrie, causing her heart to skip a beat.

Unsure of what to say, she asked, "Do you need a ride?"

"Nah, my crib isn't far. It's a nice night for a walk."

The way he smirked at her, exposing his dimples even with limited front porch lighting, simultaneously warmed and broke her heart. He didn't look at her the way he once did. He didn't even look at her the way he looked at her before everything became dark and scary at the hospital. He wasn't standoffish, nor was he cold. He was *different*, like the kid you only see in gym class.

"What… What happened to you? Like, who are you now?"

Kelvin shrugged. "I'm trying to figure that out. Do me a favor… Tell Ryan that I know and not to send me a lame-ass text. He'll know where to find me."

Carrie wanted to cry. The Kelvin she knew, the one who was her perfect match, was gone. The version he was transforming into was surprisingly and weirdly more appealing, but she knew he no longer had space for her. She sadly nodded before replying, "Okay."

"Good night, Carrie."

"Good night, Kelvin."

# CLOSURE



While most eighteen-year-olds were out enjoying the summer night, Jonathan was lying in bed, softly tossing a baseball to himself. Seeing Vanity again and not having the talk he wanted brought down his mood.

The lights in his room were off, but the television was on and muted. Although the A/C was on, he could hear Damian engaging in games of three-on-three street basketball games, where the basketball hoop was nailed onto a street light pole just outside Jonathan's window.

That was the norm in the inner city. Sure, hanging up and nailing basketball hoops, crakes, and other things onto street light poles was against city ordinances. But in a city like Providence, Rhode Island, as long as you weren't causing bodily harm to another person, having an out-of-control house party, having a domestic dispute, experiencing an emergency, or selling or using drugs, the police weren't going to come.

Suddenly, Jonathan's cell phone chimed, breaking Jonathan's consecutive streak of 2,504 times without dropping the ball. He held onto the baseball with his left hand and started to gently pat beside him on his mattress for his cell phone. Once he felt the steel of his phone, he gripped it and held it up in front of him.

He quickly sat up in bed, shocked at what he'd been staring at–a text message from Vanity.

> Hey, you up?

Yeah.

> ...

> ...

I'm sorry about earlier. You caught me by surprise.

I know. It's okay. I'm sorry.

Don't apologize. And you're right about what you said.

Right about what part?

> About almost everything.

It doesn't feel good to be right.

I know, but that's life. When do you leave?

In a few days.

Come outside.

What?

Come outside.

Okay.

Jonathan quickly hopped out of bed, half sprinted out of his bedroom, through the house, and opened the front door. And there she was, standing, dressed in jeans and a tan T-shirt. She had just gotten out of the shower and didn't bother drying her hair as it formed wet spots on the shoulder and upper back part of her shirt.

Despite the low lighting outside Jonathan's house, he could see her drowning eyes perfectly. She wasn't wearing any makeup. This wasn't keeping up an image or attending a social gathering. She was bare, raw, and vulnerable. She didn't have her walls up–no games to be played. This is the Vanity he knew. This is the Vanity he thought was tailor-made for him.

He stepped out onto the porch, closed the door behind him, and stood in front of her. Her eyes scanned his exposed biceps and chest from his muscle shirt before meeting his eyes.

"I'm sorry, Jonathan," she said.

"I'm sorry, too."

Without saying anything else, they hugged each other tightly for what seemed to be an eternity, but for them, it wasn't long enough.

"Okay, I gotta go before my parents get up and don't see me at home. I just - I just needed to see you. I don't know why."

"I'm glad you came."

"Take care of yourself, Jonathan."

"You too, Vanity."

Vanity turned around and walked down the front porch without turning around. Jonathan didn't need to see it to know. He felt it. He knew she had started to cry. He didn't care that his stepbrother and his friends were playing basketball outside, on the opposite side of the house, and could potentially see him. Bare feet and all, he sprinted after her and reached her before she made it to her. With one hand, he gently reached out and grabbed her wrist, spun her around, and kissed her.

Vanity melted into Jonathan's arms and kissed him back. It was a soft kiss that intensified with passion like the one they shared when they decided to become an official couple after she left Ryan in the dust.

The funny thing about kisses is that they can be illusionary. While Jonathan's emotions poured out through that kiss, he felt a new jolt. Maybe he can still talk to Boston College and URI. He was one of the nation's most sought-after high school players. Maybe it wasn't too late.

As for Vanity, this was the perfect goodbye to an ending chapter in her life.

"Thank you for that, Jonathan." Her voice had

become a bit raspy. Maybe it was from fighting back the tears that were going to come, or maybe it was feeling a bit chilly with her wet hair.

Jonathan didn't like the sound of her voice.

"Maybe we can -" he attempted to convince her to try the long-distance thing before she interrupted him, placing her hand on his chest.

"No. We made our choices. We have to live with them," she said, fighting back tears again.

"What if they're the wrong choices?"

Vanity smiled slantedly at Jonathan and shrugged her shoulders. She stood up on her tippy toes and quickly tap-kissed him on the lips.

"Goodbye, Jonathan."

Vanity turned around. And without looking back, she got into her car and slowly drove off.

# THE GIRL



In his song Wet Dreamz, J. Cole discusses meeting a girl in math class. I, too, met the girl in school, but I met her in the fifth-period Spanish class. It was 2001, during my sophomore year of high school, and Lissette caught my attention.

I spent all of my freshman year and the first quarter of my second year at Central High, and I never saw her before. So, I know when she walked into Ms. Sanchez's class, I knew she was a new transfer or had just moved into Providence.

Her wavy black hair fell to her shoulder blades, and her full lips were perfect—at least, that's what I thought. The combination of her fair skin, natural pink-colored lips, and full brown eyes with a hint of honey that slanted at the edges almost floored me.

Although we were friendly with mutual people, we

didn't hang in the same circle. The people I hung with were more rough around the edges. One of my best friends used to sell weed. The rest of my friends were just like me: kids from single families and lower-income households who higher-class people viewed as criminals and thugs. Although most of us weren't criminals, we understood why someone did that: because we understood the desperation in needing an extra dollar, we understood the need not to have mom work two and three jobs.

Lissette's circle consisted of those who didn't need to worry about these things. She hung around with her older sister's friends, a crew of pretty girls who hung around popular seniors who got into nightclubs during the weekend. Ergo, she went to nightclubs on occasional weekends.

So, of course, it was my luck that whenever I saw her in the hallways, she was either with her sister, her friends, or some older guy in school from that crew. One almost common thing was that pretty girls always attracted older boys in school. So, of course, it was just my luck that our senior star center fielder on our team started to date her.

Fait connected us. My old teammate (her boyfriend) had been spotted with another girl after the club during the Memorial Day weekend, and we were finishing our regular season against our rivals, Classical. I don't know if she was trying to make her ex-boyfriend jealous, but after I hit a game-tying homerun late in the game, she screamed out to me, "Nice hit, number 8."

I recognized her voice. How couldn't I have? We conversed and joked around a few times in Spanish and gym class before. I quickly turned my attention to where the voice was coming from. I saw her sitting on the bleachers, directly behind the fence, behind home plate, wearing her hair down and an unbuttoned jean jacket, where I saw her gold necklace's nameplate resting on her collarbone.

It was as though something had taken over me, and I lost sense of where I was. I waved and smiled at her as I continued to enter our dugout, not realizing that maybe my teammate might get angry with me. Luckily for me, that didn't happen. He was going to be graduating soon. And since I was only one of two sophomores on the varsity team (including Alex), this was my first and only year playing with that guy. Guy code and alliance weren't a violation in this instance.

We hit it off during the summertime at an outdoor backyard house party. Looking back, she had me with just one look. I like to believe our spark happened at the baseball game, and our story began with that dance at the party.

But things were far from perfect. Lissette is Dominican, which means she had a strict father who believed all teenage guys were after one thing: sex. So, for us to see one another, it felt like some mission that always involved her sister either tagging along or dropping her off to me with a time limit in case their parents asked too many questions.

Eventually, like every teenage daughter and parent dynamics, Lissette was turning sixteen, and it was best to have an open dialogue about dating rather than dating behind her parents' backs. But like every sad ending, I wasn't allowed to date her, not because of me but because of my brother Julian and my friends' bad reputation. It was more of you *who your friends are.* Lissette, not to betray her parents' trust, broke things off with me just before we started our junior year.

She really was my summer love, and the rest is history. I got together with Betsy during junior year; we had Jonathan a couple of years after high school when I was playing college ball, and soon after came Kelvin.

What most people do not know is that Betsy and I were going to have a kid before Jonathan. It was a classic prom night mistake. We got married at City Hall because we thought it was the right thing to do. Soon after came the miscarriage. And when you mix in other stressful stuff on top of a miscarriage and fear of adding more stress to my *wife*, I did the only thing I knew how to do: shut down.

I couldn't talk to her. I didn't know how. Since I went to school at Boston College, the same school Lissette attended, I again found myself in her arms. It was wrong, but it felt right. See, I always had baseball. And truthfully, Betsy was never the girl. It was Lissette. It wasn't fair to Betsy. And it wasn't fair to Lissette either.

I had a plan. It wasn't a good one, but it was a plan. I was going to come clean to Lissette about my marriage, but I was going to divorce Betsy. And, of course, the plan went to shit. Lissette didn't want to be the cause of a broken marriage, although it wasn't her fault. And when it was time to come clean to Betsy about my transgressions, she told me that she was pregnant again.

I cowered because I knew my heart belonged to

Lissette. Although I have been with Betsy longer, no woman has ever made my heart skip a beat like Lissette, yet I stuck it out with Betsy because she was carrying my baby again. The baby that would end up being Jonathan. So, when I got drafted to Miami and moved my little family away from New England, Betsy was the happiest she had ever been. To be perfectly honest, so was I.

In Betsy's case, even though she never mentioned it, the fact that I was thousands of miles away from Lissette put her at ease. But like every deep wound, you can't just put a bandage on it and expect everything to be okay. You must properly clean, treat, and stitch it up. So, when I got traded to Boston but spent most of my time at triple-A, playing in Pawtucket, all of Betsy's insecurities arose again because we were at home again, close to Lissette, and I had drenched fully into baseball because my window of being a permanent major league baseball player was closing.

The more time I spent training, coming home late, etc., the more Betsy grew wary. See, I never properly treated the wound. I had an insecure wife at a time when my professional baseball skills were finally clicking. So, I had a choice: keep doing what I was doing and risk the chance of her hating me, potentially losing my sons, or taking my foot off the pedal so I could be home more often.

It didn't take long before no other franchise wanted me. I was labeled lazy and wasted potential, but I just wanted to be there more for my sons. Losing Betsy meant losing Jonathan and Kelvin, and I'd be damned if I let that happen.

Eventually, Betsy and I did divorce, and she found her person. I thought I did, too, when I met Amir's mother, but I guess I fell out of love just as quickly as I fell into it.

I can see something happening with Jonathan and Kelvin. I hadn't seen Vanity in a while. Jonathan has been a bit edgier than usual, and Kelvin has been dealing with his own love triangle. Maybe it's time my boys learned the truth about me so they can avoid some of the mistakes I made.

# CHAPTER TWENTY-FOUR

Start Of The Rally

Kelvin had been distracted all day following a brief meeting with Coach Apple. In the meeting, Coach Apple confirmed that Jackson had approached him *with concerns* about Kelvin. However, he informed Kelvin that he had never mentioned putting his shortstop position up for grabs. Now that Kelvin has disclosed his health information with him and learned his doctor cleared him for workouts but *not* playing in actual games, he'll need to have a plan B just in case Kelvin isn't cleared to play by April.

*I fell for the trap.*

Kelvin internally kicked himself for falling for Jackson's games. Jackson knew if Kelvin heard the whispers about his status of being next year's starting shortstop, being the straight shooter that he is, he'd approach Coach Apple himself, potentially benching himself without knowing. But like everything that has come his way since meeting Dr. Johnson, Kelvin shrugged off Coach Apple's awkward meeting.

This new and improved Kelvin happened instantly since meeting Dr. Johnson. It felt as though Dr. Johnson was the last piece to the puzzle. Kelvin had put everything into perspective. Dr. Woo had told him that he was going to die of his condition sooner or later, undoubtedly. Dr. Johnson didn't flat-out call Dr. Woo a liar, understanding the statistics. However, the data was based on older people but confirmed Kelvin's life would never be the same because of the uncertainties in his condition. Mixing in how people treated him, feeling alone, learning how to navigate and differentiate headaches, sleepless nights, *de ja vu* nightmares, and internally figuring out who he would be had left him with a giant chip on his shoulder. He was in Jonathan's shadows all his life, always the little brother to the future major leaguer. The chip on his shoulder was now to prove everyone wrong that he could come out of this stronger.

His journey to mental toughness had its ups and downs. Some days were worse than others, often questioning whether he'll ever be cleared to play baseball again. If so, would he be cleared before the Sping's season for a final chance to get into a D-1 school? Today was a good day. The distraction he'd been dealing with all morning had been good. When he arrived home from last night's party, he received a surprising text from Analis. The two stayed up all night texting while

Analis attended to house guests of out-of-state family members over for the weekend.

"Who's the girl?" Julian asked, watching Kelvin take his phone out of his gym shorts.

Kelvin quickly glanced at Julian with a dear in-the-headlights look as he sat on the bench-press bench after finishing his set. "Huh?" Kelvin asked with a smirk. He wore a teal tank top with his grey gym shorts.

Julian smirked back, crossing his arms in his all-black attire of knee-high gym shorts and a tank top. "Huh? You've been smirking and texting every time you finish a set. Only a girl can do that to a guy."

Kelvin quickly pocketed his phone, stood up, and allowed Julian to lie on the bench press bench. He then circled the bench and stood before the barbell, waiting for Julian to start his set.

"So, you're not gonna tell me who's the girl?" Julian asked, glancing up at his nephew, ready to spot him.

"It's just a friend."

"Uhuh," Julian replied, unconvinced.

Julian grabbed the barbell and raised it off the rack.

"Spot me when I get to eight," Julian said before lowering the barbell to his chest with two hundred and ten pounds of added weight.

Kelvin glanced around the empty franchise gym. It wasn't uncommon for the gym to be empty on an early summer Saturday afternoon. Most people were at the beach, enjoying the short New England summer; some were shopping or at brunches and barbecues.

A couple of hours later, Kelvin returned home, showered, and dressed in olive-green shorts and a fitted white T-shirt. Jonathan had gone home to finish packing for Miami, Betsy was at work, and Sandy and Julian were attending Amir's 8U All-Star tournament thirty minutes away, leaving Kelvin with the house all to himself.

He sat at the kitchen island, drinking a glass of water. And although he couldn't feel it, his foot wouldn't stop tapping the floor.

*Why am I nervous?*

He didn't know why. All he knew was that he was nervous. It was unusual to him since he talked for Analis for an entire ride from New York, was confronted by her at a baseball game, danced with her at a graduation party, and spent all night texting with her.

Sandy and Julian always told him that nerves are a good thing. It meant that you cared and didn't want to fail. When you feel your stomach turning in a quiet sense of excitement on top of the nerves, resulting in a feeling you have never felt before, it means you're onto something special.

Is this what this is? Special?

Kelvin's cell phone buzzed in his pocket, almost causing him to jump off the stool, nearly spilling his water on the kitchen island counter.

He quickly dug into his pocket and pulled out his cell phone, reading Analis' text message on the screen:

> I'm outside.

His heart rate quickened as he hurried toward the front door. When he opened the door, to his surprise, Analis stood a foot away from the front door.

*Damn, she looks good.*

Analis wore an in-style, fashionable oversized powdered blue T-shirt with a unique Guns N Roses design, blue jeans, and white sneakers. Her hair was perfectly slicked back into a ponytail, and she wore lip gloss and big gold hoop earrings.

They smiled at one another for a few seconds before Analis sprung herself into Kelvin's arms, wrapping her arms around his neck. Kelvin embraced the surprise hug and wrapped his arms around her waist, catching a great whiff of the coconut scent from her conditioner.

"Machado," Analis said to Kelvin after the obvious *chemistry* hug.

"Analis Ruiz," Kelvin replied with a smirk.

Kelvin glanced behind Analis, where he could see Analis' older sister, Rosey, sitting in the passenger seat of a white four-door Honda Accord next to a dark-skinned young man, sitting in the driver's seat.

"Is that your sister from the train ride?"

"Yeah. She broke up with that guy after we got home that night. I guess I underestimated her."

"Got it. You hungry?"

"I could eat. What do you have in mind?"

# CHAPTER TWENTY-FIVE

<u>Base hit</u>

Sandy insisted on getting Kelvin his own bank account and atm card. They were monitored, of course.

*Take the card and pay for her. Don't spend any more than a hundred dollars.* Kelvin heard his father's voice echo in his brain as Rosey's *guy friend*, Jamal, parked in an empty parking spot on *Mulligan's Island*. Although he had been driving since meeting him, Kelvin could tell Jamal was on the taller side. He guessed six-two, maybe six-three, with a short, evened haircut and a light-faded full goatee.

The song playing in Jamal's car snapped Kelvin into reality. His eyebrows furrowed, and he stared at the dashboard screen displaying the song playing: A Boogie With The Hoodie. The lyrics brought him back to the memory of his weird dream when his life was hanging in the balance.

"Are you okay?" Analis asked, snapping Kelvin back into reality.

Kelvin rotated his head. Analis had been staring at him, puzzled.

"Yeah… Yeah, I'm good."

"The place is packed," Rosey said from the front passenger seat, flipping closed the visor after finishing checking her makeup. "The food must be good."

"Let's go," Analis said enthusiastically, opening her side of the door.

Mulligan's Island is a tropical-themed mini-golf venue with a par-3 golf course, driving ranges, batting cages, a section for beach volleyball located between the batting cages and mini-golf section, and an entire 8-hole pitch-and-putt section just before reaching the parking lot.

Today, the pitch-and-putt was closed and replaced with over two dozen food trucks. The day was perfect: eighty-three degrees and sunny. Jamal wore camo shorts, a grey T-shirt with some lettering Kelvin hadn't gotten a chance to read yet, and black sneakers. Rosey looked utterly out of place, wearing a white pinstripe sundress and silver sandals.

*Now I can tell who's the flashiest out of the two sisters.*

The four separated into two pairs. This sure felt like a date for not talking about it or asking her out on one.

"I never knew they had food trucks here," Analis said, rotating her head, trying to read the different food trucks' names.

"Yeah, they have these here every week."

"Which one do you wanna try first?"

"I say the tacos. Always go with something you're familiar with before trying something you never had."

A small smile curled on Analis's face. "I agree… But before we do that, I wanna ask you something." She rotated her head again, taking in the scenery of kids running around, couples of all ages enjoying quality time with one another, and groups of teens hanging out. She pivoted and stood in front of Kelvin. "Are you good, Kelvin?"

*Kelvin.* She called him Kelvin and not Machado, which indicated just how much she thought about their late-night texting marathon after Kelvin shared some of the things he'd been through.

"Like, are you really good?" She asked again with more emphasis.

He didn't know how loaded the question was as she stared into his eyes. His heart skipped a beat, and her gaze melted into his. She wasn't his girlfriend, but she wasn't staring at him like a friend would. He liked this girl. He really did; as far as he knew, this wasn't an actual date. Should he have talked about it first? Should he have disclosed every single detail the night before, answering her unanswered question that no, he wasn't good. What if she chose to distance herself like Carrie did? Why could he handle Carrie distancing herself but was afraid of Analis doing the same? Fear. Although he hadn't known her much, he was lucky to have met his intellectual equal at such a young age.

We never know when we will meet our intellectual equals. Young men at Kelvin's age rarely plan for it and instead, spend their youth using girls for fun. Most men in their mid-twenties push back when the idea creeps into their minds, afraid of missing out on some illusionary extravagant time of their lives where they'll regret not having as much meaningless sex as possible before settling down, potentially alienating and hurting the person for them. And finally, a good portion of men well into their thirties still live their lives as if they were in their early twenties; creating this façade of taking someone seriously would put an end to happiness, where in reality, they know they had let the one get away because of their shenanigans.

Surprisingly, at this young age, Kelvin understood he wasn't his father, he wasn't his uncle Julian, and he wasn't his brother. Somehow, he understood Analis was unique, and he was afraid of losing her.

Before she could see his brain spiraling, he chose the half-truth. "Yeah, I'm good."

Last night, between the apparent talks of likes, dislikes, fond memories, and jokes, Kelvin answered Analis' questions about what had transpired as best he could. He went into detail about the day he went to the hospital, feeling lost and confused at the information thrown his way, waking up the following day to get an MRI, then suddenly blacking out, and not remembering what had transpired between the time of his blackout and waking up in a different room with the drain attached to his head.

He had purposely left some critical details out: Dr. Woo's death sentence, Dr. Johnson's skepticism, but not ruling it out, and Carrie calling him a sick person. The verbal wounds were still fresh. And no matter how strong the bandages were, he didn't know if the wounds could turn to scabs and scars. Pushing the news far deep in the back of his head was the only logical way to live out the rest of his teenage years with some normalcy. And he prayed that no other soul would catch wind of his fragility. Emotionally, he could not handle it. At least not now.

———

A couple of hours later, everyone's bellies were full. The afternoon had turned into the evening. A DJ had set up on stage, playing today's popular music that made even middle-aged people who had been drinking dance. The evening July sky reminded Kelvin of his twilight skied dream when he was fighting for his life. He and Jamal had left the girls to get them ice cream and found themself standing in a long line.

"So, Rosey and Analis tell me that you're a good baseball player," Jamal told Kelvin, breaking an awkward silence.

Kelvin had been zoned out, his arms crossed, glancing around the environment. He noticed a familiar face or two, half expecting to be approached since this was his first public outing.

"Huh? Oh yeah. I play at West. You play?" Kelvin replied, shifting all his concentration forward, watching satisfied customers at the front of the line walking off with their ice cream.

"No. I never swung a baseball bat. I'd probably embarrass myself if I did. Basketball was my sport."

"Oh. Where did you play?"

"I played for my high school in Massachusetts. I only play in rec leagues when I have the chance."

"Mass? What school do you go to now?"

"I'm a junior at Brown."

Before Kelvin could answer, a familiar voice disrupted him–

"Oh shit, look who it is," Jackson sarcastically hollered in Kelvin's direction, holding hands with a slim blonde girl he'd never seen before, wearing a crop top shirt and shorts. Kelvin squinted his eyes at Jackson's Notre Dame T-shirt before settling his glare at Jackson's quote-unquote posse, consisting of a couple of the seniors who had just graduated and, surprisingly, Ryan.

Unsure of what to do, Jamal took a step to the side, allowing Jackson and company to approach Kelvin.

"What's going on, Kelvin?" Jackson asked, eyeing Kelvin, staring at his Notre Dame shirt. "Yeah, they gave me a last-minute offer. This is where I'm headed now."

"Good for you," Kelvin replied, finally resting his glare on Ryan.

"I texted you last night," Ryan added, stepping through his friends and finally standing beside Jackson.

"I was busy."

"Busy like you are now? What's going on with you?"

"I don't know. Maybe I don't like bitch-ass people who go around talking behind my back."

Ryan furrowed his eyebrows at Kelvin, tilting his head in confusion. As he tried to stare into Kelvin's eyes, he studied his posture, which was now standoffish. Although two feet were between them, the once close friends couldn't have been further apart.

"What are you talking about?" Ryan asked with his voice innocently concerned.

Kelvin was too consumed with anger. For all he knew, Ryan had conspired with Jackson. And who could blame him? Before they both made the varsity team as sophomores, Ryan played shortstop for the JV team and his middle school. Maybe Ryan wanted the coveted spot back during his senior year.

"I know what you did, Ryan. Just letting you know that I ain't going anywhere, and you ain't gonna have my spot." Kelvin muttered.

"Serious, what?" Ryan asked, lost and confused.

Jackson couldn't contain himself, grinning from ear to ear. "Ryan, he's just mad that he'll never see the field again."

"Fuck you say?" Kelvin asked before taking a step forward and pushed Jackson back with full extension in both arms. Jackson's friends, including Ryan, stepped forward in a mixture of shock and anger, but Jamal forcefully wrapped his arms around Kelvin with one arm around his neck. Onlookers standing in line and walking, passing by, stopped to observe the potential fight.

"Whoa, whoa. Let's not get arrested tonight. Come on. Come on."

Jamal backpedaled with one arm around Kelvin's neck until feeling Kelvin's body relax. When Jamal finally let go of Kelvin, he asked, "Are you okay?"

Kelvin shrugged off the sensation of Jamal's arms still around his neck. "Yeah, I'm good."

"Look, I don't know what's happening, but we are having a good time with the girls. I haven't known Analis for long, but she's not gonna like this. Go for a walk, cool off, and meet us by my car if you want you and Analis to work out."

———

Half an hour later, Kelvin met Analis, Rosey, and Jamal by the entrance of the miniature golf course. They were already holding colored golf clubs. Analis held two in her hands: a yellow one for her and a red one for Kelvin. While Kelvin was out cooling off, the three took advantage and decided to pay for a round of miniature golf.

"Hey, what took you so long?" Analis asked, handing Kelvin his club.

"Sorry. A couple of teammates started talking to me. I lost track of time."

"Good thing Jamal got the ice cream you promised to get," Rosey sarcastically said.

"Babe, come on. Leave him alone. See, I told you too that he saw some people he hadn't seen in a while, and I told him I'll bring the ice cream to you." Jamal added in, wrapping an arm around Rosey's shoulder.

Kelvin and Jamal exchanged a quick, understanding glance. Jamal displayed guy code without even talking about it by making a harmless excuse for Kelvin's whereabouts. Short enough to slip by Rosey but not fast enough for Analis. Although he had never met Kelvin, he wasn't oblivious to his background, having heard some chatter about his brain condition.

"Let's split up in twos—me and you against one another, and these two against each other," Analis said, lightly bumping her shoulder into Kelvin, disguising the suspicion on her face.

"You think we have the time to do that?"

Both Jamal and Rosey rotated their heads toward the food truck event.

"Well, it looks like everyone is over there, and we have the course to ourselves. So I'm thinking, yeah, we have the time," Jamal stated, grabbing Rosey's hand and guiding her past Kelvin and Analis. "We'll determine the ultimate winner when we see our scorecards."

"Babe, we don't have scorecards," Rosey stated through a sigh.

Jamal dug into his pockets, pulled out four squared scorecards the size of flashcards used for school, and handed two to Kelvin before completely walking by Kelvin and Analis.

"Yeah, we do."

Rosey shook her head, making fun of how prepared and organized Jamal always was.

The first hole was relatively easy. It only took Kelvin three tries to get his ball in the hole, while it took Analis four tries. They barely spoke during the first mini-course, spending their time laughing at how terrible they were at this. But despite the laughter, Analis sensed Kelvin's energy had shifted.

"Machado," Analis said to Kelvin as the two walked toward the second mini-course.

"Yeah?"

"When I asked you if you were good, why did you lie to me?"

Since returning from his walk, Kelvin avoided extended eye contact with Analis. Now, resting his gaze on Rosey and Jamal as they finished the second mini-course, he rotated his head right and met Analis' eyes.

"Look, we don't know each other that long, but we talked for three hours on a train, chilled together at my cousin's party, and talked even more. We talked all night last night about everything, and we've been talking all day. I even watched you in your baseball element. So, I think I know you enough to know when your energy shifts. Right?"

"Right," Kelvin replied with a nod.

"So, what's up with you?"

"You want the whole truth?"

"I'll quit this game and make my sister make Jamal leave you here so you can walk home," Analis sarcastically stated. She and Kelvin silently stared at one another as if they were playing a game of whoever blinked first would lose.

"… I'm dying."

Analis was left expressionless and appeared to be losing color from her skin by the second, trying to take in what Kelvin had just said.

"At least that's what one specialist told me. The others don't know how I'm, A, alive, and B, alive and functioning like normal humans. And the last one, my current neurologist, is optimistic even though he can't rule anything out," Kelvin added, watching Analis' eyes quickly shift from left to right and right to left, looking like two small bugs trapped in a mason jar.

Still at a loss for words, Analis cleared her throat, trying to think of something to say.

"I'm sorry I didn't mention this last night," Kelvin said. "I didn't know how to even say it."

"I uh… Wow… I uh…" Analis still struggled to find the proper words as she looked into Kelvin's eyes. Suddenly, the bright-eyed, confident Kelvin had a sunken look. Kelvin broke eye contact and stepped onto the second mini-course. He dropped his ball on the turf grass as he prepared to take his shot and said, "Don't worry about it. It's nothing."

Analis put a hand on Kelvin, stopping him from putting the ball.

"It's not nothing, Kelvin," Analis softly said, finally finding her words. I'm sorry that I reacted in a way that made you feel some type of way… The thing is, this is huge. Like, how are you functioning?"

"I don't know. I know this is huge, but can I ask you not to treat me like this a huge deal, please?"

"… Yeah, sure… But can I ask you why?"

Kelvin broke contact, bent his knees and back slightly, and readied himself again to hit the ball.

"Tiger Kelves gets ready," Kelvin said, mimicking a sports analyst tone. He then measured the ball with his club before putting the ball. The ball started to travel at a good pace on the tufted grass before losing its momentum on the incline part of the second mini-course, making him realize that he should have struck the ball harder. "Damn."

"Kelvin?" Analis softly said with a hint of worry in her tone.

"Come on. It's your turn. Your sister and Jamal are already on number four."

Analis took a step onto the grassed tuft and put her

ball down. "Are you going to answer my question before my shot or after?"

"I don't wanna scare you off," Kelvin blurted out.

*Shit. Why did I say that? Now she's gonna think I'm weird.*

Analis furrowed her eyebrows. She stared into Kelvin's eyes, almost forcing eye contact.

"Scare me off? Why would you think that?"

Kelvin glanced behind Analis, hoping lines were starting to form behind them, but no one was in sight. Before he could answer, Analis put her hand on Kelvin's forearm.

"Hey, whatever you're holding in, I get it... But eventually, you're going to have to let it out, or it'll drive you crazy."

"I'm afraid that I won't be able to play baseball anymore. I've only been cleared to train and work out, but I'm being held back from playing in games... I can't go to the *Perfect Game* Tournament in Georgia with my travel ball team. That's where most of the scouts go. That's where most of the kids get their offers from schools and get major league scouts to look at them... It's like, fuck, my last chance to get noticed ahead of my senior year, if I even get to play during my senior year... If I don't, then what? Baseball is all know."

Analis sadly smirked. "What about life, Kelvin?"

"What about it?"

"Baseball is all you know. Have you thought of a plan B-?"

"I never let my mind get to that place."

"I get it... Tunnel vision. Eye on the prize. But what I mean is, have you thought of a certain hobby that you flourish at that can be a great post-career when you retire from baseball that could come in handy just in case you can't play?"

"No."

"Well, you should."

Analis quickly got in position to put the ball and hit it further than Kelvin. The ball traveled over the incline part, traveled the rest of the mini-course, and fell into the hole for a hole-in-one. Analis raised her hands in awe, with a mixture of excitement and shock on her face.

"Ohhhhh, look at that Tiger Kelves," she hollered, smiling from ear to ear.

Kelvin stared at Analis with a smirk, watching her trot on the tufted grass before picking her ball back up. He admired her beauty, confidence, wit, and honesty. Although they were starting to get to know one another, he admired how she challenged him to face himself in the mirror. When you wrap that all in one, you have the perfect girl in front of you, strutting her stuff, acting like she has just beaten you on the PGA Tour.

"Don't even bother scoring that. You're already behind me," She sarcastically hollered at Kelvin, stepping off the second mini-course's exit.

Kelvin playfully shook his head, walking toward his ball to take his second shot, thinking, *I'm falling in love with this girl. But how can I bring her into my world when everything is unraveling?*

# CHAPTER TWENTY-SIX

Change Up

Kelvin was getting physically stronger. Going to the gym every single morning was paying off. His shoulders were a little broader, his quadriceps and calves were more muscular, his biceps were larger, his forearms were more defined, and his jaw was more chiseled.

During the evenings, as the summer days came and went, Kelvin spent his time at Alex Sr's (Alex's dad) indoor baseball training facility for numerous reasons: Sandy not being at his facility every evening because of Amir's games and not having people at the facility to train with him at that time of the hour. And when he did get one of the trainers to have a session with him, Kelvin felt the fear in their body language. It was that fear of *what if Sandy's kid pushed himself too hard and collapsed on my watch.*

Training at Alex's was easier. Alex was one of the few who treated him like a man and not this fragile chandelier. Most importantly, Alex Sr pushed him hard. He constantly yelled *use your hips, quicker hands than that, sit on the throw, hit it where you want.* He even taught Kelvin how to push the ball during an at-bat when the pitcher threw him a pitch at a specific location.

When Kelvin first walked into Alex Sr's facility, he was a kid whose potential was in jeopardy. As the summer reached into August, Kelvin was an unquestionable baseball stud who couldn't publicly display his skills, making him feel like a caged animal. Thinking to himself, it was no wonder Alex was *playing pro ball in DR.*

---

A few weeks have passed, and nothing has changed with Kelvin's status on whether he could play baseball. His travel ball 17-U team made it to the semi-finals in the Georgia Perfect game tournament, and his teammate, Clay, instantly received an offer from *Boston College* and a private workout session with the *Toronto Blue Jays.*

Kelvin was genuinely happy for Clay. Although attending different high schools, Clay at Lasalle and Kelvin at Metropolitan West, the two had been playing travel ball together since they were thirteen. A day after Clay received his *verbal* offer, his friend and the team's catcher, Duce, received a verbal offer from Oklahoma

State, which was a massive deal in itself because rarely did North East Coast players get noticed by West Coast schools since the west coast states are loaded with talented kids who take advantage of being able to play in winter because of the weather. At the same time, North East Coast kids resort to indoor training.

As the summer days and weeks passed, Kelvin unexpectedly spent more time with Analis. Despite the obvious chemistry, *the talk* still hadn't happened. *Are we dating? Are we friends? What are we? Will we ever be more than friends?* Kelvin wanted to be Analis' boyfriend so badly, but he didn't trust his new imperfections around her. *What will she think when I suddenly get sad or mad when I think about baseball? How would she react when I get nervous about my next MRI? How long can I hide my sudden mood changes? And why can't I say yes when she wants to pull up and watch me hit balls off the machine by myself?*

Everything could be so simple if he could get out of his head.

The *guy's summer*, which he had assumed would happen, never came to fruition. Gregory was also playing travel ball with the team all summer. Although the team didn't play every day, they practiced every other day. Then, when you mixed in a girlfriend here and there, mini-family vacations, and the fact that Kelvin had put distance between himself and his friends, he hadn't seen Gregory in a while. Alex and Anthony were still playing baseball in the Dominican Republic and wouldn't return until late August, just before school started. Jason had entered the transfer portal and transferred to PC, where he and Damian had started their late summer basketball training camps for their school.

Analis was escape. She didn't know it. And as unfair as it sounded, she was an escape from the fact that almost every single one of his peers was headed or trending into bright collegian careers while his future seemed grim. During Metropolitan West's playoff run, Kelvin was the hottest hitter on the team, leading the team in home runs, hits, RBIs, stolen bases, and OPS. Defensively, he led the team in fielding percentage without committing a single error. This summer's Georgia's Perfect Game Tournament was supposed to be when he cemented his place as one of the country's best high school baseball players and received offers from powerhouse schools like Jonathan did a year ago.

A wise man once said, "Baseball is a cruel sport." You can feel the highest adrenaline in the top half of an inning, only to feel like your heart has been ripped out in the bottom half. A pitcher could be pitching a shutout with the season on the line, only to have his third baseman commit an error. Baseball is a cruel sport because, after the error, the lights-out pitcher gives up the devastating game-changing home run.

Like the cruel sport America's pastime is, Kelvin reached a point where he couldn't disguise the inevitable. Analis was no fool. When you spend enough time with someone, you learn their quirks, likes, dislikes, types of smiles, and when they're hiding something.

"When are you going to ask my sister out?" Rosey flat-out asked Kelvin, snapping him out of his trans.

Kelvin had accepted Analis' open invitation to the

bowling alley. Tonight, one of the rare nights the guy's crew was utterly free, Kelvin asked Analis if his brother and friends could come.

Sure.

Analis replied in a text that didn't consist of further questions or emojis.

The bowling alley had dimmed the lights and turned on their neon-colored lights, giving it a night-club feel as music blasted through its speakers. As usual, Jonathan, Damian, Jason, Gregory, and Clay had turned the entire bowling experience into a competition. Analis's friends were up to the challenge, turning everything into a boys vs. girls event. Although everyone was having fun, Rosey couldn't help but notice two people off their *A-game*, Analis and Kelvin.

Kelvin turned his head to look Rosey in the eyes. She sat so close to him he could smell the coconut scent from her conditioner.

"I know you like her. So why are you being so weird tonight?" Rosey asked, not bothering to lower her voice due to the volume of the music.

"Is it that obvious that I'm not myself right now?"

"Maybe you are being yourself. I don't know you well enough to know if you're not being yourself." Rosey fired back with a smirk. There were times when Analis and Rosey would resemble each other much more, and tonight was one of those nights. "But my sister seems to know you enough to know that you're acting weird," Rosey added.

"She said I was acting weird?" Kelvin asked, shifting his body entirely to his right.

"Of course. What's up with you? You got a girl or something?"

"No."

"You like her?"

"Does she like me?"

"I asked you first."

Analis was up to bowl next. She wore a white shirt with blue jeans that looked like they were styled in the 90s, which was a new trend again. Her hair was perfectly slicked into a bun, and she wore a pair of gold hooped earrings. Kelvin watched Analis laugh and smile from ear to ear as she grabbed a bowling ball.

"Look, my sister is fire. And I'm not just saying it because she's my sister. She really is fire. She's smart and funny, and she doesn't take any bullshit. She's not gonna be single forever. So if you like her like I think you do, ask her out, and stop being so weird. She doesn't like when people switch up on her. It makes your new self seem like your true self." Rosey added, tapping Kelvin's leg before standing up and walking away.

Analis managed to knock down only three pins in her bowl. When she turned around, her girlfriends cheered her with screams and laughs. Kelvin's crew did the same. Through all the laughs and hi-fives, Analis met Kelvin's eyes, sitting by himself. With a simple nod to her left, Kelvin understood it was time to talk.

*My mind was unraveling. The worst part about it was that I wasn't in control. I learned that I'm a control freak. At the beginning of this ordeal, I was able to ease my mind in the hospital somewhat. Maybe it was because I couldn't worry about the unknown. I didn't know the end result, and I didn't know anyone going through what I was going through.*

*During my appointments at the memory clinic and speech pathology, since I had developed a small stuttering problem post-aneurysm, I didn't panic because I let my mind travel into baseball. Again, I couldn't stress the unknown. But everything changed as soon as I was verbally restricted from playing the sport I love. I started having the same De Ja Vu nightmare of crying, sitting on a hospital bed, and saying goodbye to everyone I love.*

*I became insomniac. I pushed myself hard at the gym in the morning, grinded in my baseball workouts, and put up a fake smile, pretending everything was all good. Ryan, Carrie, and some teammates saw and treated me differently. Although I shouldn't have cared, I did. I don't know why, but I did. My parents pretended to treat me like the same old me, but I still noticed they still chose their words carefully with me. As for Jonathan, he was about to leave. As I navigated this new me, the only person who never switched up on me was about to leave me alone.*

*I understand that we evolve in life, and changes are inevitable. But lately, I've been asking, why me? Why did I have to go through these life-altering changes, and who decided I could handle them? The irony is that we desire growth, but when the obstacles seem insurmountable, we would instead return to our cocoons. That's me in a nutshell.*

*I'm a control freak and probably a coward, too. I didn't know that about myself until recently. I went from a promising kid with all the tools to someone who couldn't handle living without all the positive reinforcement I had gotten from being that efficient, positive, quick, athletic, sharp kid who gets all his things done, stressing how my health had let me down. It was like my mental toughness and emotions were at different spectrums heading into a collision course. My way of dealing with something as someone who feels he's not doing well with the changes is to shut down. I don't want to do this anymore. I'm making everyone unhappy, I'm pushing people away, and I have to go.*

Analis was at a loss for words, trying to understand how I could feel like this when, on the surface, I've always appeared to feel okay. We've been outside for half an hour in the semi-empty parking while everyone was inside bowling and having a great time. She leaned against the hood of Jamal's car with her arms crossed, trying to process what was coming out of my mouth. Her brown eyes bounced left to right, then right to left, looking like two small bugs trapped in a mason jar.

"Um... Wow,... I didn't know you were holding all of this in," Analis said.

I could tell she wanted to say more, but I threw a lot at her and understood that being speechless was normal.

"Also, I convinced my parents to let me finish out my senior year at Central," I added before Analis pressed his palms on the hood of the car, sprung herself off, and wrapped her arms around me. It was the first time she'd hugged me with so much emotion. She didn't have to say anything else. I wrapped my arms around her waist, resting my chin on her shoulder, catching the aroma of her perfume. We hugged for several minutes without saying a word. Through the silence, I felt her empathy.

"I wish you can understand that you're much more than a baseball player," Analis said.

She finally unwrapped her arms around my neck, and I let go of her, and our eyes met.

"But only you can make yourself understand that... We've been chilling together for a while, and ninety percent of our conversations weren't focused on baseball. I get it. It's what you love. It's what you do or did, but it's not who you are... But only you can see that for yourself," Analis said. "And as for all this, I have to go talk?" Analis lightly punched me in the chest before continuing. "What is that all about?"

"I meant that maybe-"

"Nothing!" She interrupted me, bulging her eyes. "That's you in your head... Here's what you're going to do... You're going to let yourself feel like you're doing right now and not constantly fight yourself. If that means you have to put distance between everyone around so you can figure your shit out, so be it. I have my own stuff going on, too. I have to move back on campus, school is starting soon, and my life will be a lot more busier, but I am one phone call or text away if you ever get those whole I have to go moments in your head."

She displayed the perfect combination of empathy, reassurance, and toughness. My heart rate heart picked up a bit. We were the only two standing at close range in the parking lot. The light pole next to Jamal's car made me feel like we were in one of those Romcoms from the 90s that my mother loves so much. I wanted to kiss her. I mean, I've been wanting to kiss her, but right then and there, I wanted to kiss her. I felt like it was finally time. It was time for the truth. It was time to reveal that the other reason why I've been so weird around her lately was because I wanted to be more than just friends with her. I didn't just like her; I was in love with her, and the thought of rejection from her would probably crush me.

So, the kiss attempt was a bad idea because the timing was probably off. I spilled my guts about how mentally I wasn't right; she reassured me, and my response was to kiss her. No... It's not a good idea. Plus, what if she didn't want to kiss me back?

Get out of your head, Kelvin. Just tell her how you feel.

Shit, my heart rate picked up again as I leaned on Jamal's car next to her, with a direct view of the bowling alley's front door. Now I knew what Eminem was talking about when he said his palms were sweaty from the nerves in that song. It was finally time.

"Analis," I said, trying to disguise the nerves in my tone. "Yeah?"

Suddenly, the bowling alley's door flew open. My brother, Rosey, Jamal, Jason, and the rest of our friends walked out full of energy. I couldn't quite hear the chatter, but I could tell Clay had the best bowling score, and Damian was the last person out, talking with one of Analis' friends.

With the moment ruined, although our crews weren't yet approaching us as they stood just outside the front door, engaged in animated conversations, I went with one of the truths, but not THE TRUTH, "I appreciate you, Analis."

Analis nudged me with her elbow the way a friend would and said, "I appreciate you too, Machado."

# CHAPTER TWENTY-SEVEN

<u>Watch the signs</u>

The next day, Analis invited Kelvin to his cousin Christna's cookout. The backyard looked identical to what Kelvin had seen during her graduation party. The pavilion still covered an outdoor couch-like seating area that happened to be on top of outdoor hardwood flooring. To the left, when you first walk into the backyard from the driveway, there is a spacious outdoor deck accessorized with a stainless steel grill and a medium-sized outdoor dining table. In the middle of the yard, between the deck and the pavilion, there was an open concrete space now occupied by about thirty-five to forty people, ranging from twelve years old to into their seventies, seated in lawn chairs, steel chairs, and stools, eating and drinking, engaged in conversation.

Kelvin sat in a vacant chair outside the pavilion, drinking a soda from a clear plastic cup. He wondered if his travel ball team was currently winning their second game in their last tournament of the summer. No matter how many solo sessions, weight training, journaling, or hanging out with Analis, the absence of being present on the baseball diamond always crept into his mind. What colored cleats would he wear with the white and purple pinstripes uniform, and what mental notes would he have on opposing pitchers and hitters as he readied himself for ground balls? After the double headers were done for the day, where would the team go out to eat? Would they hang around the hotel pool or challenge one another in video games after scrubbing their jerseys?

Analis abruptly sat beside Kelvin, breaking his trance. Blinking away the fog in his eyes, he couldn't help but notice how much more noticeable the freckles she had on her cheeks were. She was dressed in light blue jeans and a teal sleeveless crop top. In the golden embrace of sunlight, her eyes transformed from deep pools of dark brown into glistening orbs of caramel.

Shielding her eyes from the sunlight with her hand, she asked, "What's up with you, Machado?"

*Oh, nothing. That I'm definitely in love with you, and it might be bothering me more than not playing baseball. I almost told you last night, but I can't tell you right now after telling you that my future seems grim, and I'm struggling to get out of my head. For a while, I thought I was good, but it turns out that I'm not. It isn't fair to you.*

"Nothing," Kelvin replied.

*A lie.*

"I've been journaling," Kelvin added, rotating his body so he could face Analis.

*The truth.*

"Really?" She asked, rotating her body as well.

"Yeah. I've been doing it for a while. I just haven't told anyone. I wrote one this morning about my upcoming MRI."

"Oh."

"Yeah."

He brought his soda cup to his mouth and nervously laughed into it before taking a sip.

"And you're nervous?" She leaned a bit forward, landing her hand on his knee.

Last night was a significant breakthrough for Kelvin. Analis had told him long ago that whatever he'd been fighting to keep in, he'd eventually have to let it out and let himself feel. There were obvious sparks between the two of them. Now, more than ever. With one touch of his knee, he understood that he may have said more without saying how he felt about her.

"No. I'm not nervous... I'm just sad," He said, taking a silent inhale of the late summer air.

"Why?" Analis' eyebrows arched.

"I don't have that feeling of anticipation for the first time. I think our talk made me suddenly at peace that I might never play again... It feels like a bad breakup that ended on good terms, if that makes any sense."

Analis didn't know what to say. She really could not reply to that. So she hung her head for a few seconds, taking in the sudden sadness. This was the opposite of the result that she anticipated. She ordered herself to buck the hell up and lifted her head before anyone in the cookout could see her. She smiled at him.

"Come on. Let's go," She said, rising to her feet.

"What? Where are we going?" Kelvin replied, gazing at her.

"If this is a breakup that ended on good terms, which I don't think it is, who says you can't reminisce on old times?... I'm going to have Christina get a hold of your brother and meet me at the front of the house."

---

Analis had stopped at her house to change into something more comfortable. Kelvin didn't wait more than ten minutes in the car before Analis stepped out of her house wearing lower-thigh-high spandex-like shorts and comfy sneakers.

On the way to Metropolitan West's baseball field, Analis' playlist started playing Jessie Reyez's song *Jeans*, which talks about how perfect her mate fits her. As if last night and their moment at the cookout weren't enough, watching her hair blow in the wind and singing carefree added another layer of attraction to her.

When Analis parked on the dirt lot of Metropolitan West High, Kelvin was wary, but Analis quickly turned off the ignition and stepped out of the car before Kelvin had time to ask a question. She started her trot through the lot, leaving Kelvin behind, knowing he'd be trailing her soon enough.

After sitting in the car for ten seconds, Kelvin

stepped out and jogged slowly after Analis. As soon as he jogged out of the dirty lot, the school's baseball view was in view. What had shocked him were the people occupying the field: Jonathan, Gregory, Clay, Darius, and Anthony, all dressed in gym shorts and T-shirts, were all putting their cleats on, tossing baseballs around, and setting up the protective net a few feet before the pitcher's mound.

Surprisingly, Anthony returned home early from the Dominican Republic, where he had spent the entire summer playing professionally alongside Alex. In contrast to Kelvin and Jonathan, Alex was light-skinned with greenish eyes and a head full of curly black hair, which he styled into a taper-faded haircut. The muscular-legged and broad-shouldered Anthony was the first of the group to spot Kelvin walking toward them.

"YOOOOOOO," Anthony hollered at the top of his lungs as he finished slipping on his cleats.

"What are ya doing?" Kelvin asked, continuing his walk, almost reaching the dugout.

"Your cleats, glove, and bat are in the dugout. Put 'em on, bitch," Jonathan said, standing behind the protective net.

"What's going on?"

Gregory greeted Kelvin with their traditional travel ball team handshake. "We are going to play a home run derby, and then we're going to play of Oppo," Gregory said.

"Oppo?"

"Yeah. Who can hit the ball on the opposite field since we all claim we're the best oppo hitters?"

Suddenly, the loud sound of a group of females

approaching the field made Kelvin turn his head. He was immediately surprised to see Rosey and Analis' group of friends approaching the field from the same dirt lot he just walked from, each holding softball gloves in their hands.

Kelvin rotated his body again, landing his eyes on Analis, who was now greeting Jonathan and Clay with a hug near the pitcher's mound.

"Come on. You hit first," Gregory said, tapping Kelvin on his chest.

———————————

After putting on his cleats, batting gloves, and helmet and warming up, Kelvin approached home plate.

"Ayo, what's his walk-up song?" Darius yelled out, standing behind the protective net by the pitcher's mound, where a portable speaker stood, blasting music.

Clay stood in the outfield with Rosey and her friends, wearing gloves in their hands, while Jonathan was standing in his shortstop position, Gregory at third base, and Anthony at first base. Analis stood two feet behind home plate, wearing an oversized catcher's helmet and mask, with an oversized catcher's glove in her left hand.

"Wait! I know. It should be Devastated!" Analis yelled out.

"What's that?" Darius asked.

"Joey Badass. His song Devastated. Put it in your phone."

Kelvin looked back at Analis, who looked ridiculous

in Anthony's catcher's mask and glove, but he felt she couldn't have looked more perfect. He smiled, knowing the song very well.

"It fits, right?" Analis said, smirking and adjusting her facemask so she could see Kelvin.

"Yeah," Kelvin replied with a wide smile.

# JOURNAL ENTRY

*I had baseball... And now I found the Girl. But do I go after her?*

I haven't journaled in a while, mainly because if I actually write these words, they become true. Lately, I've been feeling like Jonathan when it comes to my father. I love my father, and I get along better with him than Jonathan gets along with him. When they're together, just the two, there's a lot of awkward silence. I wouldn't call it tension, but there is a lot that is said through their nonverbals.

Throughout our lives, we heard the, "You two are just like your father," "I remember when your father was your age, he was just like you," or, my favorite from older uncles, "Tu papa no era fácil." There was always a gratified emphasis in that last statement. Ironically, the statements came from divorced, single, and trying to hold on to their youth despite their age, uncles.

Normally, you'd feel the same, being a 17-18-year-old kid, but it hits differently when you have a younger sister and a single mother for most of your life. Although I was young when my mom met and married Mike, I could somehow tell the look she gave my dad when he came by to pick me and Jonathan up was different than the way she looked at Mike. I don't doubt that she loves Mike, but that first love hits differently. I guess it hits even harder when you marry and have children with that first love.

I could be totally wrong and be imagining all this in my head. One thing I know for certain is that my dad is a smooth guy. He's charismatic and charming with an alpha-male aura. It landed my mom, Amir's mom, and the woman he recently dated before their relationship crashed and burned because my dad once again couldn't stay faithful.

*You two are just like your father. Meaning what?*

Is it Jonathan's charms? Is it my quiet, stand-offish personality that gets mistaken for strength? Or is it that we both show signs of lying and deceiving? Jonathan wasn't transparent with Vanity about Miami. Somehow, I landed the girl every guy wanted in school, Carrie, and managed to let another girl capture my heart. Were these beginning signs that I'll inherit my father's vices?

Most guys would say it's a good trait to have. Maybe, I guess. But when you're raised with a conscience, the way my mother raised me, your heart breaks when you break someone else's.

Lately, Carrie has been texting me again and

checking up on me, and I don't know why I find it odd. Other than meeting Analis, I've always been open with her about everything. Honestly, I think we connected easier because although she had been living in Cranston, she was sort of an outsider like me. She and her family moved here from New Jersey when she was in seventh grade. So, like me, she didn't belong to any clicks. She was well-liked. And because she was an out-of-towner and boys didn't know who she was until high school, it made her that much more desirable. They didn't have to worry about if a certain guy had kissed her first in junior high or went out with her as a freshman, etc.

Our initial bond was unexpected but natural, sort of like mine and Analis'. Or even worse, according to stories like my parents. I don't know if I'm supposed to feel and think how I do since I'm only 17, but I can't help but think pulling back from Analis is probably the right thing to do. I care about her a lot, and I can't fake being just her friend anymore, but I don't think I can trust myself either.

How do I know that I won't follow in my dad's footsteps? On the surface, it looked like he really loved Amir's mother, a woman who still treated me and Jonathan like we were her own kids, and he still cheated. I cared about Carrie a lot, and somehow, I gave my heart to someone else. I care about Analis even more, and it's safe to say that I'm actually in love with her. If I echo these words to my brother, my father, Gregory, and even Anthony, they'd ask me if I even know what being in love is.

Honestly, I can't put it in words, so maybe I don't

even know what being in love is. What I do know is that Analis has been solid with me since day one. When almost everyone treated me differently during the hardest time of my life, she didn't. She challenges me, pushes me, and when my mind starts to spiral, she doesn't judge me. When I start to pull back because I'm terrified of my future, she reels me back in. In a short amount of time, she's like my best friend.

*How is that even possible?*

So, I'm faced with another decision. It's not a decision about my health, my baseball future, my future school future. It's a decision about my heart... I now know what people mean when they talk about this as a once-in-a-lifetime feeling. I now know what Joey Badass felt when he did the *Fallin'* song and the true meaning of Justin Nozuka's *Nova* song.

Do I finally man the fuck up and tell Analis how I feel and ask her to be with me, potentially risking losing arguably the most important friendship of my life, disguising my obvious inherited red flags and the future heartache I bring?

*A kid like me isn't supposed to be thinking this way so early in his life. But when you're pretty much given an expiration date, your thought process changes.*

Or do I play it safe, protect our friendship, and risk watching her potentially meet someone better suited for her?

# THE JOURNAL

*Miami*

## Jonathan and Sandy

"Wow, I can't believe this place is still open, let alone taste the same," Sandy said, using his thumb to wipe the corner of his mouth.

"How could you eat soup when it's hot outside?" Jonathan asked, tossing his napkin on his empty plate.

The two had arrived in Miami a few hours ago, wearing shorts and T-shirts. After dropping off Jonathan's belongings in his dorm room, they desperately needed to get something to eat, and Sandy had used his *father's executive* decision to eat at La Camaronera Seafood Joint and Fish Market, a privately owned mom-and-pop seafood restaurant founded by a family of Cuban fishermen.

La Camaronera is located in a small plaza. A

cartoonish neon sign and brash colors lead you into this seafood restaurant, a fairly stark contrast to the industrial, well-lit, chrome-framed dining room that awaits indoors. The place has a utilitarian, canteen-like feel; local art and murals liven things up, and casual diners crowd over simple tables and chairs. It's a busy Latin cuisine that you don't immediately think of. It's an authentic, bustling, lively, casual dining room where everyone enjoys seafood and does not worry too much about photos and online likes.

Sandy leaned back in his chair and said, "This is the best seafood soup you will ever have."

"If you say so."

Sandy sensed his son's mood. It wasn't as chipper as he'd expected. Usually, it could have been the long trip or the hunger that set into the two of them, but Sandy knew better.

"What's up with you?"

Jonathan stared past his father, watching cars park through La Camaronera's wall-sized windows. This wasn't California, the sunshine state, but the sun was brighter than he'd expected.

"So, you're not going to answer me?" Sandy asked, sitting up straight.

"I read one of your journals, Dad."

Sandy slanted his head in confusion. "You what?"

"I read one of your journals... I gotta say. I think I understand myself a bit better now."

"You mean after always hearing how you're just like your father?"

Jonathan almost felt embarrassed that he shared this information with his father.

"Yeah... I wanted to understand how I could let go of someone like Vanity like that the way..." He couldn't finish his sentence. He didn't know how without affecting his father. He lowered his head, fumbling through his words. "What I mean is-"

"What you mean is you now understand how you could let go of someone like Vanity like I let go of your mom."

Jonathan lifted his head back up, looked his father in the eyes, and nodded.

"Then I'm happy you read my journal."

"But me and Vanity aren't anything like you and Mom."

"You sure about that?" Sandy asked.

Of course, there were similarities. Like Jonathan and Vanity, Betsy and Sandy were expecting a baby well before they were ready at an early age. And just like his parents, overnight, there weren't parents to be anymore. The difference was that Vanity wasn't Jonathan's Betsy. A few nights ago, when he kissed her goodbye, he felt Vanity was his Lissette. So, instead of telling his father the entire truth, he lied.

"I'm sure about that, Dad... Why don't you go back after Lissette?"

Sandy opened his eyes wide in shock. Blindsided by Jonathan's knowledge of that name, Sandy reached for his glass of water and took a long drink.

"I didn't mean to blame you for what happened between you and Mom, but now I understand. You should go after her–Lissette."

"How long have you known?"

"A few days after Kelvin got discharged from the

hospital. You always told us how writing kept you sane… I'm like Mom. The way I cope is by making sure everyone else is good. I smothered Kelvin. And since you barely talked, I read your journals to make sure that you were good. That's when I read about her."

"What about you, Jonathan? Are you good?"

"I am now. Kelvin is doing better, and I accept what happened between me and Vanity. No need to beat myself over it, the way you have been beating yourself up all these years."

Sandy chuckled. He chuckled like Jonathan chuckled when one of his character flaws was exposed.

"Why are you scared, Dad?" Jonathan asked with a hint of challenge in his tone.

Sandy smirked, narrowing his eyes at his son. Oh, how much he is like him. A young Sandy, for sure. He is strong, confident, and charming through his vulnerabilities.

"I'm going to tell you a quick story, explaining why it isn't that simple. Then you can never ask me again. Got it?" Sandy said, leaning forward.

"I can't promise anything," Jonathan sarcastically replied.

"Jonathan."

"Fine. Okay. Go ahead."

"Okay. Even if Lissette was single and interested, I can't go after her. I can't because of your mother."

"I don't get it," Jonathan replied, confused. "Mom is remarried. You each had a whole other kid."

"I know. Listen, When I rekindled things with Lissette back in Boston College, I really hurt your mother. I didn't know how bad it was until I got traded to Boston, where our unresolved issues and her rightful insecurities went from zero to a hundred... See, she could have taken half of my money, the house, the car, you and your brother. But she didn't. She walked away from me with her dignity and only asked me to be a full-time father to you and your brother because she didn't want me to do the same my father did to me, which was being a part-time father... On top of that, I didn't know it yet, but your grandmother had committed fraud against me."

"What?" Jonathan said, feeling his voice rising.

"Yeah. When I went to school, she had taken out credit cards in my name, and I couldn't afford to keep up with the payments. I was just a ball player. Maybe she believed I would make it big in the pros, and I'd let what she did slide, paying off the debt. But when things didn't go according to plan, and I was trying to support a family, and I needed to take out a loan for the first time in my life because I was so used to paying everything cash, and I got denied because of bad credit, guess who was there for me?"

Jonathan didn't answer. He felt his eyes water up a bit because, deep down, he knew the answer.

"Your mother. She helped me out. Not with money, but steered me in the right direction. When I started to get depressed because my career was over, guess who told me to finish my degree and use my writing talents? Your mother. Even though we were divorced, she became my best friend. Your grandparents are a major reason I'm sometimes closed off to many people. I love your grandparents. Of course, I wasn't going to pursue legal actions against your grandmother. I forgave her, but I didn't forget. The same applies to your grandfather for being absent a lot. I don't trust people outside of my circle. But those are issues that I have to deal with or live with. But your mother, boy. She's something else. She's the best person I know. And I'm happy that she found Mike. I really am. And I know she had Junelie, and I had Amir, but I can't just run off and pursue someone that I hurt her with."

Jonathan took a deep breath. "Dad, I feel you. But the things you wrote about Lissette. That isn't just any other girl. You said Mom is the best person you know. Still, you were gonna choose this Lissette over her. It's been like, what, nineteen years? Rhode Island is small. I know who she is. Her son is a sophomore who plays for East. And don't even ask me how I know. You know I know people at East. My point is that she's single. And I feel what you said, but Mom got her happy ending. Why do you feel like you can't have one?"

Sandy smirked at his son. Knowing that Jonathan no longer held a grudge against him warmed his heart. But it saddened him because they were so alike and could have deep conversations but were now about to be separated by thousands of miles.

Sandy raised his hand, singling for the waitress to bring the check. "That's a conversation for another day. But I'll tell you what. If you make time in the busy schedule you're about to have by video chatting with me at least twice a week, I'll tell you all about it."

"Deal."

# CHAPTER TWENTY-EIGHT

Full Count

Kelvin couldn't stop the heel of his right foot from smacking against the examination table, anticipating Dr. Johnson. He nervously looked around the office where he first met his neurologist this past summer. A few weeks have gone by. Jonathan had moved and quickly settled himself at Miami University, Analis moved back on campus, Kelvin's transfer paperwork had been approved to attend Central High School, and he now awaited results from a week-old MRI.

Sandy cleared his afternoon schedule so he could take Kelvin to his appointment. He leaned against the wall with his arms crossed, glancing at and reading pamphlet covers about the human brain shelved on the office walls.

"Would you relax?" Sandy softly directed Kelvin.

"He's taking forever," Kelvin replied with his palms pressed against the top of the examination table, making the thin white paper sheet crumble.

"Worrying about time or what he will tell you isn't change a thing... Think of it as a three-two change-up with a guy on second and first base open. Sit back and wait."

"Really? A baseball analogy?"

"It's the only way to make you understand... You tend to be out of front on that 3-2 change-up, anticipating a heater, knowing they're not going to throw you a fastball with a base open."

"Oh, here comes the criticism."

Snady's glare landed on Kelvin.

"Since when was it okay to get baseball criticism again?" Kelvin asked, finally keeping his foot still.

"Since I have a feeling this doctor will clear you to play. I think there's enough time for you to jump on a Fall-Ball team. I'll ask Alex if he has room on his squad."

"What?"

"You heard what I said, Kelvin... I've been thinking, and you've been following directions and taking care of yourself. I see that you're physically stronger. You've been running, lifting with a spotter, and making sure you are breathing correctly during your reps. Alex has been sending me videos of you putting in work in the cage and fielding work. Physically, you're ready."

"I hear a but coming."

"But this doctor has to clear you first officially, and you have to sign a contract."

Kelvin furrowed his eyebrows. "A control?"

"Yeah. A contract with me that says that baseball isn't everything."

Kelvin rolled his eyes. "Now you sound like Analis."

Sandy sprung himself off against the wall. "Why? What does she say?"

"That I should consider a plan B."

"She's right. Kelvin, when we're young, we think we will play forever. But when you look at the average retirement age in the pros, it's about thirty-six, maybe thirty-seven years old. The special players are the ones who play into their forties if injuries don't end their careers early. So if you're a mid-level player retiring in your mid-thirties, you didn't get the huge contracts or endorsements. How are you supposed to live off your earnings when you have to pay your agent and manager, provide for your family, and so on? Every ball player should plan for plan B, even when they're playing... Unfortunately, I didn't make it far, but I had a good plan B. That plan B helped me provide for you and your brothers with everything you needed."

"Do you love writing like you loved playing baseball?"

"I do, but it's a different kind of love because I get to help make dreams come true... Our stories aren't written yet. You can go on and play baseball for more than ten years at the professional level and become an analyst after you retire. Or, you play college ball and figure out that you want to be a nurse or find a trade that you end up loving, or you might end up being a coach or something, like Alex... All I'm saying is that you need to sign this contract because I will not let you mope around for the rest of your life. My job is to make sure that you end up being the best version of yourself. I failed at a lot of things in life, relationships, marriage, communication, but I won't fail you." Sandy's voice started to crack, trying to fight back tears. "You understand me, Kelvin Machado?"

Kelvin started to wipe away his tears with his forearms. "Yes, sir."

Sandy walked across the room, lightly grabbed Kelvin's shirt collar, and pulled him close into his bear hug. Kelvin wrapped his arms around his father like he did countless times as a kid before he got too cool to express male affection towards his father as he reached adolescence.

"Dad, are we huggers again?"

Sandy and Kelvin started to laugh as father and son stopped hugging.

"I got something to tell you," Sandy said.

"What?"

"Dr. Johnson told your mother the news over the phone."

"What news?"

"Your MRI showed that your AVM is still there, but the treatment is working because your AVM is shrinking. And he cleared you to play. We have to go to your mother's after we leave here," Sandy informed Kelvin with a smirk.

*I can play again? Oh shit, I can play again. I've been waiting to hear these words for what felt to be an eternity. I didn't know if I was, but I felt myself smiling. I thought I'd* be crying tears of joy, but I guess my robotic self was all cried out.

I must have had a dumb-ass look on my face because my father narrowed his eyes in confusion.

"What's wrong with you?" Sandy asked.

"Nothing," Kelvin replied, shaking off the shock, quickly turning his blank expression into a grin.

*I suddenly understood the saying of having that special someone to share your highs and lows with because after my father told me that I could play again while we waited on Dr. Johnson, I wanted to pull out my phone and text Analis. The problem was that we fell out of sync lately. She was doing all her first week on campus things. Some of our texts went unanswered, and some were responded too late. During our last two phone calls, she politely rushed me off the phone because she needed to either do something or attend something. I wasn't surprised and expected it. I'm still in high school, and she was a college woman now living on campus. It was dumb of me to think she'd always actually be available to me.*

*We all say things that we genuinely mean on the spot. However, one thing that this whole process has taught me is that life is unpredictable. Things change by the second, and we have to adapt. So, at that very moment, with every single urge in my body telling me to pull out my phone and text Analis the news, I decided to let her be as I heard the light knock on the door before Dr. Johnson finally walked in.*

# CHAPTER TWENTY-NINE

<u>Eighth Inning</u>

On Labor Day, the evening before schools in Providence welcomed its students, Kelvin knew he had to do something. The summer days have shortened, causing the street lights to come on earlier. The walk from Sandy's house to Metropolitan West High School was only a ten-minute walk. En route to the school, Kelvin wondered why when, as soon as the calendar turned into September, there was always a cool breeze in the evening air. He wore a pair of grey sweatpants and turf baseball cleats, which looked like a regular pair of sneakers to the average eye.

As Kelvin turned right on the quiet, steep, hilly street of Metropolitan Avenue, he had a direct view of the school's football and baseball fields. The field lights were on, and Kelvin could see Amanda, Ryan's girlfriend, and the school's star softball player, standing on the dirt two feet before the pitchers' mound behind a sturdy protected net, throwing batting practice pitches to Ryan.

Kelvin momentarily paused and took a deep breath as Ryan launched line-drive hits into the outfield. He continued his walk down the steep street where the football team was wrapping up their team practice on their state-of-the-art tuft field just before reaching the baseball field. He opened the gated door directly next to the home team dugout like he'd done for the past three years, glancing at the empty bleachers.

Amanda is the traditional All-American, Caucasian, pretty, seventeen-year-old female with long blonde hair, hazel eyes, freckles, and a well-endowed chest. She wore her hair in a ponytail, and she and Ryan wore gym shorts and grey T-shirts.

Ryan noticed Kelvin and stepped out of the batter's box, causing Amanda to turn around and focus on Kelvin.

"I came to apologize," Kelvin told Ryan, walking towards home plate. "Hi, Amanda."

"Hey," Amanda replied, standing awkwardly, unsure of what to do after Kelvin and Ryan's falling out at the food trucks. She debated approaching Kelvin and Ryan in case of a surprise altercation since Kelvin had been uncharacteristically on edge but decided to stay put.

Ryan dropped his bat on the batter's box dirt and stood tall as Kelvin approached.

"I heard you were getting bigger. They weren't lying."

Kelvin reached Ryan and stood face-to-face with him as Ryan started to take off his batting gloves.

"Yeah. I've been putting in work," Kelvin replied.

"I could tell."

"Listen, my bad about what happened. I'm sorry."

"Which part?" Ryan asked, darting his eyes into Kelvin's.

"That's fair. Um, I'm sorry for everything. I really am from thinking you played me with Jackson. I'm sorry for pushing you away before transferring from school without telling you. You deserve more than that. I haven't been a good friend."

"Yeah, you've been pretty shitty," Ryan replied with a smirk.

Kelvin held his grin as he nodded his head.

"So, why Central, though?" Ryan asked. "You felt that out of place here?"

"That obvious?"

"Yeah."

"Well, it's not because of the whole racial thing if that's what you're thinking. I came here instead of East cause of you. The thing is, everyone I became friends with wasn't my real friend. They're yours. You played Little League and Middle School ball with everyone here. I didn't. So, I felt the resentment from the guys the day I took over a spot that the team felt should have been someone else's. I heard the whispers when Carrie and I got together. It was like I was with someone I shouldn't have been with. Then this past year was just weird with Vanity leaving Jackson for my brother, and we still got some of Jackson's boys on the squad who don't vibe with me. I know that other than you, I don't have real friends here."

"Yes, you do!" Amanda yelled out, softly tossing a ball in Kelvin's direction.

"I mean, other than you, too, Amanda," Kelvin replied, correcting himself, glancing at Amanda with a smirk. "We still boys?" Kelvin asked Ryan, closing his fist and holding it up chest high.

Ryan closed his fist and lightly tapped Kelvin's fist with his. "Yeah, we're still boys... Do you want to hang out here a little longer to play a home run derby? You look like you're big enough now to handle my bat."

Kelvin laughed. "Okay. You go first since you're already warmed up."

# CHAPTER THIRTY

9th Inning

The calendar year turned into October, and the travel fall ball was wrapping up in two weeks. Kelvin had been playing on Alex Sr's team alongside Alex, out dueling one another, rotating positions at second base and shortstop. Even better news to Kelvin: Alex returned later than he was supposed to from the Dominican Republic after the five-day grace period, forcing Park East to transfer him to the nearest high school. Since he had no desire to attend Metropolitan West, he used his father's Providence address. He decided to go to Central High School to play baseball alongside Kelvin.

They had played four weekend tournaments this fall and won all four. Alex was projected to get drafted in the first round of the MLB draft if he elected to skip college, and playing alongside him brought the best out of Kelvin. The teams Kelvin and Alex had played, which contained other rival Rhode Island high school baseball players, started to buzz, saying that because of Kelvin and Alex, Central High School would be a dark horse for the State Championship.

Having taken so many classes at Metropolitan West High, the only subjects Kelvin needed to graduate were Gym and English, so life as a senior was smooth for Kelvin. He utilized his free time at the gym with *Tió* Julian and Alex. His indoor training with his father and Alex Sr was his sanctuary whenever his mind drifted off into a dark place since he was still trying to get acclimated with some of his sudden headaches post-surgery.

Everything seemed to work in Kelvin's favor, but something was missing. His heart still longed for that person he wanted to share everything with. He thought distance and less speaking time would make him realize that what he felt for Analis was just a crush, but he was wrong. Not speaking with her nightly made him miss her even more. Sure, they texted, chatted, and occasionally video-chatted as friends, but it only made him wish he had kissed her that night outside the bowling alley.

When Kelvin had a two-homerun performance in the semifinals, because of Analis' busy schedule, it took Kelvin three days to share the news with her. Although Analis was ecstatic over the video chat, his news felt watered down by that time.

It was now Friday night, and some kids had gone home for the weekend. Others had stayed behind for

URI campus and off-campus parties, while the rest attended a Multicultural Student event put together by their Student Services Center. Tonight's event was a Latinx event in collaboration with the URI Spanish department for the closing of Latinx Hispanic Heritage Month.

Kelvin received a surprise invite from Vanity, who decided to attend URI instead of Rutgers. When Kelvin asked Sandy about these events, Sandy encouraged him to go. So, here he was with Alex and Jason, who wanted to visit friends he had stayed in touch with after transferring to PC. The trio witnessed students' outstanding performances, from cultural dances to poetry, short stage plays, and singing.

Everyone trickled outside on campus when the event concluded, engaging in separate conversations. Alex caught up with an old high school teammate, and Kelvin decided to walk toward the campus baseball field. However, he was immediately stopped in his tracks by a dark-complexioned man who appeared to be in his early forties. "Kelvin Machado," the man said, touching Kelvin's shoulder.

When Kelvin turned around, he noticed the dark-skinned man wearing a URI baseball cap.

"Yeah?" Kelvin replied.

"Derek James," he said, extending his hand. Derek stood a couple of inches taller than Kelvin and had the body of a former athlete who had taken a couple of months off from training: broad shoulders, wide chest, and back with a bit of a pudgy midsection. "I saw your game at Central High School for your brother's senior night," Derek added.

Kelvin squinted his eyes, trying to decipher where he'd met Derek before as he shook his hand.

"I'm sorry, but I don't remember you."

"We never met. I'm URI's infield coach. I'm hearing you've been tearing it up this fall."

Kelvin's look quickly turned from a squint to wide-eyed, excitedly shaking Derek's hand.

"Thank you, sir."

"I heard about your health scare, too. How are you?"

"Better. A lot better."

"Are you sure?" Derek's tone was skeptical. "I talked to your old coach and your potential coach at Central. As far as they know, you haven't been medically cleared to play yet, but you're playing travel ball."

"Wait. You talked to my coaches?"

"Yes."

"Oh. I mean, I have been cleared. I can get it in writing, too."

"Good. In the meantime, if I were you, I would look into an independent study here at URI. You can start taking that now, even though you're still in high school. You get college credits that fit your major."

"Okay. But why are you telling me this?" Kelvin asked. His mind was racing, trying to understand why Derek had been talking to his coaches and looking into his medical status.

"Kelvin, even though we're a D1 school, we haven't had the best teams. I'm being elevated to head coach, and I want the rest of this country to respect this program. I like your baseball mind. I need that. What

I'm saying is that I need your help building this program."

Kelvin was taken aback. "Like as a coach or a player?" He replied, furrowing his eyebrows in confusion.

"I can't say yet. I'm not sure of your medical status until I see the clearance on paper if you can play or not. But I do know that I want you here... We have plenty of time to talk. I know your father is a professor here. I'll stop by his office on Monday and talk to him. Enjoy the rest of your night, Kelvin. It is nice to meet you formally."

Kelvin and Derek shook hands again before Derek walked away. Kelvin watched Derek walk away in awe, still trying to process what had happened. *Did I get an offer to come to URI?* He took a satisfactory deep inhale of the night's air and started to walk again but immediately stopped at the sight of *her.*

Although the night's temperature had dropped into the low fifties, the Multicultural Center still had a dozen round tables and seats outside. The bright yellow sidewalk light created a sense of intimacy for those still outside. Analis sat with friends at the furthest table from the Multicultural building, where the light shone the brightest. She wore dark blue jeans, gold hooped earrings, and a black varsity jacket.

He didn't hesitate. Kelvin approached Analis' table with a profound new sense of confidence. He didn't know if it was because he physically felt the best he'd ever felt, because he may have just received that elusive college offer, or because he loved his attire, which consisted of light blue fitted jeans and a matching jean jacket over a light grey hoodie.

Like many times before, his heart skipped a beat as he inched closer and said, "Analis Ruiz."

Analis quickly looked to her right and immediately blinked away her shock with a smile. "Machado?" She replied, rising off her seat. "What are you doing here?" She asked before hugging Kelvin.

"Vanity invited me to this event."

"Who?" Analis asked, rotating her body at an angle to introduce Kelvin to her group of friends.

"The rich girl down the halls who dorms with Jalise," A caramel-skinned, big-boned girl sitting next to Analis added.

"Oh… Right, she's your brother's ex, right?" Analis asked, redirecting her attention to Kelvin.

"Yeah."

"Well, this is Jalise, Raymond, Victor, Maria, and Carmen," Analis introduced, pointing at each of them with her index finger. "Everyone, this is Kelvin," she added.

"Hi," Kelvin said, waving at the table. "Can we talk in private?" he asked Analis.

"Sure."

---

"Wait? Are you serious?" Analis asked with enthusiasm. She and Kelvin had been sitting in the bleachers next to each other, facing the turf baseball field. The field's light had been on, and Kelvin couldn't help but visualize playing on that very field.

"Yeah. I'm still in shock."

"But what does he mean by needing your help?"

"I don't know yet."

"You gotta take it, Machado."

Kelvin crossed his arms, rested them on his knees, and rested his head on his forearms. "Would you be okay with me coming here too?"

"What? Of course. Why wouldn't I?"

*It's time.*

Kelvin lifted his head and looked into Analis' eyes.

"Because I want to be more than just friends with you."

"What?" Analise said, widening her eyes.

"I like you. I've been feeling you since the night we met on the train, and to be honest, I think I more than like you. It's the biggest reason why I've acted weird with you because I didn't know how to tell you... I can't even believe I'm actually saying this right now."

Analis slowly nodded a few times, taking in what Kelvin just revealed.

*Shit. She's not talking. She's not talking. Say something else.*

"I didn't tell you because I was nervous that you wouldn't feel the same, and I didn't wanna mess up our friendship. Because I'd rather have you as a friend than not have you at all."

Analis smirked before Kelvin could nervously ramble on. She shifted her body to the right, leaned in, and planted a soft kiss on Kelvin's lips. Kelvin softly cupped Analis' face with both hands, kissing her back. The kiss was nothing short of magical. The soft tendernesses warmed both of their hearts. But then, Kelvin pulled back.

"But I don't think I can be with you right now," he

said to her as they softly pressed their foreheads against each other.

"I know," Analis said. "You're still working on yourself."

"Yeah. Like, I'm still trying to figure out who I am and who I'm going to be... I don't want to bring you into my world when I'm still not a hundred percent mentally stable. I still have my bad days."

"I understand... But I knew you liked me," Analis said with a smirk.

She and Kelvin each pulled their heads back, sitting up straight.

"You did?" Kelvin asked.

"Of course. I'm not blind. I noticed the way you look at me. I appreciate the way you always treat me."

"Damn. Why do I regret just saying that right now isn't a good time?"

"Because your mind and heart want one thing, but your conscience knows best. It's a good trait to have, Machado... Trust me. If it's meant to be, it will be."

Analis stood up and stared at the sky before focusing on Kelvin.

"Where are your boys?" Analis asked.

"Jason is with old teammates, and my boy Alex is somewhere with a friend."

"I guess it's just me and you then."

Analis extended her hand and pulled Kelvin up to his feet.

"Come on. Let's go for a walk."

"Okay."

Kelvin and Analis walked off the bleachers and began to walk side by side through the campus.

"So what comes next, Machado?" Analis asked.

Kelvin looked at Analis and smiled before shrugging his shoulders. She smiled back. Truthfully, he didn't know what came next nor what his future held. One thing he knew for sure was that he just turned down the chance to be with the girl of his dreams. Maybe it was for the best; perhaps it wasn't. But right now, all that mattered was that he felt the same butterflies he'd felt the night he met the girl on the train. And as far as he knew, that feeling would never go away.

# EPILOGUE

Game 2

Jonathan had been making a name for himself on the baseball diamond in practice and scrimmages against other state colleges. One of the many perks of attending school in South Florida was that he could practice all fall and winter before spring came around. Despite the most respected senior on the team being a shortstop, Jonathan was well-received by all of his teammates instead of being the guy looking to derail the dream senior season of the captain of the team.

One thing Jonathan quickly understood about his teammates was that positions were earned. Everyone on the team put in two a days. Lifting, hitting drills, sprints, fielding, throwing. These were daily routines. It was the ultimate environment of breathing and eating baseball.

On this Saturday evening in October, while everyone was watching the Miami Hurricanes football team host rival Florida State, Jonathan entered the school's weight room and saw *her*.

He'd only seen this caramel-skinned, long black braided hair, full lips, hazel-eyed beauty twice on campus. She took his breath away each time without even looking his way. After asking around, he discovered her name was Emily of Orlando, Florida. The half-black and half-Puerto Rican was an All-American freshman point guard whose schedule was about to get busier as practice times increased because the start of the season was looming.

Emily wore thigh-high, white, and orange Miami Hurricanes gym shorts and a black sports bar, drenched in sweat as she finished her last few reps on the straight leg raise machine. Jonathan must have looked like an imbecile, staring at her, standing at the gym's doorway. Before he looked worse, he redirected his gaze toward the dumbbells as he entered the gym.

Jonathan tried to resist the urge to look her way again. They were the only two in the gym. She was a star basketball player; he was on the baseball team, and making a female uncomfortable was the last thing he wanted to do. But she was just too damn beautiful.

*Is this how they make em down here in Florida?*

Jonathan was now a couple of feet away from her, making his way down the gym aisle en route to the dumbbell rack. He couldn't resist and decided to sneak a glance at her. Just at that very moment, as Emily rested in the seated position in the straight leg raise machine, her hazel eyes met Jonathan's, making his heart skip a beat.

The Baseball and A Girl saga isn't over. And Kelvin's story isn't over by a long shot.

TURN THE PAGE TO START READING A SNEAK PEEK TO **GAME TWO**.

# GAME TWO

JOHNATHAN
November 2$^{nd}$

Deleting text messages has become the norm lately. I mean, how would you explain daily messages from an ex-girlfriend when you're currently seeing someone? It doesn't matter if we haven't seen one another since the summer, and it doesn't matter that we're in two different parts of the country. Thanksgiving was around the corner, and I would return home for three days. We could talk then. Until then, I need to make sure Emily doesn't see these.

I don't hide things from Emily. But right now, deception is arguably the best route to go.

*Why can't I just cut off Vanity for good and ask her not to text me anymore? Umm, maybe because you feel guilty at the fact that your absence pushed her into that abortion, and the thought of you ending the patched-up friendship over someone you just met worries you because you fear what she may do next.*

Things have been hectic at school lately surrounding the latest controversy. Three members of the baseball team have been busted for using PEDs (performance-enhancing drugs). The entire team had to be retested, and I've been stressing over the results. Not because I'm dirty, but because we all got together at Anthony's mom's house and had some of his homemade protein cookies.

It's easy for your mind to spiral when three of your confirmed dirty teammates claim they have no idea how PEDs could have gotten into their bodies. *If you didn't knowingly take them, how'd they get in your system? You start to question what you ate. Could it have been the type of protein Anthony used?* If that's the case, the entire program will drain.

The question running through my mind was, who was the source? Rumor has it that someone in the school had alerted the NCAA about our team, specifically my three teammates. Who was the source, and why was they doing this?

According to whispers from our athletic department, our coach knew what was going on and would be terminated any day now. A new guy will run this team if we're not suspended for the year.

Some of the NCAA's decisions will depend on how honest the clean players are during interviews. We know we'll be asked if we knew something or saw something.

As I lay on the beach chair, using my hand to shield my phone from the sun's glare so I could read and properly delete Vanity's text message, I was gutted by her question.

Are you okay?

I swipe left using my thumb, deleting the text message, and watch my now girlfriend, Emily, wearing a peach bikini, walk out of the South Beach water as Halle Berry did in that James Bond movie. The four o'clock sun isn't as bright during this time of the year, but Emily still glows like poetry in motion. She looks like a Goddess. Her abs started to form a 4-pack, while her arms displayed some definition. Her wet black hair, split between her trapezoids, rested on her back and just above each breast. Her naturally thick yet toned legs displayed the definition in her quads with every step on the sand towards me.

"Hey, you okay?" She says, trying to read me.

I swing my legs over the beach chair, digging my feet in the sand as I sit up, making room for her to sit beside me. I look at my new girlfriend in the eyes, who convinced me to escape campus to enjoy a private beach day. As she wraps her towel just above her breast, I go with the half-truth.

"Yeah, I'm good."

"Why don't I believe you?"

We're still getting to know one another, but she isn't stupid. Of course, she knows everything isn't all good with me.

The truth is, as of yesterday, I know my teammates were lying when they said they don't understand how the PEDs got into their system, and I know of one more person who's been cheating. But how do I say this during my interview without jeopardizing the entire program? I sigh and give her a crooked smile.

"I need to tell you something, but you can't say anything to anyone," I tell her.

Her eyes rest on mine, making my heart pang. With her soothing voice, she says to me, "I got you."

# GAME TWO

**KELVIN**
November 15<sup>th</sup>

Things have been weird again. Health-wise and personal life-wise. Thank God that school has been a breeze. Because of the increase in headaches and my parents hovering over me because of my latest Emergency Room CT scan that showed edema in my brain, I need something to go smoothly in my life. Fall Ball has finished. And although I've kept up with my training regimens with my dad at his facility and with Alex and his dad's facility, fewer games means more free time. More free time for someone like me means more time to be in my head.

Since kissing and telling Analis how I feel about her, we haven't seen each other as often. Maybe it was for the best because the couple of times we chilled, things were awkward. Perhaps it was me again in my head, but it was as though we both purposely made it a point not to touch that subject, resulting in small talk, forced jokes, and meaningless conversations on television shows, movies, and music.

These were the conversations we were supposed to have as teens. Just because life flipped my life on its head doesn't mean everyone needs to have important conversations with me. There isn't anything wrong with talking about whether you're anticipating the next Dune movie in a few months and what we think about that new Lessons in Chemistry show.

Truthfully, I wanted to have another deep conversation—not about my health or my mental state. I think… No, not, I think. I know what conversation we need to have—the conversation about us. I honestly don't want to wait anymore. I want to be her man.

So, here I am, driving this Friday night to URI to surprise Analis, with Rosey in the passenger seat. She thinks this is the most romantic thing anyone has ever done for her sister.

I put on my best pair of sneakers and my dopest jeans–sweater combination. I have a fresh haircut, diamond stud earrings, and expensive cologne.

I wanted to call Analis and set up a time to pull up and talk, but after speaking with Rosey, she thought this was a better way. They're sisters, so she knows her better than I do. Her support and ultra-confidence have made me feel good about this plan.

I'm a minute away from URI, and my heart races with excitement, nerves, and anticipation. The music has been blasting in the car, but I lost track of what's been playing since we got off the highway.

I'm wondering what she will be wearing. Will I

catch her outside or in her dorm room, and how will she react? Will she hug me, kiss me like last month, or both?

I'm a hundred feet from the campus, but something is suddenly weird. It's more than odd–something is wrong. I grip the steering wheel tightly as my vision comes and goes. It was as if I was blanking uncontrollably at a hundred miles an hour. I suddenly begin to sweat, feeling my foot easing off the gas pedal.

I suddenly can't see entirely, but somehow, I manage to pull over and park the car. I don't know how, but I do. The music is deafening, and my vision is a charcoal-colored blur. I desperately reach for my doorknob and open the door. I'm struggling to breathe, and I can hear the faint screams from Rosey.

What the fuck is happening to me?

I feel myself drop. I don't know where, but I drop. I feel the thud. The charcoal-colored blur in my vision was starting to become pitch black as I heard Rosey scream, "Oh My God, he's having a seizure!"

# DISCUSSION WITH THE AUTHOR

Q & A's

**Q - Why tell this story?**

**A -** I believe it sends an important message. Most of the time, your plans aren't God's plans. Life is going to throw you curveballs, and you need to be able to adapt and have a strong mentality if you're going to be able to make it through life. You need to have a plan B, C, and D in life. There isn't any time to complain about the cards you were dealt. Each second is valuable. I was fortunate enough to learn the hard way at an early age. It'd be wrong of me not to pass this message along to the younger generation.

**Q—You mentioned that you were 20 years old when you went through what Kelvin went through at the book's introduction. How accurate was your experience when your AVM ruptured in the story?**

**A -** It was very accurate. In the book, Kelvin had a regretful night before waking up the next morning with that headache because he knew he should have pursued Analis more. I had a regretful Valentine's Day night, not pursuing what I wanted, before waking up the next morning with a headache. I remember telling my mother the next morning that I wasn't going to class, and I took a nap. I woke up and went to work at Rhode Island Hospital, but ended up telling my supervisor that I needed to go to the emergency room, where everything happened, just like in the book–the CT scan, the responses of the young nurse, and on-call neurologists, my confusion and denial because I was feeling physically fine.

**Q - How was it reliving some of these memories?**

**A -** Surprisingly, therapeutic. I just now decided to go public with my condition. Like Kelvin, I am a reserved person. So, I rarely talk with people about my past, especially this part of my life. As a result, I rarely talk about it at all. Whenever I shared my story, especially with those in the medical field, I was always told how lucky I was to be living alive and, as far as they know, functioning perfectly fine. Writing this book was the first time I got to sit back and relieve every single moment of my journey, although every moment didn't make it into this book.

**Q - Why is that? Why was this the first time you got to relieve every single moment?**

**A -** Because I didn't have the luxury of doing so during or after my recovery. Unlike Kelvin, my father doesn't live in the States, and my income relied on to make ends meet. I was fortunate to have a job that gave me excellent health insurance, preventing me from paying tons of medical bills, but I needed to keep working as soon as possible in order to keep that job. Yes, I thought about things during my downtime and lived in my head a lot, but those were short periods of time. Then, when I got a hundred better, I was nearly an engaged man in my late twenties, and I guess there wasn't a need to go back in time and relieve those moments.

**Q - Did doctors really tell you that you were going to die?**

**A -** Yes. I especially remember sitting in the real Dr. Woo's office. My older brother had driven me there, and we sat side by side, speechless. Just like in this story, he told me that people with my condition do not live to see age 28, let alone live past 30 years of age. I remember him going into specifics about the dangers of playing sports with my condition. I used to play tons of pick-up basketball games and pick-up baseball games, and he warned me that catching an accidental elbow blow to the head or an accident bump to the head could cause imminent death. He went into further detail about how he had never seen the size of my AVM on anyone else and that I was undoubtedly going to die, and the only way to live longer was to change my entire physical lifestyle, which sent me into a quiet depression.

**Q - Is it safe to say that Kelvin is based on you?**

**A -** Not quite. Although we have personality similarities, Kelvin's story is not done, far from it. Mine isn't either. As we dive deep into Kelvin's life as he enters adulthood, his path, choices, and results will differ significantly from mine. And although my path has led me through different professions, Kelvin is just a teenager, adapting to his new life. I've already adapted. I have a good idea of what I am destined for. Kelvin doesn't yet.

**Q - Does this mean there will be a sequel to this book?**

**A -** Yes. There will be at least two more books. We've only scratched the surface with Kelvin and haven't begun to scratch the surface on Jonathan.

**Q - How do you feel now?**

**A -** Good. I feel good.

**Q - What was the deciding factor in writing this book in the young adult genre?**

**A -** I have a teenage niece, and I have teenage nephews. I have a seven-year-old son who is wise beyond his years. My niece and nephews are at a point in their lives where they will face adversities and have to have adult conversations. That's why it was important for me to show the contrast between how Kelvin handled things, especially when pursuing a relationship with Analis, and how Jonathan handled his situation with Vanity. Kelvin was wise enough to understand that he needed a friend and had an adult conversation with Analis instead of swallowing his pride, which further potentially complicated his life and maybe derailed Analis' grades. Obviously, Jonathan is focusing on baseball more than his girlfriend. I'm not advocating for young men not to have girlfriends or put them on the back burner at all. But many times, I've seen young athletes, males and females choose to put their young love life above everything else, jeopardizing their future, and end up heartbroken and regretful. It's okay to take your time and choose YOU, especially when you're young with the whole world in front of you. Then, when life throws you a curve ball like it did to me and like it did to Kelvin, you have to learn how to pivot because your second choice could indeed be your first choice. You just needed to go through this particular adversity for you to see it.

**Q - What can we expect from the next book?**

**A** - More of Jonathan, that's for sure. The brothers alternate chapters throughout the book, making it a dual-main-character novel.

**Q - Last comments for those reading this book...**

**A -** Appreciate every single moment of life. I know we live in a social media world but enjoy the present. Don't follow trends, be your own trend. I know the future can be scary, but don't let the fear of striking hold you back from something greater. Fear is an illusion that only needs to be understood. It's a limitation we self-consciously put in our brains. Once you can conquer that, you can do anything you want.

# ACKNOWLEDGMENTS

There are so many people to thank and not enough words to express my gratitude, but I will still try my hardest.

I want to first thank my wife and sons for their patience. We have busy lives–day jobs, schools, baseball, etc.- and thank you for giving me the space I needed to complete this novel. I love you, Mrs. Canó. Thank you for being the most incredible woman I ever met. To my boys, sometimes I wish I could freeze time so you guys won't grow up so fast. Keep being the kind, funny, independent, athletic, thoughtful kids you are. I love you guys.

Thank you to my mother. I am a first-generation American-born Dominican. Most of us carry the burden of our parents' struggles. Whatever they failed at is engraved in our brains, and we're fed that *American Dream* destination plan–go to school, college, become a lawyer, a doctor, a fireman, get married, buy a house, have some kids, and retire. I thank my mother for NOT feeding me this and allowing me to dream about MY Fantasy, which is being whatever I want to be, and not killing the dreamer in me, no matter how unrealistic my dreams may be to someone else.

A special thank you to everyone involved with this novel and my first novel, Identical: My Big Brother

Carlos "Loso" Perez, for designing the covers, my special readers, my brother Edwin Silverio, Brook Tyra, fellow author Sip Rodriguez, my wife, Michele Canó, and Kaitlyn Arraial. One of my oldest friends, Rafael "Pito" Medina, for taking my very first headshot and being one of my closest confidants when I was recovering from my ruptured brain AVM.

A massive thank you to my editor, Haydee Disla. Amiga, this is our second book. The first, Identical, was a learning experience. We learned from our mistakes and applied our schools to this one. And like Rafael, you were one of the few people in my inner circle when I was going through the horrors of my ruptured brain AVM. You made sure to call me every Friday night to lift my spirits, and when I was in that dark place and didn't pick up, you left me a message to lift my spirits. I'm forever indebted to you.

Francelin Ruiz. If I'm the real Kelvin, you are the real Jonathan and company. You drove me to the hospital that day and hadn't left my side since. And even though we rarely spend time together because we now have our own grown lives, what's understood doesn't need to be said. We will always be brothers.

My friends Ermy Guzman, Jeffery Castro, Jona Cedeño, Heny Puro, Cesar Ricardo, and Rafael Gutiér-rez, thank you for your friendship and support over the years.

Victor Ramos, my friend and mentor, I appreciate you. I appreciate your vision, talent, and work ethic, and I admire your passion. The best thing about you is your heart. Whenever I have a question or need help, you are always a text away and never fail to help in any way you can. I appreciate you, my friend.

Finally, in this order, Mabel Diclo, Tiffany Black, Edmicelly Xavier, and Dahiana Torres.

When I started this writing journey, it all started with a short scene written in my Blackberry notes. I sent it to the other person I knew in showbiz, Mabel Diclo, an old friend from junior high school. She loved it and forwarded it to her roommate, an actress, and then Edmicelly Peña, who advised me to base the entire story on the dialogue of the scene. Little did I know, Edmicelly would turn out to be one of the best friends I'd ever have. Next comes Tiffany Black, who was friends with Edmicelly. She guided me to the proper writing software and programs without meeting me to further expand as a writer.

And finally, Dahiana Torres. We have known one another since we were fifteen years old. We have been neighbors, friends, and, at times, very close friends. We called you D, not just because of your first name, but because you played basketball for our school's girl's team, and you were a tremendous defender. We bonded by playing pickup basketball in front of our houses. You were the only girl playing with all the guys in the neighborhood. We grew even closer by venting, sharing secrets and feelings, and talking to one another late at night during high school.

Life has taken us on separate paths only to bring us closer on a couple of occasions as we grew older. One of them was the film we worked on together, me as a writer and you as the director. And it was there that you taught me the most valuable lesson anyone has ever taught me–hard work.

I admit that there was a time when I half-assed a couple of things because I was new to this business, and I felt overwhelmed. Now I realize I was not ready to tell that story, but it PUSHED me. You pushed, pushed, pushed, and got on my ass. Your name was on that project, and you'd be damned if you looked bad. You were still the same in your face, D, who was unafraid to tell anyone what they didn't want to hear. I still remember your words: "Ricky, if you really want this, you will have to work and sacrifice. Only YOU can want that for yourself."

I saw you grind every single day on that project, post-production, and even got on my ass when it came to promotion. I didn't realize that watching you at the time was teaching me something valuable that I'd apply more than a decade later. And from the bottom of my heart, thank you, D. Thank you, my old friend.

# ABOUT THE AUTHOR

Ricky Cano was born on August 25th, 1985, in the Bronx, New York. Early in his life, Ricky moved around a lot. He lived in the Dominican Republic; Norristown, Pennsylvania; Miami, Florida; back to New York City; Providence, Rhode Island, where he spent most of his adolescence before finally settling in Cranston, Rhode Island, well into adulthood.

Ricky enjoyed a range of hobbies and participated in many different sports, from Baseball to Basketball, Soccer, Boxing, and even Martial Arts, while living in Miami. Despite being a gifted athlete with a collegian promise, Ricky had to give up on his athletics dreams by the time he was sixteen to help his mother, a single mother of three, make ends meet. He took on many positions, from a fast-food chain employee, a busboy & dishwasher at a diner, and a call center rep, before online buying was an option. Later, he tackled many positions while working at the State's most prominent and busiest hospital before becoming a first responder.

On February 15th, 2006, just as his young, unbalanced life seemed to be settling in, Ricky was prepping to try out for his collegian baseball team when his life was derailed. A massive brain aneurysm had occurred due to a ruptured AVM, a brain condition he was unaware he was living with since he was born. Since the AVM was located deep in his left brain, a spot doctors deemed too dangerous to operate on, Ricky was treated, then sent home twelve days later with a date to return for a massive radiation surgery.

Despite the radiation surgery, Ricky was given pretty much a death date; as Neurologist Dr. Woo stated, "People with your type of condition rarely make it to see twenty-eight, let alone thirty." Over the next five years, Ricky turned to writing, the one thing that has never let him down. He started writing at twelve, beginning with notebooks while his teachers lectured in class. That led to short stories on his mother's home desktop. Over the next five years, Ricky had a second radiation surgery and a handful of procedures. He successfully wrote a screenplay at age twenty-five about the tumultuous times during his aneurysm and recovery from the first surgery without prior screenplay lessons.

Seeing his creation on the big screen during the Boston International Film Festival fueled Ricky's passion for writing. Along with a trusted friend, he successfully wrote a second film and cast himself as the lead while also co-directing a large cast. Over the next year, just before his 27th birthday, doctors determined that Ricky was one hundred percent cured of the brain condition that had threatened his life. His Neurologist said, "You're my miracle man."

Over the next three years, Ricky wrote several screenplays and pilots, was cast in a couple of films by other local directors as an actor, married, and became a father for the first time. However, he soon learned that the Hollywood business is challenging. Despite receiving great feedback over the next five years, he couldn't quite sell any of his pilots or feature film screenplays. The now father of two sons turned his attention to novel writing. He picked out his latest pilot and show, Identical, and converted it into a hybrid book with a screenplay and a traditional novel format. His goal for this book is simple. "The book will sell the show. If it doesn't, I'll be a bestseller. I'm going to make it. I don't know how, but I am going to make it.

Catch Ricky on Instagram at Ricky_TheWriter_Cano, on X at RickyCano25, and on TikTok at @rcano885

www.ingramcontent.com/pod-product-compliance
Lightning Source LLC
Chambersburg PA
CBHW031139160726
47991CB00004B/1479